THE NETHERWELL HORROR

LEE MOUNTFORD

For my beautiful wife, Michelle. And amazing daughters, Ella and Sophie.

FREE BOOK

Sign up to my mailing list for a free horror book...

Want more scary stories? Sign up to my mailing list and receive your free copy of *The Nightmare Collection - Vol 1* directly to your email address.

This novel-length short story collection is sure to have you sleeping with the lights on.

Sign up now.

www.leemountford.com

1

HE WAS SCARED. Terrified.

Just what the hell have I gotten myself into?

The air was cold, even though the cave at the base of the cliff offered some protection from the lashing rain outside. Waves from the sea crashed and roared, and the wind howled into the large natural chamber. Flickering flames of torchlight illuminated the area, which was both high and wide, and had stalagmites and stalactites spearing through the ground and ceiling. The rocky walls were sparsely decorated with spray-painted graffiti, a sign that youths used this cave as a place to congregate, and the litter on the ground—food wrappers, empty bottles of alcohol, and even, disgustingly, used condoms—were also a testament to that.

The man could smell salt from the sea and worried that the water would soon come rushing inside and start to flood the cave. Thankfully, however, the tide levels seemed low enough not to pose any danger, and the waves simply hit the sloping beach outside before gradually drifting back out. Another swell of seawater crashed onto the pebbles, and then the chaotic process repeated itself over and over again.

It was almost loud enough to drown out the sound of chanting from the man's brethren, as well as the terrified cries of those who were to be sacrificed.

Almost drowned out their screams... but not quite. And it turned his stomach.

The man hadn't meant for any of this to happen. He certainly hadn't intended to join a fucking *cult*! He'd just wanted to find a place to finally lay down some roots and meet a girl to fall in love with.

He wanted to put his life back together.

And here, in this strange town, the man thought he'd found all of those things. But then it had all changed. The woman he loved—at least he *thought* he loved—opened his eyes to something new. Something strange. At first, it was intriguing, even if part of him knew that getting involved was a mistake. The whole thing was just so life-changing that he couldn't help himself. He was resistant and sceptical at first, of course, but the things he'd seen in such a short space of time had changed his outlook in short order. Then, he found himself begging to be a part of it all, to learn more.

In doing so, he'd never realised what would be demanded of him.

The man then felt a hand on his shoulder. It was her: the siren that had brought him into this new and terrifying world in the first place.

'It's time,' she whispered, just loudly enough for him to hear over the waves and sobbing.

The three people who were bound and kneeling on the floor of the cave looked absolutely terror stricken. As well they should. They knew what was coming. They begged, which was only natural, but knew what was coming. The two men and lone woman who now pleaded were all members of the Order, but none were willing to give up their lives for it. Their loyalty didn't *quite* stretch that far. In the end, though, that choice had not been theirs to make

'Please,' the woman begged. Her voice was quiet, almost inaudible as a savage wave crashed to the pebbled beach outside.

No one would listen to her, the man knew.

His throat felt dry. This girl's face was a picture of fear. And seeing one so young—early twenties at best—look so scared was an upsetting thing.

But there was something else to her expression, as well. The realisation that an unpreventable death was only moments away. Not acceptance, because how could one accept something like that? No, this was more like a terrible understanding that nothing would save her now.

Nothing.

Her death, and the death of the two men with her, would take place tonight. And it would be the start of something both horrifying and incredible.

A strong wind blew through the cave again, and the dark robes of the gathered members of the Order all billowed and flapped. All of these people were completely covered and hidden by the heavy material they wore. The man's own garment, like that of most of the other members, was a thick robe of a dark grey colour. Dull and unremarkable, it was woven of itchy fabric that irritated the skin. He felt like he was wearing an old burlap sack with a large hood that covered most of his face.

Only a handful of those present had different robes. Theirs were made of silk and were blood red, with elegant black patterns embossed on edges of the hood, the arms, and the base.

These people were the Elders, and they scared the hell out of him. Thankfully, however, that *other* person wasn't present at this time. That other *thing*. The man had seen it before, always dressed in simple black cloth with a high collar, like a priest. That thing was even given distance and respect by the Elders themselves. The man was certain that when that dark presence—there was no other term for it—stared at him, it was looking directly into his soul. Still, just the fact that the Elders were present now was enough to scare him.

These victims, with hands tied behind their backs, had short chains around their necks and ankles, holding them in place. The iron chains were fixed to baseplates that had been bolted to the floor.

Escape was impossible.

The lives of the chosen would be forfeited in order to start something beyond imagination. Their blood was needed. As was their flesh. As were their souls.

But it was more than that. It wasn't just the sacrifices that were important. It was *where* they would be sacrificed. This cave was special, as were the clifftops above it, though he wasn't entirely sure why.

Three circular symbols had been drawn onto the rocky surface of the ground, and each of the chosen were placed within one. These symbols had initially been made in chalk, then tried again with the blood of the elders, and lastly redrawn with a liquid much darker and more viscous. What that liquid was, exactly, the man had no idea. But he did know a little of the markings themselves, and their meaning. The geometry of them—and *geometry* was the correct term—was special. The three rings, with other etchings within, were all confined inside a larger, circular seal, that had also been drawn in the same way.

The Seal of Moloch.

Other than the chosen three, no one else stood inside

the outer seal. Instead, they all gathered around its perimeter.

Once fully desecrated and drained of life, the bodies of the sacrificed would stay in this cave, inside their respective symbols, for a short time. That would allow death to permeate into the ground and very air around them. The bodies would be found in due time, of course. But that was apparently of no concern to the Order. By then, things would have already been set in motion.

Another crash from the waves outside made the man jump. He noticed one of the Elders start to approach him and it was a struggle for him to keep from shaking.

The Elder then lifted up an arm and held out a knife.

Not shiny and sharp, but dull and rusted, with a thin blade that had a slight curve to it. The instrument used to start the killing did not need to be anything special, it only needed to inflict as much pain as possible.

'Do what is required of you, my son,' the Elder said. The man felt tears well up inside of him.

I'm not a murderer. I'm not a murderer. I'm not a murderer.

But if he didn't do what was asked, and fully commit to the Order, then he knew full well what would happen. He would replace one of the chosen. *He* would then be the one shackled within the maddening seal in the centre of the cave, as all others watched on. It was *his* life that would be painfully taken from him. It was *his* body that would be sickeningly desecrated. And *his* soul that would... the man could scarcely even think about it. He knew the price of failure. They had told him he was special, destined for greatness, but that didn't mean he could disobey their will.

The man locked eyes with the female sacrifice chained to the floor. Her brown hair was wild, and dirt streaked her plump, naked body. She had large, dark eyes, and they bored into him, pleading for mercy. The man knew, should their roles be reversed, the woman would have no hesitation in taking hold of the blade and gutting him. He knew she would enjoy every moment of it.

The Order had no shortage of blind devotees. But it seemed the devotion of these three did not extend quite so far as to give up their lives in the name of the 'Truth.'

Still, just because the woman would have indeed killed him if given the chance, did that justify what he had to do?

'Now!' the elder yelled in a voice that was both sudden and almost deafening, easily overpowering the cacophony of the roaring sea outside.

The scared man felt his bladder loosen. He raised his hand and took hold of the handle of the blade.

I'm not a murderer. I'm not a murderer. I'm not a murderer.

'Very good, my son,' the Elder said. 'Now... do it.'

2

THE MORNING AIR felt revitalising to Jim Taylor as he walked across the stony beach. The breeze had a bite to it, a sting, but it made him feel alive.

After he had gotten up that morning just before dawn had broken, as was typical for him, Jim's joints felt stiff. His body, a shell of what it once was, ached like this every morning, and was a symptom of his advancing years. Years seemed to advance at an ever-quickening pace.

At seventy-three, Jim didn't know how long he had left before he was finally reunited with his sweet Ada. And, just after waking—when he ached the most—was when he tended to think it would happen sooner rather than later. However, after heading off for his morning walk, things tended to look different. Jim's body loosened. Hell, he'd even recently started some light jogging once a week.

Jim loved the early mornings—it was the perfect time of day. The red of the dawn sky was beautiful, especially when looking out over the sea. The sound of the waves was relaxing and peaceful. He was usually the only one out and about at such an early hour, and he enjoyed the solitude of it all. It was times like this, walking alone and taking in the natural beauty of the world, that Jim felt like he could live forever.

Well, maybe not forever, but long enough. There was another girl in his life now that he couldn't bear to leave behind.

Jess.

She bounded across the beach up ahead of him, sprinting over wet pebbles and barking in delight. She would even trot into the shallow waters, going just deep enough for the sea to come up to the white fur of her chest.

The Border Collie was thirteen years old, and therefore quite advanced in age in her own right, though you couldn't tell that from looking at her. White and black, with one brown eye and one blue eye from a pigment defect, she was full of life and energy whenever they went out for a walk. A hint of arthritis had developed in the old girl recently, something Jim had in common with her, but she didn't let it hold her back. Jim heard her bark again, and he watched as she sprinted off up the beach towards the base of twin cliffs that looked out over the sea.

Between those cliffs, which jutted out into the sea like pincers, was a small river that cut into the land and ran back up through Netherwell Bay, separating two sides of the town. At low tide, you could walk the riverbed, which Jess loved to do. Today, however, Jim would need to use the footpaths and cross one of the many bridges farther up in order to get back to his own side.

The stick Jim walked with—a thick, polished wooden one, with a formed handle and brass base—helped him navigate the uneven beach that was a mix of browns and greys thanks to the stones that littered it. There were a few patches of exposed sand, which was muddy given the rain overnight, but the majority was wet stone pebbles, and therefore slippery underfoot. That meant Jim had to move a little slower and more carefully than usual. Still, he wasn't concerned about Jess running off. She was well trained and loyal. The dog would often wander ahead to play and do her own thing, but she would always return. Jim had a feeling he knew where his furry companion was running off to now: the cave at the base of the cliffs, dug into the nearest one to him.

Hollows Cove, as it was known.

The natural void in the face of the cliff was a place Jess loved to explore. Jim wasn't keen on letting her, truth be told, given it was often full of rubbish left behind by gangs of young troublemakers. He remembered one morning when Jess had run into the cave and disturbed a group of youths who had apparently slept there after partying through the night. Jim had seen the remains of a fire on the beach outside, as well as scores of empty bottles. It seemed like these kids had enjoyed a good night, though they were having a terrible morning after being woken up by Jess' barking. They looked pale and ill and were all clearly suffering from terrible hangovers—even though none of them looked old enough to drink. Jim had commanded Jess back to his side, then left the group to their suffering.

That was the only time he'd ever found the cave inhabited during his walks, however, so he always let Jess explore as she wanted to. She wasn't the kind of dog to bring back anything she found, so he didn't worry about her picking up anything disgusting. And given the rain the previous night, which Jim could still smell in the air, he knew for certain the cave would be empty now.

Jess' barking suddenly became frantic.

Furrowing his brow, Jim pushed himself on quicker, still

being careful not to fall. At his age, that could be dangerous. Soon, the cliff base came into view, and he saw the yawning opening of the cave in its surface. Squinting, he could make out the sight of Jess bounding out, barking as she did. She looked over to him, barked some more, spun in a circle, then darted back inside. She had found something, Jim knew, but her tone wasn't excitable, as it often was upon making a discovery. The barks were loud and urgent.

He moved quicker.

'What have you found, girl?'

It took Jim another couple of minutes to reach the cave. He didn't even have to enter to see what it was she had found. The gory remains were clearly visible, sitting centrally in the wide-open space of Hollows Cove. Red chunks of meat and flesh were strewn about a rocky ground that also glistened with blood.

Jim's heart missed a beat, and everything stood still as his mind tried to process what he was seeing.

Then he turned to his side and vomited while forcing his eyes shut. However, in his mind's eye, he could still see those horrible details he'd quickly taken in before turning away.

A hand severed at the wrist, with short, blue-painted fingernails... on what fingers remained. A foot. A torso with the white ribs poking through the flesh and the skin stripped clean. Three heads sat on the ground, mouths open, eyes missing, and all facing each other. Intestines were draped between the heads, connecting them like points on a string-map.

Jim managed to pause his retching and call Jess back to him, fearful that they were both in danger, and that her barking would alert whoever did this to their presence. The dog wouldn't come at first, instead standing just before the hideous mess, growling at it relentlessly.

'Jess!' Jim screamed in a tone he had never used with the animal before. Jess looked to him, ears pulled back to her head, then turned again to the nightmarish scene. She barked once more, but eventually relented and returned to her owner.

Jim didn't want to wait around any longer. His heart was pounding in his chest, and a cold sweat had broken out over his skin.

He'd never been one to carry a mobile phone before, thinking it a useless piece of modern technology, but he dearly wished he had one on him now. As it was, he needed to leave, find a phone, and then call the police.

He was a former army man, and had seen many things in his time, such as death, murder, mutilation, and more. But this?

This was different.

It was just like what had happened in Netherwell Bay all those years ago, when Jim was a young man. He recognised it instantly after seeing the horrific desecration in the cave, and after spotting those fucking symbols on the ground.

This was evil. And it was back.

3

'I'M NOT DOING IT, MARK,' Beth Davis said. She had her arms folded tightly cross her chest and glared down at the man who was shaking his head in annoyance.

Mark Pritchard was the Editor-in-Chief of the local newspaper where Beth worked, *The Daily Enquirer*, and he sighed in frustration.

'Yes, you are,' he stated.

The short, skinny man was seated behind a desk that overflowed with paper, folders, and even takeaway food packaging. The office they were in was a large one—too large, considering the meagre size of the open-plan work-space outside that the rest of the team had to share. The office had a low L-shaped leather sofa and glass coffee table in one corner, with Mark's desk central to the back wall. The chair behind the desk was framed by a large, arched window that overlooked the town of Ashford.

At thirty-five, Mark was a year Beth's junior, yet he had quickly risen to the position of Editor-in-Chief, despite working at the paper for three years less than Beth. And despite being—in her opinion—utterly useless at his job.

Being the son of the majority shareholder obviously had its benefits.

Mark was balding, and what little hair he did have was cut short atop a thin, weasel-like face. When he smiled, the gesture seemed to lack warmth or happiness. Instead, it always came across as a creepy sneer to Beth, hindered by discoloured and crooked teeth. When standing, and not hiding behind his desk, the man was only five-foot-four, and Beth often wondered if that was why he tried to order others around and belittle them, as if trying to make up for something.

This little Napoleon had been captaining the once respectable newspaper down the toilet for years, chasing the basest stories, which were to be reported with little-to-no objectivity. Sensationalism was his mantra.

Although, Beth had to wonder if that was exclusive to her newspaper, or the state of her industry in general.

'Look, just sit down, will you?' Mark asked as he gestured to the chair on the other side of his desk.

'No, I choose to stand,' Beth stated, still keeping her arms crossed. She liked looking down over Mark and could tell it made him uncomfortable. Even if the man stood she would still have had a few inches on him, and was maybe even a little broader than him as well. Beth didn't consider herself obese, but she certainly wasn't supermodel-thin, and was proud of that fact. She stood at five-nine and had long brown hair that, if not styled for work engagements, was usually maintained in a functional bun. Her slightly cherubic face was always made up with a light layer of foundation and subtle make-up, to help hide the smattering of freckles across her cheeks. But Beth's most striking feature was her bright blue eyes. That day, she wore a simple blue blouse, black trousers, and heels, something she considered professional but not too uncomfortable or flamboyant. Mark, on the other hand, was dressed in tight jeans and a dark-blue blazer over a white shirt. The shirt had been unbuttoned down to his chest, allowing his bare, pale skin below to be seen. He probably thought it looked hip and 'smart-casual,' but in Beth's eyes he just looked like he was trying too hard.

'I don't understand what your problem is. Why do you keep fighting me on this stuff?' Mark asked in an exasperated tone.

Beth shook her head. He knew why. She'd made her position on this very clear before. And yet, here they were again, singing the same song and doing the same dance. Earlier that day Mark had demanded she change a story she'd written that was due to go out in tomorrow's edition. Beth had spent months investigating reports of fake expense claims by a local member of parliament. A story, Beth soon found out, that had legs. One slight problem, however, was that Beth's source had money and gambling issues of his own. A public figure himself, the man was still ready to waive the right to anonymity and be named in the story to help prove his case.

Mark, however, had gotten friendly with the government official in question over the last year, and Beth was well aware that 'Little Napoleon' saw the friendship as a way to move up the social ladder. And despite Mark's claims to the contrary, Beth knew full-well the reason he wanted to change the narrative of the story—to instead focus on her witness and his money troubles—was to protect his new friend.

Beth's story had originally remained as impartial as she could have possibly made it. She had indeed highlighted the money troubles of the witness, as they were relevant, but the other evidence was solid. Mark, instead, wanted to change it into a hit piece that actually protected the MP. He also felt that shining a light on a local businessman who could not be trusted with money was a 'good public service.'

'I fight you on this stuff because it's unethical,' Beth said.

'It makes for a better story,' Mark replied. 'It will sell more copies and also get more clicks on the website.'

'But it isn't the truth! You want me to say that my witness is at risk of losing his home.'

'He is.'

'No, he isn't! It hasn't gotten to that stage yet. Not by a long shot.'

Mark closed his eyes, then gripped the bridge of his nose. He let out a sigh. 'You're just splitting hairs,' he said.

'It isn't splitting hairs, Mark!' Beth shouted, feeling another surge of anger.

Mark's face flushed red and his beady eyes quickly flicked to look behind her, off through the open door and out into the bullpen. Beth had answered back to him —*loudly*—and she knew that he hated being seen as weak.

'Quiet down!' he scolded with a snarl, but any show of intimidation he was trying to make was ruined by his obvious embarrassment.

Beth then felt a discreet vibration from her trouser pocket, indicating someone was calling her mobile phone. There was no way she could answer now, however, not in the middle of this.

'I'm not changing the story, Mark,' Beth stated, calmly this time, but with a certain edge and defiance.

Mark shook his head, took a moment, then slowly got to his feet. He leaned forward as he pressed his fists into the surface of the desk. He shot her a scowl and leaned in closer still. But Beth was not going to wilt away from this man. She wasn't afraid of him. Instead, she took a step forward, causing him to shrink back a little in surprise.

'Anything to add?' she asked.

He took a moment to answer, then nodded. 'Yes,' he said. 'I think it's best you take some time off.'

'What?' Beth asked, incredulous 'Are you firing me?'

'That's not what I said,' Mark replied, raising his palms defensively. 'But, bottom line, the story *is* going to change before it runs tomorrow. So, perhaps you are best served taking a few days—hell, a few weeks—to get your head where it needs to be. You could even look to see if anything else comes up that would suit you better. Might be that this paper isn't the best place for you anymore.'

He wasn't wrong in that regard. Beth's father would be rolling in his grave if he could see the state of the so-called journalism here. She wanted to argue back, to defy Mark and stay around here out of spite, if nothing else. But, at the same time, she also wanted to tell him where to stick his job.

'This place is going to go down the shitter, Mark,' Beth told him. 'And you're the one doing the flushing. You are out of your depth and flounder around like a spoiled child.'

'Get out of my office, Beth,' Mark said, gritting his teeth. 'Before I *do* fire you.'

And that challenge was enough. Beth had plenty of money saved up to last a few months without a job, and this could be the kick she dearly needed to move on to something better. She hated leaving a job half-finished, which was what this felt like, but what other choice did she have? Give this slimly little toad the benefit of breaking her?

Not a chance.

'You won't get to fire me, Mark,' Beth said, leaning in closer to him, putting her own hands on the desk as well. Mark pulled back farther. 'Because I quit.'

He didn't get the chance to add anything else. Beth simply stood back up to her full height, cast him a last scowl, then turned and left his office. She made her way over to her desk and started to collect her belongings. Erland Cowell—a researcher, and one of her closest friends at the paper—cast her a confused look and mouthed, 'Are you alright?' Beth shook her head but did not go over to speak to him. Right now, she just wanted to be out of the building.

She was done with this place. It was time to find a fresh adventure.

4

BETH THREW her box of her collected possessions onto the passenger seat of her Ford Kuga SUV, then walked around to the driver's side. She got in, closed the door behind her, and let her head fall back to the headrest. A long exhale escaped her.

God, how she needed a drink right now. The day hadn't gone as Beth had imagined when waking up that morning.

She was just about to fish her keys out of her pocket and start the engine, when she remembered the call she had missed during her meeting with Mark. After retrieving her mobile phone, she quickly unlocked it and checked the call log, where she noticed a number and area code she didn't recognise. Beth also had a voicemail waiting to be listened to. She debated waiting until she was home before listening. After all, if it was something to do with work, or one of the stories she was working on, there was little she could do to help, and she didn't feel up to a conversation outlining why she had just quit her job. Still, the fact that it was from a number she didn't recognise piqued her interest, so she swiped the screen of her smartphone across to the voicemail app and hit dial. After navigating through an automated menu, the message started to play. The voice that spoke was one Beth hadn't heard for four years. But it was one she recognised all too well.

'Beth, it's me... Josh.'

It was her brother. And he sounded panicked.

'Sorry for calling out of the blue, but I didn't know who else to turn to. I'm in trouble, Sis. I mean real trouble. And I need help. Something... something has happened. I've gotten caught up in something, and I don't know what to...' his voice trailed off, and Beth heard him start to sob. 'I need your help. Please. I'm in a town called Netherwell Bay. There is something wrong with this place. I can't go to the police. I don't know what to do, Sis. Please... I need help.' He started to cry again. Beth couldn't remember ever hearing Josh cry as an adult before. Not even at their own father's funeral. The message then suddenly cut off and an automated voice took over: 'To return the call, press one. To save the message, press two. To delete, press three.'

Beth was too stunned to press anything.

She hadn't seen or spoken to Josh in years. He wasn't exactly one for taking on responsibility or staying close to people, let alone asking anyone for help. Beth had last seen him on the day of their father's funeral, and prior to that hadn't spoken to him for a number of years. In fact, she had been a little surprised Josh had actually turned up to say goodbye to their father. After the service, however, Josh had swiftly left again. Beth had no idea what he was doing with his life now, or where he was living. Until this message.

She was well aware that Josh was no angel, and had often landed himself in trouble over the years she had known him. However, he'd always been able to worm or charm his way out of it. Beth had never, ever, heard him scared. It just wasn't part of his makeup. She wasn't even sure he cared enough about anything or anyone to allow fear to register. Yet, on the voicemail she had just listened to, he not only sounded fearful, but absolutely desperate.

The automated voice then repeated its options to her, seeming impatient for a response. Beth chose to redial the number—which was a landline, not a mobile one. As it dialled, she realised that Josh was fortunate she had kept the same mobile phone number for all these years. In truth, she was a little surprised he still had her number in the first place.

Beth listened to the ringing tone as the call awaited connection at the other end. And it continued to ring. And ring. And ring.

She let the call continue for a few minutes, but ended it when she realised no one was going to pick up. Strangely, it didn't give her the option to leave a message of her own. It just rang on and on.

She felt a sense of urgency begin to rise in her gut. She quickly searched the mysterious number online, and the results showed that the call had come from a public payphone in a place called Netherwell Bay.

Why the hell is he using a payphone? And where the hell is Netherwell Bay?

She was more than a little surprised people even used public payphones anymore. Did Josh not have access to a mobile or house-phone of his own? Or was there a need to use something he couldn't be linked to?

Beth decided that trying the number again would likely prove fruitless, so she saved his voicemail and contemplated what she could do. With no way of contacting Josh directly to find out what was going on, there was perhaps only one option.

Beth used her phone again, this time to Google Netherwell Bay. Knowing that the UK had many towns with the same name, she also used the area code from Josh's call to narrow down the search. She quickly found the place she was looking for.

The first website she clicked on described a small, coastal settlement in the North East region of the country. The few pictures on the site showed a fishing town that time seemed to have forgotten. Given Josh was one for living the fast life, Beth couldn't fathom what the draw of this place was to him.

Unless, of course, it was a woman.

She punched the route to Netherwell Bay into the route-planner application on her phone and saw that the drive would take a little over five hours—but only if she didn't hit any major traffic.

Was she really considering travelling all that way, on such short notice, just to help a person—brother or not—that hadn't bothered to keep in touch over the years? Did he even deserve her help?

Josh had ignored her for years. Beth, for her part, had initially tried to maintain a relationship with him. She'd tried damn hard, always texting and calling, desperate to be a good big sister. But a person can only be ignored for so long before they give up completely.

The sensible thing for Beth to do would be to wait for Josh to call back, which he likely would, and then offer any help she could from a distance.

But that wasn't where her mind was going.

Like it or not, he was still family. The only family she had left on this earth. Her father had always impressed upon her the importance of family. It was important to him, *hugely* important, given he did not know his own parents.

That seemed to push him harder to look after his own kids. Beth was grateful for that, and it broke her heart knowing her father had watched his own son become estranged only a few years after losing his wife. Beth saw it as her responsibility to try and hold the family together as best she could and make her father proud, so she really tried with Josh. However, she knew that her father went to his grave with a broken heart.

Josh's tone during the short message had scared Beth. He was obviously afraid, and that meant the trouble he was in was serious. Given what had just happened with her job —namely that she didn't have one anymore—she had nothing holding her back. Even if the trip called for an overnight stay, the only thing stopping Beth was her own reservations.

And, like it or not, she still felt responsible for her younger brother. That, above all else, was what helped her reach a decision.

She would need to go home first and pack some things. Beth's job as a journalist had taught her that a short trip could quickly turn into something more prolonged.

Given it was just before lunchtime, Beth figured she could be in Netherwell Bay before dusk, even if she allowed for a couple of food and restroom breaks on the way.

'What the hell am I getting myself into?' she asked out loud. For a day that had already started out strangely, things had just taken a very unexpected turn.

But Beth's mind was made up. Josh was family. And she resolved to help him.

5

THE LONG TRIP was finally taking its toll on Beth. Her eyes felt heavy and itchy, a consequence of focusing too hard on the road ahead without having taken a break in the last two hours.

She had finally left the motorway a little over an hour ago and was now winding through the secondary roads of the countryside, with rolling fields and hills either side of her.

Her neck felt stiff and her lower back ached.

Beth just wanted the drive to be over. Her car was a spacious one, and well maintained, but even the most comfortable cars could only stave off the aches and cramp of being stuck in the same seated position for so long. The sound of AC/DC blared from the car's sound system and Beth tapped her fingernails on the steering wheel along to the quick rhythm of the band's music.

After initially making the decision to head to Netherwell Bay, Beth had first returned home to pack some clothes and make sure her flat was secure. It had crossed her mind to look into booking accommodation ahead of time, but she'd decided against it, reasoning that she would be able to find somewhere suitable upon arrival, if it was needed. So, after grabbing a quick bite to eat and changing into some jeans, some comfortable Converse, and a beige, long-sleeved blouse, Beth had left for a town that—until earlier that day —she had never heard of before.

Four hours of driving—even broken up with a couple of toilet breaks—was taxing. Beth checked the built-in satellite navigation system that displayed on the dashboard, and, thankfully, it showed just over an hour of the journey still remaining.

The home stretch.

Beth had spoken to Erland Cowell when he had called to check up on her. He was good at his job, and a good friend, but Beth was aware he carried a little bit of a torch for her. Something that was not reciprocated. He was handsome enough, and had auburn hair and stubble that was indicative of his Scottish roots, but she just wasn't in the market for anyone. During the call, she told him what had happened with Mark, and also that she'd quit. Erland was shocked, and offered to fight her cause, but she'd told him not to. No sense in both of them losing their jobs. Erland had insisted that if there was anything he could do for her, she should just let him know. Beth told him she would, and that she would keep in touch. She meant it, too. These days her industry was full of underhanded and untrustworthy people, so she refused to let good colleagues just fade away into the past.

Beth had also tried calling the number of the payphone in Netherwell Bay a few times during her drive, but each time had yielded the same results: endless ringing until she grew annoyed and ended the call herself.

Beth sighed, feeling like she was losing a fight with

fatigue. She tried the number again, using her hands-free setup so she could concentrate on steering the car. She figured that calling again would help break the monotony of the drive, if nothing else. It rang a couple of times, and then, to Beth's surprise, the call actually connected.

A voice answered, one that was clearly not her brother's. It sounded aged and gravelly.

'Hello? Who the bloody hell is this?'

The curt tone took Beth off guard. 'Hi,' she eventually said. 'I had a missed call from this number, so I was just calling it back.'

'Well, this is a phonebox, love. Whoever rang you ain't here anymore. Is it you that's been calling this phone all day?'

Beth paused for a moment. 'Yes... I guess that was me. As I say, I had a missed call—'

'And as *I* say, whoever it was ain't here anymore. This phonebox is right outside my house, and I'm trying to enjoy some quiet time in my garden. Hard to do with this thing ringing all day. Didn't even think it was still connected. Goodbye. And stop calling.'

'Wait!' Beth quickly said. 'I promise not to bother you anymore, but can I ask, did you see anyone using that phone earlier today? Around lunchtime? I think it would have been a man in his early thirties. Dark hair, fairly tall?'

'Didn't see anyone!' the grouchy man snapped. 'Now bugger off!'

The line went dead.

Beth took a moment, shocked and slightly amused at the man she had just spoken to. 'Charming,' she muttered. Beth had a feeling Netherwell Bay would not be a welcoming place. From the little information she had found online, the fishing town was fairly small and, despite having a somewhat interesting layout, not a place that attracted tourists. Beth had been to small, out-of-the-way places before in her line of work, and they tended to be isolated and insular. And —as clichéd as it was to say—the locals generally tended to be wary and distrusting of outsiders. Was that the kind of general welcome she had in store? Or had the man she'd just spoken to been something of an oddball and not representative of the town at large?

She would find out soon enough. Beth raised a hand and started to massage the back of her neck, trying to work out a kink that was developing. After the call with the rude man had ended, AC/DC had again begun to thunder out their fast riffs and high vocals. Beth found herself nodding along to the music. She liked the band well enough and had one or two of their albums loaded onto her phone, but the last time she'd heard them would have been... four years ago. And it was the same album that she was now playing.

FOUR YEARS PRIOR...

The day had been a hellish one for Beth.

Saying goodbye to her father, the man she loved and respected more than any other in the world, was heartbreaking. The ceremony at the church had been mercifully brief, yet it still felt like an eternity for her. Beth couldn't stop crying through it all. Worse was the crematorium, where she had to sit in the front row and watch as her father's coffin disappeared into a chamber hidden behind a small red curtain. The coffin was pulled along on a quiet conveyor belt as it passed into its final resting place, where Beth knew full well that the body of her father would start to burn.

A great man, who had taught her so much, reduced to nothing more than ash and dust.

The wake afterward was sparsely attended.

Beth had organised a gathering in a local pub and a few friends and extended family followed along after the funeral. It wasn't anything fancy, her father wouldn't have wanted that, but the people there were pleasant and kind with their commiserations and well-wishes. And, in truth, when the funeral and cremation was over with, Beth felt a palpable sense of relief. Her body actually seemed lighter since the previously terrifying idea of saying goodbye to her father was done with.

She was still crushed, of course—just as she had been when her mother had died all those years ago. But this was different. Beth was an adult now. The idea of death was different than it had been for her as a child, though it was no less terrifying.

The pub was a well-to-do country public house, with a rustic interior made up of low ceilings held in place by exposed timber beams, polished wooden floors, a large ornate fireplace, and plush seating. Beth had paid for some food to be served that people seemed to be enjoying. But as Beth looked around those present, she searched for someone in particular. Someone whom she had not expected to turn up to the funeral. Someone who had surprised her.

Her brother, Josh.

Beth had been floored earlier that day when he'd turned up. She had been standing outside of the church, greeting people as they arrived, only to see an old, beat-up car come to a stop close to her. Josh got out. He was dressed in an ill-fitting suit, and his long black hair had been brushed and slicked back. Josh saw her and smiled—the same charming, effortless grin he'd always had. He'd then made his way over.

'Hey, Sis,' he had said, stopping a few paces before her.

Beth had no idea how to respond at first. She truly hadn't been expecting him to turn up. Though she had tried texting and calling him, Beth had no idea if the number she was calling was still current. In the end, she doubted he was even getting her messages. It killed her to think that Josh may not have actually known that his own father was dead. Evidently, however, he did.

'You got my messages, then?' was all Beth could think to ask.

Josh's smile faltered, and he nodded. 'Yeah.'

'Ever think of calling me back? I've been struggling, you know, and it would have been nice to know ahead of time that you were coming.'

He shrugged. It wasn't an arrogant or careless gesture, more an awkward one. 'Sorry,' was all he offered.

There was a long moment of silence. The physical distance between them may have only been a few feet, but to Beth it felt like they were separated by an immense and impenetrable void.

'Was it quick?' Josh had asked.

'Cancer. Took about five months after he was diagnosed.'

'Shame.'

More silence. Other people had arrived, and Beth's attention was split as she turned to greet them. Josh had used the opportunity to disappear inside and escape further judgement from his sister.

After that, Beth had kept a close eye on him during the funeral and cremation. He looked sad, though as far as Beth could tell he didn't shed a tear.

Now that everything was over with, however, she felt the

need to speak to him again. Perhaps clear the air. She was fully aware that anything confrontational or accusatory would send him running for the hills again. Josh had always classed himself as a 'free bird'—his own words—but Beth knew full well it was just his aversion to responsibility. He was also not someone who handled criticism well.

Still, she dearly wanted to speak with him, just to make sure he was doing okay. She wanted to let her little brother know that she was there for him if he needed her.

Taking a long drink from her glass of wine—her fourth of the evening—Beth looked around for him, but it didn't take her long to realise he was not among those gathered anymore. She approached Mr. and Mrs. Askwith, an elderly couple who had lived next door to her father.

'I don't suppose you have seen, Josh, have you?' she asked them.

Mrs. Askwith—a small, five-foot-four lady with grey hair and biting wit—answered first. 'He wasn't what I expected, dear. Your father told us a bit about him, but I thought he'd be a little more... presentable. First time we've met him, you know. Didn't say an awful lot.'

Her husband, a tall gentleman with a kind smile, raised a hand and gently took hold of her arm. 'That wasn't what Beth asked, was it, sweetheart?' He then turned his attention to Beth. 'I did see him heading outside a moment ago. Perhaps he stepped out for a cigarette?'

'Thank you,' Beth said. She had a feeling he hadn't simply stepped outside for that. Beth finished her drink in a single mouthful and walked quickly outside. She headed to the front of the pub, which was set back from the main road by a private car park. It was starting to grow dark, but Beth quickly spotted the car Josh had arrived in. Her eyes were drawn by the white smoke that rolled out from the half-open driver's-side window. The engine was running and she could hear the steady hum of rock music.

Josh was sitting inside, with his head resting back, eyes closed, and a cigarette pinched between his lips. Beth approached him and tapped the glass of the partly open window. Josh's eyes snapped open in surprise and the cigarette fell from his mouth.

'Shit,' he said, coughing smoke and frantically trying to find the dropped stimulant. He eventually retrieved it and chucked out of the window before looking up with an annoyed expression to see who had disturbed him. Upon seeing Beth, however, Josh's features immediately softened.

'Hey, Sis,' he said. 'You scared the hell out of me.'

'Were you sleeping?' Beth asked.

Josh shook his head. 'Just relaxing. I needed to get out of there. Too stuffy.'

'You weren't about to just drive off without saying goodbye again, were you?'

Josh's silence confirmed Beth's suspicion. Anger suddenly bubbled up inside of her. *How can he be so selfish and cold?* 'You really are a piece of work, you know that?'

'Don't be like that, Sis,' he said and cast his eyes down to his hands fidgeting in his lap.

'Be like what?! Don't be honest? What do you expect me to say, Josh? You've been nothing but a ghost to me, and to Dad, for years now. I've tried to keep in touch, to keep us a family, but you just don't give a shit. You just don't care!'

He quickly turned his head to face her. 'I *do* care, Beth. I love you.'

Beth laughed, humourless and cold. 'You care about yourself, Josh, and that's about it. And you only love yourself. You know what, Dad's dead now, and you've paid your respects. Nothing keeping you here anymore. So just run away like you always do.'

'Beth, I...' he started, but then trailed off.

Beth shook her head. 'Just go.'

He looked genuinely hurt, but Beth didn't care anymore. She didn't want to hear any excuses. She was tired of them, and she just wanted him gone.

Josh put the car into gear.

'I'm sorry I'm such a fuck up,' he said. 'But I do love you, Sis. I always will.'

With that, he pulled the car out of the car park and headed off down the road. The sound of AC/DC faded away as Josh drove out of Beth's life yet again.

PRESENT DAY...

It took Beth a moment to realise that tears had welled up in her eyes, and one had escaped down her cheek. The memory of her father's funeral, and her last interaction with Josh, brought with it a lot of anger and sadness. He was right in what he'd said, of course: he *was* a fuck up. But then she thought back to the message he had left her earlier that day, and the fear in his voice.

Beth was reminded of Josh as a ten-year-old boy, and the time he had investigated into a hornets' nest which he'd assumed was old and abandoned. He'd kicked it, not thinking of the consequences, and was then chased all the way home by angry, flying insects, getting stung a few times on the way. With their parents out at work, it fell upon Beth to look after him and apply ointment to the stings, which she gladly did. She then held him until the crying stopped.

The role of the older sibling was one she had always

taken seriously when they were kids, and one she tried to uphold as an adult. She could even pinpoint when the changes in Josh started: when he was fourteen. He'd been the one to find their mother, dead. It shook him up, affected him deeply. Since then, the role of protective older sister was one she struggled with more and more as he pushed her away.

Until now, perhaps.

The hard-rock band continued to blare out from the car's speakers for the rest of the trip. And, just over an hour later, the voice on her sat-nav system came to life, indicating she was nearing her destination.

The road Beth was on had narrowed in a little, allowing just enough space for a car to pass from the opposite direction. She continued forward, up a gradual incline that went on for a few miles, until eventually she reached the peak. There, things levelled out a little, before again falling away into a steep drop. The winding road then ran to a built-up area—a fishing town that was bathed in the gloom of dark clouds. The expanse of the sea—rolling off into the horizon —was visible beyond the buildings of the settlement.

Beth had arrived in Netherwell Bay.

6

THE ROAD ahead dipped down sharply and narrowed even more, making it practically a single lane now. Up ahead, Beth saw a small lay-by on her left-hand side, and she quickly pulled into it rather than just heading straight into town.

She wanted to get her bearings first and take a moment to assess the situation, and so she switched off the engine and stepped out of the vehicle while stretching her legs and back. The air was crisp and clean and felt good in her lungs. She could hear seagulls singing and squawking overhead.

There was a single wooden bench in the lay-by, and on the backrest of the bench was a small plaque commemorating a couple named Walter and Doreen. Beth had no idea who the couple were, but the message of a loving man and wife who would be long remembered, as the plaque read, was touching. From this vantage point, and at such a high altitude from the rest of the town, Beth was greeted to a fantastic view over most of Netherwell Bay.

To her far right on the opposite side of the road was a series of eighteenth-century terraced houses, which ran partway down the steep bank. Each dwelling was stepped in order to keep up with the severity of the slope. The left-hand side of the road, the side she now stood on, was a lush green, with wild grass and trees. That side fell away drastically to meet a small river that cut through the town from the sea. A low and simple wooden-rail fence was all that separated Beth and her vehicle from a grassy drop into the water.

The road she had been travelling on, and the only one into the village as far as she could tell, continued down, and at the bottom she could see a larger built-up area. Red and grey pan-tile roofs were mounted on tall, thin terraced buildings. The walls of the structures were finished in dull red and grey bricks, or white and pastel renders. The streets were narrow, and the levels inconsistent, with steps, drops, and rises in the town's formation. Natural rock walls interspersed with houses cut into rising ground levels, highlighting the fact that the town was etched into a natural and irregular landmass: a mixture of rising cliffs, dipping valleys, and a river that cut through it all.

Where the winding watercourse sliced into the town was evidence of a harbour, with moored boats and narrow wooden walkways. The area was sheltered by raised land on both sides, held back by man-made retaining walls of grey brick and stone. Either side of the river's entrance, and jutting out into the sea, large cliffs could be seen. Two long, stone breakwaters extended from the lower face of these cliffs, running round to meet each other and closing together at their ends like pincers. They left only enough room for small boats to pass between, creating an enclosed body of water.

A steady hum of the waves could be heard beyond the breakwaters, and small fishing boats bobbed up and down on the current of the vast body of water that ran off to the horizon. Beth could detect that distinctly salty sea smell of a coastal town.

Netherwell Bay was obviously a vastly different place than back home, and Beth instantly felt alienated, despite the quaint, old-world aesthetic that poured from the vista ahead. Hell, there was even smoke belching from several chimneys, something she hadn't seen since she was a child, given most homes in the UK were now heated via a gas supply, not by the burning of coals or logs on a fire.

Beth scanned the town, focusing on the built-up area predominately to the right-hand side—from her perspective —of the river. The area seemed to be the hub of Netherwell Bay: a large, tightly packed cluster of buildings. Beth could see houses, shops, even a large pub that overlooked the sea. With no real idea of where to start, this seemed the most logical place.

Beth considered her options.

She could simply start asking questions, trying to find out if anyone here knew or had seen her brother. But that could be risky, especially as she wasn't yet sure just what kind of trouble Josh was in. If the wrong person overheard her asking the wrong kind of question, Beth knew she could put her brother in danger. Paranoid? Perhaps, but it was still a risk.

The other option was to take it slow, get a lay of the land, then see what she could pick up. But that route would take time, and given how scared Josh had sounded in his message, time might not be something he had much of.

Lastly, Beth thought about locating that payphone, the one Josh had called from, to see if she could glean anything from the area around it. The irritable man she'd spoken to may not have seen Josh make the call, but somebody else might have.

Still undecided, she turned back to her car, ready to head deeper into town. She would decide her course of action on the way. However, before she entered the vehicle, a sound caught her attention: a steady tapping, coming from her right, barely audible over the rhythm of the sea.

Beth looked over to one of the houses that lined the road on the opposite side. The one that drew her focus was a fairly nondescript townhouse with brown brickwork, wooden window frames, and a red-tiled roof. It was sand-wiched in-between terraced houses either side, and the source of the sound was emitting from this dwelling, from an upstairs window that had a low sill.

Someone was standing just behind the window, close to it, and was gently rapping their knuckles against the glass, as if to get Beth's attention. When Beth looked closer, her breath caught in her throat.

Whoever this person was, male or female, they were completely naked, allowing Beth to see their mottled and blistered skin. They were also severely malnourished, and scars ran from each shoulder joint and met at the sternum, where a single, raw incision continued down to the abdomen, creating a Y shape on the chest. The person had no genitalia, simply an open wound in its place, indicating something had been cut off... or cut out. The face of the tapping stranger was hidden by stained and dirty bandages that wrapped around their head completely. Other than the tapping on the window, the only other movement from this figure was a quick and constant twitching of its limbs and head, as if they were in the middle of some kind of epileptic fit.

The person continued their steady knocking, and Beth

—in horror—let out a gasp. She instinctively backed away. As she did, her heel caught the edge of the footpath behind her and she fell to the grass, landing on her back. The fall didn't hurt, only startled her, and Beth quickly sat upright and looked up again to the window. The mysterious knocking figure was gone. Beth rose to her feet, feeling her heart pound in her chest, and studied the window closely.

Nothing.

If anyone had indeed been standing there in the first place, they had disappeared quickly. Too quickly. Especially considering Beth had only averted her gaze for a moment.

Beth instinctively looked around to see if there was anyone else present on the street who could make sense of what was going on. But she was alone.

She shivered and could feel goosebumps form on the back of her arms. She quickly got back into the car and decided to head into town while trying to ignore what she had just seen... if, in fact, it had been anything at all. She'd never been one to have hallucinations, but how could she rationally explain what had been up in that window? The state of the body was horrific and more resembled a corpse than a living person.

Putting the car into gear and taking quick, panicked breaths, Beth revved the engine and pulled out of the lay-by, casting a look back up to the window as she did. Still nothing. No deformed, painfully thin figure up there trying to get her attention anymore. She tried to calm herself.

'That was just in your head, Beth,' she told herself. 'Has to be. Just relax.'

She focused on the road ahead, forcing the image of that thing from her mind. Beth had to keep her wits about her when rolling down the steep hill. If an oncoming car came up at speed, she wouldn't have the room to move over and let it pass. Rain started to fall, light for now, but Beth could tell it could easily turn into a downpour, given the dark clouds.

The level of the road she was on sunk below the bank of grass to her right and the houses to her left, which towered over her, making her feel enclosed and claustrophobic. And she was still panicked at that horrible vision behind the window. The road then bent round slightly to the right and began to level out, signalling Beth had entered the town centre.

The way ahead was still narrow, and had buildings either side, though now these buildings had changed from simple townhouses to a mix of commercial and public structures as well. To her right was a large, striking building, constructed from smooth stone blockwork. It stood two stories high and had tall, thin windows with wooden frames and arched heads. A circular window was set into a small gable peak to the front of the building, indicating an inhabited room within the attic space. Black, cast-iron guttering and downpipes complemented the grey slate roof, and there were iron railings to the front that separated the structure from the public footpath before it. A brass plaque was mounted on the wall by the door, and Beth could just make out what it read: Netherwell Bay Heritage Centre.

Other buildings close to it were built from red brick, and still others were layered with white renders, while some were constructed from sandstone block. The variation and mismatched materials lent a quaint, old-world quality to the town, added to by narrow alleyways between buildings, some barely wide enough for a person to walk through. The road and paths were cobbled, and Beth bounced in her seat as she made slow progress along the winding, uneven road, that as yet had offered no off-branches or side roads. Just a long, single route ahead. There were a few people milling around, drifting into quaint shops or gossiping in clusters. Most turned to look at Beth as she slowly passed them, eyeing her vehicle suspiciously. Parked cars either side of the road made her progress even slower, some not pulled over far enough to leave a comfortable space for her to pass.

Beth could see high cliffs beyond the buildings ahead of her. They dominated her view and loomed over the town. Eventually, some turn-offs from the main road opened up, but Beth ignored them and kept going. The way ahead widened out a little. To her left, the buildings faded away, and the thoroughfare ended up running parallel with the river she had previously been adjacent to, though Beth could barely see the water given the size of the drop just beyond the protective railings. On the other side of the river, more houses ran up a hill, this one steeper than the one Beth had just descended. The houses there looked even older than those Beth had already passed. They were also smaller and single storey, with severely worn and weathered brickwork. Beth looked over to that side of the river and saw that it curved away from her at the top. She had a feeling that the road there led up to the plateau of one of the great cliffs that overlooked the sea.

When she turned her attention back to the way ahead, Beth could see the road bloom out farther, creating a large, open, cobbled space that acted as a turning circle. This was, it seemed, the end of the line, as just beyond the edge of the circular space—that reminded Beth of a large courtyard flanked by buildings—was a low stone wall. After a short drop, there was a pebble beach running out to the sea. The open area she found herself on, however, was rife with activity. People were huddled together, looking out to the beach.

Beth also saw a few news vans and camera crews. Something was going on.

A row of parking spaces abutted the low stone wall, of which most were taken. A few, however, remained free, and Beth—with no other route to take—eased herself into one, creeping slowly past the crowd. She parked the car and gave herself a moment to get her bearings, and to try and make sense of the activity outside. But her attention was quickly drawn to the beach beyond the stone wall to her far left. She finally realised what the people gathered here were staring at.

Her stomach tightened as she was able to make out a police presence a few hundred metres away: cars, vans, and a few officers dressed in thick high-visibility coats. The beach curved around the face of one of the great cliffs. Whatever was going on with the police, most of it was blocked from view by the the cliff. However, Beth could tell what was going on was serious. Both from the number of police vehicles—which, given the lack of access, must have driven up the beach from somewhere else—but also because that area of beach was cordoned off with tape.

Beth had a terrible feeling about it all. Her mind ran to Josh. Could something have happened to him?

Please, God, don't let him be dead.

Beth watched the police's movements for a few minutes, but she could see nothing of any further interest. In fact, the officers present moved around very slowly, aimlessly, as if simply standing guard. Beth's guess was that the crime scene had been here for a while now, and most of the important work had likely been done already. The news crews, too, seemed to be just waiting, with no reports currently being filmed.

Going onto the beach to try and talk with the police

would be useless, Beth knew, as they would tell her nothing. However, the gathered crowd might reveal more information. Beth disembarked from the car, pulled her coat tight, and walked closer to the pockets of people while trying to listen in to conversations. Not many were talking, but she did hear that the police had been out there since early morning. A few people even started to slope off, seemingly having had their fill. Before Beth could ask anyone anything, however, the heavens opened, and that light rain quickly started to lash down heavily. The crowd then began to fully disperse, and the camera crews jumped back into their vehicles.

Damn it.

Beth needed to get out of this rain, at least for now. She noticed one of the buildings close to her—the one with white render and slate roof tiles—had a large painted sign on its gable face that read the Trout and Lobster.

It was a pub, evidently, and quite a large one. A small glass of wine sounded just the thing to calm Beth's nerves until the rain passed. And The Trout and Lobster suddenly seemed like the perfect place to start her investigation proper. Beth cast one last look back out to the police on the beach before running inside of the pub.

7

AFTER MOVING through a small draft lobby and into the main area of the pub, Beth was greeted by a blast of warmth from a ceiling-mounted heating unit above her. She stood under the comforting, hot air, letting it radiate into her bones and dry her a little, and allowed herself to take in her surroundings. It was fair to say that the interior aesthetic of this place was in desperate need of attention. A single word summed it up perfectly: gaudy.

While spacious enough, with high ceilings held up by intermittent brick pillars, it was the decoration that left a lot to be desired.

The wallpaper looked to have once been a plush red, with golden sea-shell imprints, though the colours looked to have faded considerably. The floors were bare-timber boards, but they didn't appear to have been treated in a long time, and were stained and discoloured. But the worst of it was the maritime decorations that hung on the walls and ceilings: mounted fish, ship-wheels, and nets draped from the ceiling that were littered with fake starfish and shellfish. A large steel anchor even dominated a wall to Beth's left. It wasn't the fact that these items were all maritime that put Beth off. That all made sense, considering the kind of town she was in. However, it was the sheer *quantity* of them. It was too much.

Alright, we get it, this is a coastal town pub.

The whole pub had an unmistakable smell of cigarette smoke that was almost overbearing. Beth knew it would cling to her long after she had left this place.

Straight ahead was a large seating area with lots of empty tables and booths. In fact, there was only a single family of three present there—a man, woman, and toddler —all eating a meal. Beth reasoned that this was the restaurant section of the establishment. Beyond that, she could see a drinking area up ahead. The width of the pub narrowed in that space. Stools were lined up against the bar, there were small, circular tables in a central area, and a few fabric-lined benches were pressed against the wall opposite the bar. This area, though smaller than the restaurant section, was considerably busier, and all of the noise and chatter seemed to be coming from there—especially from a group of gathered men near the bar, all laughing and swearing with abandon. Billows of thick cigarette and cigar smoke rolled from the drinking space, and it was clear that the pub was an establishment that chose to the ignore the 'no smoking in a public place' law. A few of the patrons looked over and stared at Beth, but she steeled herself, having been in places she was not welcome many times before. It was part of her job. Well, her *former* job. She made her way over to the bar, though the walk felt like an eternity as she passed through the practically empty restaurant section while everyone watched. She sidled up to a bar stool, the conversation notably muted as she did. Beth ignored it and caught the barman's—or bar-*boy's*— attention with as friendly a smile as she could muster.

The thin young lad serving barely looked over sixteen— and given it was a weekday, should probably have been in school. A thin layer of dark fuzz lined his top lip, and pimples were scattered across his rosy cheeks. His dark hair was messy, sticking up at the back, and he looked as if he'd just rolled out of bed. He gave Beth a shy smile, showing braces behind his lips, and cautiously approached her.

'C... can I get you something?' he asked. Beth knew she would likely need to drive again today, so she really shouldn't be drinking at all. But she reasoned that one little beverage couldn't hurt, nor would it impede her judgment or reflexes too much.

'I'll have a small, dry white wine please,' she replied, still holding her smile. The barboy nodded, then turned away to fix her drink. Still feeling eyes on her, Beth cast a glance to her right. Beside her, a small, frail-looking old man sat at the bar, perched on a stool. He was sipping a tumbler of amber-coloured liquid and kept his eyes firmly on his drink, minding his own business. But beyond him, leaning up against the bar, was a group of four men, all roughly in their late thirties and early forties. The leader of them, who had been the loudest, was a short-haired brute with a thick neck and white t-shirt that was far too small to contain his wide arms and bulging beer-belly. He made no effort to hide his admiring gaze. The man wore a chunky gold chain around his neck and had tattoos covering his forearms. Beth locked eyes with him for a moment and he flashed her an ugly smile, making it painfully clear he liked what he saw. Beth simply averted her gaze away from him, looking over at the rest of the patrons instead.

There was another old gentleman sitting on the bench

against the back wall, and he was joined by a younger man; they bore a striking resemblance to each other. The older of the two was dressed in an old, checkered shirt with burgundy trousers. His aged face was a mixture of deep wrinkles and thick tufts of white hair that sprouted from random places. He had wild, bushy eyebrows and a thick, grey stubble. Without question, Beth knew that the man had once been a fisherman. The person next to him, the younger of the two, shared many of the same characteristics, such as a rather square-shaped face and thick hair—though his hair still had streaks of black mixed in with the grey. He wore waders with a black, long-sleeved vest beneath.

Father and son, Beth assumed. A small, sandy-coloured Terrier dog lay asleep at their feet.

The bar-boy set down Beth's drink. 'One pound, fifteen pence, please, ma'am,' he said, trying to sound polite. Beth nearly fell off her stool. Back home, the same drink would have cost well over five pounds. She handed him the money and took her change.

'Thank you,' she said, and took a sip. She kept her expression neutral, holding off a grimace, but knew instantly *why* the prices here were so cheap.

The chatter between the drinkers soon picked back up. Beth kept her ears open, listening for anything that could lead her to Josh, or something relating to what was going on outside.

It didn't take her long.

Beth's attention was quickly drawn to the group of men at the bar, where her thuggish admirer was holding court.

'I heard it was a mess. Guts everywhere.'

'Can't believe they still don't know who it was that got cut up,' another added.

The ringleader smiled and shook his head. 'Police know

who is dead, I reckon, it just won't be common knowledge yet. They certainly ain't told the press. I was speaking to the reporters outside and they don't seem to have a clue yet.' The man speaking then looked over to Beth once more and, with a smug grin, added, 'So they won't know who the killer is, either.'

Beth didn't look back at him—didn't allow herself a reaction—even though she felt a deep sense of dread building. Evidently someone had been killed, and in a rather gruesome fashion, it would seem—though the group of men were talking about it with such glee that they could have just as easily been talking about a game of football.

Was it Josh? Was that why he called this morning, because he was in fear for his life? Or, if not him, was he somehow involved in a murder? Was that the reason he had sounded so panicked?

Despite his troubles in life, Beth would have never thought Josh was capable of killing. But his message, begging Beth to come to the place, coupled with the apparent murder she was now learning about, couldn't have just been a coincidence.

Could it?

She took another sip of her wine... a sip that turned into a long mouthful of the vinegar-tinged drink. Then the glass was empty.

'I'll have another,' Beth said to the boy behind the bar. His eyebrows were raised in slight surprise at seeing how quickly she'd finished her drink. But he dutifully prepared her another and set it on the table, again taking her payment and giving change.

This second wine was a mistake, Beth knew, and would likely put her over the limit to drive, but she felt her dread rising further, threatening to turn into full-blown anxiety.

She needed to calm herself to think clearly. Perhaps alcohol wasn't the best thing for that, but it was all she had on hand.

'Christ, you're a good drinker, aren't you, love?' the thug with the gold chain said to Beth. 'That went down so quick I don't think it touched the sides of your throat.'

Beth gave a well-practiced and stern smile. One that showed no humour and simply said: *fuck off and leave me alone.*

He didn't get the hint. Or, he just ignored it. 'I like your eyes,' he said, stepping around the old man that separated them, then leaning against the bar next to Beth. 'A real strong blue, ain't they?'

Yes, you fuckwit, Beth thought. *They* are *a strong blue. Is that really your best line?*

Beth was readying herself to let him down, and not particularly gently, when a side door to the bar area opened, and another older man walked in. He was wet from the rain and flanked by a dog—this one a black-and-white Border Collie.

This man was broad and relatively tall for someone his age, with grey hair that was brushed back. He bore a long, flat nose and square jaw that was softened slightly with sagging jowls. He walked with a stick, the brass bottom of which tapped on the timber floor as he entered.

'Afternoon, Jim,' the man, who now stood next to Beth said, thankfully averting his attention from her. 'Don't often see you in here anymore. Thought you'd kicked the drink?'

'I need one today,' the old man said. Beth took note of the name the thug had used.

Jim took off his waterproof coat, then approached the bar and ordered a pint of stout, which was served thick and black, like tar. He grabbed his drink and moved to a seat along the opposite wall. The sleeping Terrier awoke and, upon seeing the Collie, started to yap and bark. The larger dog simply responded with a quick growl, shutting the Terrier up instantly, and continued with its owner. The dog then lay at Jim's feet as he sat down.

'You're looking a little peaky, Jim,' the man next to Beth said. She could smell his sharp aftershave. 'You not feeling too good?'

'I'm fine, Pete,' Jim replied. 'Just wanna have a drink in peace.'

Pete held his hands up defensively, though he didn't look away from Jim, and the smile he wore was practically a sneer. 'Fair enough, old man.' Jim didn't respond, so Pete went on, 'Heard the news? About what they found over at Hollows Cove?'

The old man didn't make eye contact with Pete, but Beth noticed Jim's body stiffen up. He then shifted slightly in his seat and it was clear to Beth that he knew something.

The young bar-boy then leaned over towards Pete and whispered something Beth was just about able to make out. 'I heard it was Jim that found the bodies. He was the one that called the police.'

Pete's eyes widened, so much so that they threatened to pop out of his head. 'No fucking way!'

Beth was also a little taken back. Not because the old man was the person who had called the crime in, but because the boy had used the plural. *Bodies.*

Just what the hell was going on here?

'What?' one of the other men asked. 'What did the lad tell you, Pete?'

Pete strode away from the bar with an arrogant swagger as he stepped towards Jim. 'Is that true, Jimmy? You the one that found that mess this morning?' Jim didn't answer or make eye contact. But that was good enough for Pete. 'You did, didn't you?' The thuggish man let out a bellowing laugh. 'Shit, Jim, you gotta tell me about it! Did you recognise any of the poor fuckers?'

'I'm not in the mood to talk about it, boy,' Jim said sternly.

'But *I* am,' Pete replied, pulling a stool up to the table close to Jim. Pete took a seat, set down his drink, and laid his meaty forearms on the table's surface. 'And I want all the details.'

8

'I GOT NOTHING TO SAY, PETE,' Jim replied before he took a drink of the thick, black liquid from his glass. The frothy head left a white, bubbly layer on his upper lip.

'Come on, Jim,' the younger man pressed. 'Spill it. What was it you found? I heard the bodies were all cut up. Jeff over there,' Pete pointed to one of his friends, 'was told there was three of them. Is that right?'

'It was a mistake coming here,' Jim said, clearly agitated. He started to get to his feet and grabbed his glass. Pete shot out a hand and took hold of Jim's arm. The pub fell silent.

'No, don't leave. Just sit and talk to me, old man. No need to run off.'

'Leave me be, Pete!' Jim snapped, baring his teeth. His dog was now up on its feet and gave a low growl. Beth felt like the situation could spiral out of control at any moment. This older man clearly didn't want to talk about what he'd seen, but Pete didn't appear to care.

But Beth was interested to learn what Jim knew. Part of her wanted him to give in to Pete and divulge, if only for her own benefit. It was all far too much of a coincidence to not have anything to do with Josh's call.

'Better stop that mutt growling at me, before I kick its face off,' Pete said, curling his top lip. His own face was a picture of anger, and he glared at the snarling dog.

'Let go of my arm and she'll stop,' Jim said. He didn't wait for Pete to comply, however, and simply yanked his arm free, surprising the younger man with his speed and strength. 'Leave me be,' Jim stated, then squeezed himself past Pete and walked away towards the emptier restaurant area. His dog followed dutifully behind.

'Suit yourself,' Pete said, scowling. 'You miserable old cunt.'

Jim, with his back to them all, stopped suddenly. Beth expected him to turn around and stride back over to Pete. Thankfully, the old man eventually continued on, avoiding any further conflict. Beth sensed Pete and his friends would be quite happy escalating things to violence if they felt their fragile manhood was ever threatened.

Jim wandered to an empty booth and sat down. His dog crawled under the table. The bar area was still silent, everyone waiting to see how Pete would now react. Pete got to his feet, downed what was left of his drink, and returned to the bar. He slammed the empty glass down and barked out his order.

'Whiskey. Double.'

The young boy jumped to action and gave Pete his drink. Beth noticed the boy didn't take any money. Pete took a sip, then turned around and leaned his elbows back on the bar. Beth could feel the anger radiating from him. But Pete then cast a confident smile. 'Fuck the old clown,' he said with a laugh. 'We'll find out what happened soon enough. Nothing ever stays secret in this town. Not for long, anyway.'

There were a few chuckles, then the bar seemed to come to life again. People began to talk, though at a lower level than before, as if Pete's relatively lighthearted comments were permission for them to carry on with their conversations. It was clear to Beth that the man held quite a lot of sway here, likely through fear, and was probably best avoided if she could help it.

Then she thought again of Josh. Had he got caught up with Pete somehow? And was the thug, who at that moment cast Beth another glance, actually involved in the murders he claimed to want to know more about?

It was all conjecture, of course, but she did not return his admiring glance. Beth didn't want to be anywhere near him. The one person she did want to talk to, however, had just moved away from them, and didn't seem in the mood for chit-chat.

She considered her options as she took a mouthful of her drink, forcing herself to keep from shuddering. It truly was awful stuff. Though, in truth, the second glass had been more palatable than the first.

If she went over to Jim's table to start a conversation, in all likelihood he would tell her to get lost. But, more than that, Pete and his friends would no doubt take an interest, and she really didn't want to draw their attention. However, she couldn't let the opportunity slip. It was all she really had to go on, even if she couldn't be one-hundred-percent certain the apparent murders had anything to do with Josh.

So, if she couldn't talk to him here in the pub, then she needed to do it somewhere else.

An idea formed.

The steady rat-a-tat-tat of rain on the windows had eased, indicating the heavy storm was coming to an end outside. And Beth figured Jim would leave the pub soon.

Given what the man had seen earlier, Beth guessed that he had only come in for a drink to help calm his nerves—just like she had. That hadn't gone well for him.

Beth simply could wait outside, watch the pub, and bide her time until Jim came out. She could then either speak to him, or even watch and wait, to see where he headed. It was better than sitting here all night, and her instincts were screaming at her to act.

She quickly finished her drink, and part of her dearly wanted to order another. The taste was becoming more and more bearable now, and it had given her a pleasant buzz, but she pushed that craving to one side. Keeping her eyes away from Pete—who she could feel was still staring at her —she got up.

'Not going anywhere yet are you, love?' Pete asked. Beth just ignored him and left, walking through the restaurant area. She heard Pete mutter 'Bitch,' but ignored it, even though it was a struggle to do so. There were more important things at hand. As Beth walked, she passed Jim. The poor old man looked ashen, his eyes forlorn. He was over halfway through his drink already.

She kept going and strode outside into the open air, that smelled damp from the recent rain. There was a chill to the breeze now. The falling rain was merely a drizzle. The cobbles underfoot were damp and shiny. Only one or two stragglers remained looking out at the beach. The news crews were still huddled inside their vans, despite the weather easing.

Even with clean and brisk air in her lungs—a change from the smoky interior of the pub—Beth still felt a little fuzzy-headed. Two drinks had been a mistake, and Beth chided herself for succumbing so easily. She had to focus and try to figure out where the best place would be to wait for Jim.

She knew there were at least two entrances to the pub: the one she just left through, and the side door she had seen Jim use to enter. But the size of the building meant that watching both exits at the same time would be impossible. So, she had to pick one.

Given Jim had moved away from the bar area—and away from Pete—Beth figured he would likely follow her out of the main door she had just left through. That would mean he wouldn't have to pass Pete again, either. It was as good a guess as any, and it that way she could wait in the relative comfort and warmth of her car while scoping out the large, rendered building.

She started to walk over to her vehicle, her feet wobbling slightly on the cobbles underfoot. *Hadn't anyone in this town heard of asphalt?* Beth was certain the locals here must have had to spend a fortune each year on fixing the suspension to their cars.

The police presence was still on the beach, she noted, and the activity looked as muted and low-key as when Beth had first spotted it.

Had the bodies already been removed? It seemed likely.

As Beth got closer to her car, however, she heard something on the wind that drew her attention. A series of murmurs seemed to be coming from beyond the low stone wall which separated the parking area from the beach beyond.

Beth furrowed her brow and started to walk over to the wall that came up roughly to her knees. The drop beyond was a little more substantial, but only by a couple of feet or so, and whatever was making the sound was hidden from view. There was something about the noises that troubled her. Her concern rose the closer she got—the sounds rising and becoming more and more clear. A knot formed in her stomach as Beth realised what that noise was.

But it couldn't be.

The sound of crying children—babies—was now unmistakable, though apparently it was loud enough for only her to hear, given no one else was as close. Panic rose as Beth ran up to the wall. The cries turned into distressed screaming.

What the hell is happening to them?

Beth reached the wall and quickly leaned over to look down the short drop to the stony beech below. A shriek of horror escaped her.

This can't be real!

They weren't children. Not quite.

Though the bodies of the writhing, purple things that glistened red were of a similar size to babies, and they had roughly the same shape and appendages, it was clear they were something else entirely. Their bodies were smooth, with fingers and toes fused together, but it was the faces of these horrific monsters that so terrified Beth.

The eyes were two little black orbs, like small shark eyes, positioned on the side of the heads. They had no nose, and the only other feature on the faces was a round mouth that sat central. It stretched and contracted like the suckers on a leech. Small, jagged teeth were visible just behind the rubbery edges of the puckering maws. The child-like wails emitted from the creatures were growing louder and louder.

Beth backpedalled, unable to make sense of what she had seen.

Can't be real, can't be real, can't be real.

The image of the knocking figure in the second-storey

window from earlier sprung back into her mind. What the hell was going on here?

Beth backed up into a car behind her, and she let herself slump to the floor in horror while clutching her head in her hands. She pressed her palms over her ears in an attempt to drown out the horrific sounds. That was when she realised she was crying.

What the fuck were those things?

She didn't feel safe being so close to the wall... and what was beyond it. She had to get away from this madness. And only when safe could she try to make sense of it all. Beth forced herself to her feet, and then noticed it...

The awful cries and shrieks of the monstrous infants had ceased.

The only sounds Beth could now hear were the natural ones of the town: cars, seagulls, and the waves of the sea. After a moment's hesitation, she slowly made her way back over to the wall. Beth was sure—absolutely certain—that what she had seen was real. *And* she had heard them.

But now, with everything silent, Beth was reminded of her fall earlier after seeing the thing in the window. It had vanished quickly. And, sure enough, as Beth cautiously peeked over the wall again, all she could see was the shiny stones of the beach, and a small, skittering crab that ran over them.

No twisted, nightmarish versions of babies wriggling around together in a terrible, writhing mass.

Beth shook her head, unwilling to accept what now seemed obvious—that she had been seeing things. Twice in the space of a short time, no less.

No.

She didn't believe that. Couldn't believe it. Those things weren't just in her head. They couldn't have been.

Her heart was still racing, and she backed up again, still sobbing slightly. Something was wrong here in this town. Something was *very* wrong.

'You okay?'

The voice startled her. Beth spun around and saw that some people were gazing at her with puzzled expressions. A worried-looking old man stood closest, only a few feet away, and he had a black dog in tow.

It was Jim.

9

'I'M... I...' Beth had no idea how to answer Jim's question. Her mind was struggling to make sense of what she had just seen.

Jim frowned, seemingly sceptical of her, yet his face still carried a look of concern. 'You look a little unsteady. Why don't you sit down?' he offered, gesturing to the wall behind her. The one that Beth, only moments ago, had looked over and seen those horrible deformities. She didn't want to be anywhere near that wall.

'I'm okay,' she said finally, forcing herself to sound strong.

Jim nodded. 'Okay. Your eyes are running a little though. You been crying?'

Beth shook her head. 'No, it's just the wind in my face. It made my eyes water.'

Jim looked around, and Beth knew he was taking note of the air around him. While there was a breeze, it certainly wasn't a strong wind. 'Fair enough,' he said, but Beth could easily detect the doubt in his voice. 'I'll leave you to it.' He then turned to look down at his dog. 'Come on, Jess.'

Jim turned to walk away, but Beth quickly stopped him. 'Wait,' she said, her voice slightly raised. And, she realised, sounding slightly desperate.

Get it together.

Over the years, Beth had interviewed a lot of people, and she'd learned that one of the best ways to get them to open up was to be calm, relaxed, and understanding. The first step in gaining someone's trust was presenting yourself as someone worthy of it. Right now, she wasn't coming off in a positive light to Jim, who was looking at her with a raised eyebrow while he waited for her to continue.

'Sorry,' Beth said, trying hard to gain control. 'I've just been watching the police over there. And I was inside a few moments ago, too, and heard you talking to that pig of a man about what you found earlier today. The thought of knowing some people were killed over there,' she pointed to the cordoned-off area on the beach, 'it's a lot to take in. I must have gotten myself a little upset. I'm guessing that was where you found... whatever it was you found?'

Jim's features softened a little and he nodded. He remained silent, however. Beth had already figured the place of Jim's discovery and the police area on the beach were one in the same, but now she had confirmation.

'Must have been terrible to see,' Beth said, keeping her voice low and gentle. 'I hope you're okay?'

Jim gave her a sad smile. 'I'll be fine,' he said. 'Can't say I recognise you, though. Never seen you around. You new here?'

'Oh, I don't live in Netherwell Bay,' Beth replied with a shake of her head. 'Just visiting.'

'Visiting someone you know?' Jim asked, and Beth was suddenly aware that he was sizing her up and fishing for information. Clearly, he was still wary of her.

'No,' Beth said, thinking quickly. 'Just taking some time for myself. Wanted to get away from it all.'

'And you picked Netherwell to visit? Seems odd, lady, as there ain't a lot here.'

'Oh, I don't know,' she replied. 'I love these quaint coastal towns. They are so peaceful.' Beth cast a look over to the beach and the police. 'At least, they usually are. Can't say I expected this.'

'Your accent,' Jim went on. 'Doesn't sound local. You not from round here?'

It felt like an interrogation. Beth's best efforts to disarm the old man's defences were coming up short. He didn't trust her, that was clear.

'I... I have, I guess,' Beth answered. She knew where he was going with the question, but she couldn't think of a way to derail the conversation. And she didn't get the chance.

'So, you come all this way, to a small, forgotten, and dying place like this, just because you like little seaside towns? Is that it?'

And there it was. Beth flushed and felt incredibly stupid. She still wasn't thinking clearly after what she'd just seen.

'Well, when you put it like that it sounds—'

Jim held up a palm and cut her off. 'Listen. I don't like being lied to. There ain't nothing here for tourists. And, I'm sorry, but you saying you got upset at what you heard in the pub back there has about as much truth to it as a politician's speech. Now, to be honest, it ain't none of my business *what* you are doing here. I don't much care. But I'll tell you this: Netherwell Bay ain't a place you want to stay. So, you'd be wise to take my advice and just leave town as soon as you can. Forget whatever it is that brought you here and go.'

Beth was silent for a moment, before answering honestly, 'I can't.'

Jim nodded. 'I see. Well, if you'll excuse me, miss, I've had a hell of a day. It started badly, and then I had to spend most of it with the police. Thought a drink in this place,' he motioned to the Trout and Lobster behind him, 'might have helped, but that didn't work out too well. So now I just want to go home. If you won't take my advice, then good luck to you.'

He then turned and walked away. Beth wanted to shout after him again, to get him to stop, to try to gain his favour. But she knew it was pointless. It would come across as being too desperate, and the man's guard was already up. It was a lost cause with him... for now.

But there was still something she could do while standing around. Beth walked up to one of the news vans. It was white, with the words 'North East News' brandished across the side in blue. She knocked on the door. A woman with long blonde hair and immaculate makeup was sitting inside the passenger side. Beth instantly knew this woman was a reporter who would be featured on camera. The window lowered and the young woman greeted Beth with a smile.

'Can I help you?' the woman asked.

'Yeah, just wondering what's going on? A few people inside the pub back there are saying there have been some murders. Is that true?'

Beth had no idea how much information the reporter would be willing to share, if she even knew anything. Being one herself—for a newspaper rather than a television channel—Beth knew her kind were a funny breed. Some were happy to divulge a little information to bystanders in the hopes of learning something new. Others, if they had nothing to gain, were very tight-lipped.

'We've heard that, too, but not a whole lot more. Possibly three dead,' she replied. 'Can you tell me what you know?'

Beth shrugged. 'Just that there have been some people killed—murdered, apparently—and that it looks pretty gruesome. I don't know anything else. Just curious.'

'Well, the police aren't saying much yet. We are hoping for a statement soon, but I don't know any more than that, to be honest. We don't even have enough to run a proper story, and all we know for sure is that there's a police presence here. The murders aren't even confirmed, just what some locals are saying.'

'Okay, thank you,' Beth said, beginning to grow frustrated.

'Hey,' the woman said, suddenly digging into her pocket. 'Do me a favour, will you?' She handed Beth a card with the name Karen Porter written on it, along with a mobile phone number. 'If you do hear anything else that is of interest, will you call to let me know? We're struggling for leads here.'

'I will,' Beth said with a smile. It was a lie, of course, unless she felt the woman could help her with her own search.

Beth turned and looked back out to the beach. This time she kept her gaze away from the police, and gazed out to the sea instead.

The murders, Josh's message, the things she was seeing... something was very wrong here in Netherwell. She didn't have the first clue as to what that was, yet, but she had an awful feeling her little brother was somehow tied up in it all.

If he was still alive—and she prayed to God that he was —then Beth was going to do everything in her power to help him. She swore to herself that she wouldn't leave this place until Josh was safe. No matter what it took.

She would figure this all out for him.

10

JIM MADE his way back to his bungalow, crossing the river at the first footbridge he came to, which took him to Old Town. He then hiked up the steep bank.

The area of town on this side of the river was smaller than the main section, and was part of the original settlement. Netherwell Bay had only expanded beyond the separating watercourse decades after the first homes were built.

The incline made Jim's calves burn like it always did, but he pushed on, passing the small houses to his right. The day's events weighed heavily on him.

Even beyond the obvious. The interaction with that lady back in the town centre stuck with him, too. After first seeing her, looking pale and scared, he'd thought she had found something similar to what he had that morning.

But no, instead she had tried to feed him what was clearly a bunch of bullshit, and he was good at spotting bullshit. He had no idea why, but it was clear the woman just wanted to find out what he'd seen over in Hollows Cove.

Jim had never in all his years living here seen the lady before, and Netherwell wasn't a place that got many visitors.

Still, something had seemed familiar about her, and as soon as he heard her speak, he'd put it together.

The woman's accent was the same as young Josh's.

The two certainly had a look of each other. Brother and sister, he'd wager. And, if she were anything like him, then that meant she was trouble. If not, then the poor woman probably didn't want to know what had become of Josh.

Jim made it to the crest of the bank, where the houses to his right curved away. Suddenly, a realisation struck. That was probably why she was here—looking for her brother. He couldn't be certain, of course, and he'd made quite a lot of assumptions, but Jim figured it wasn't a bad guess.

Jim followed the curve of the houses, walking along the now level road ahead. His bungalow was towards the end of the row, and the back looked out over the grass of the clifftop, giving a majestic view of the sea. The Overview Lodge, Ms. Jacobs' bed and breakfast guest house, was situated at the far end of the street. Being three stories, it dwarfed its neighbour, separated from it by a long double driveway. The Overview Lodge, like most other buildings along the street, had a white rendered finish to the walls to protect from the driving rain and wind, and the pitched roof was a dark red tile. It had bay windows on either side of the entrance door, and those were repeated up each of the three floors. It was a grand-looking place, though it got little business. Jim knew that the only reason it still carried on was because Ms. Jacobs owned it outright.

She was a strange woman. To Jim, at least. Her smile always seemed like a condescending sneer, and she mainly kept to herself.

Jim continued on, getting closer to his home. Given all that had happened that day, it suddenly felt like an age to Jim since he had left his little house that morning. He'd followed a different route then, following the pathway down the other side of the cliff while weaving through trees and shrubbery, a much more naturalistic trail than the way he'd taken back, which had cut through the town centre. Of course, he had been massively waylaid today. Given Nethwerwell didn't have its own police force, he'd had to go out of town to give his statement. The officers had taken him and Jess to the station via a police cruiser, after he'd insisted his dog come along, and had dropped them off near the Trout and Lobster when finished, but only after grilling Jim on everything he had seen.

According to them, such an act of savage violence and murder was unheard of in Netherwell Bay. Obviously, their memory didn't stretch back very far. Or, more accurately, they were too young to know what had happened in this town all those years ago.

Because if they did know, they—like Jim—would be terrified it was happening again.

Jim reached his bungalow, which had pastel-green render, a grey slate roof, and wooden sash windows—the frames of which he'd freshly painted only this past spring. He'd kept the place in as good an order as he could, but without Ada around to give it her special touch, the house wasn't the same. It was still Jim's, though. Bought and paid for.

He unlocked the latch and stepped through the door, into the open living area. Jess brushed past his legs and trotted over to her water bowl in the kitchen, which was accessed off the living room by a door in the far wall. Jim heard the dog noisily lap up the liquid, no doubt spilling a good portion onto the tiled floor.

There was no entrance lobby, and the front door led straight into the living area itself. He'd kept the flower-patterned wallpaper that Ada loved so much, though it dearly needed replacing. A large fireplace with a chunky timber mantelpiece was fitted to the side wall, and the floor was lined with a thick blue carpet. The room was quite cluttered with Jim's books and magazines strewn about and a high leather sofa opposite the fireplace. Jim dearly loved to read and hadn't bothered buying a television after the one he'd shared with Ada broke a few years prior. The mantelpiece above the fire was lined with pictures, mostly of Ada, and her urn sat centrally on it.

A door to the right of the living room led out into a short corridor, and from there the toilet and two bedrooms could be accessed. Jim knew he should really go to the bedroom and change, feeling grubby after his day, but he just couldn't seem to muster the energy. Instead, he shuffled over to the sofa and dropped down into it, sighing as he felt the aches of his body catch up to him. A deep feeling of worry had burrowed into his gut, building constantly since that morning, to the point he felt sick.

'Hell of a day, hun,' Jim said to the brass urn on the mantelpiece. 'I have a bad feeling about what's coming.'

'WELL, I HAVE PLENTY OF ROOM,' the old woman on the other
side of the counter said to Beth. 'But that really isn't the
point. Our policy is that guests have to book ahead.'

Beth held back an exasperated sigh and tried not to
show her annoyance. 'I understand, and I'm sorry. If I'd
planned ahead better I would have booked, but this has all
been very last minute. Would you mind letting me rent a
room? I'd really appreciate it.'

The Overview Lodge. That was where Beth now found
herself.

After Beth's brief interaction with Jim, she had felt at a
loss and was unsure of her next step. With dusk setting in,
though, she knew there was no chance of her going back
home that night. That focused her mind and made the next
step simple: accommodation.

She'd spotted a small shop only a few hundred yards
away that was still open. Beth had trotted inside and spoken
to the owner, asking about any local accommodation. The
Overview Lodge was the only place the man knew of, and
he gave Beth directions. While at the shop, Beth bought a

pack of sandwiches, a few bottles of water, and a container of fruit salad, just in case this Overview had no food facilities. After a brief hesitation, she had also added a couple of bottles of strong red wine to the order.

It was a short drive to the hotel, and Beth just wanted to get a room and try to relax. Trouble was, the owner seemed intent on making things difficult. She was a small, frail looking woman with a stern face, light makeup, and grey hair pulled back in a bun. The angular glasses perched on the old woman's nose reminded Beth of a strict school-teacher who was well overdue retirement. The old woman was dressed in a long-sleeved blouse with a flowered pattern.

She had introduced herself as Ms. Jacobs, then *promptly* refused Beth's request for a room. Beth had assumed they must have been full if the woman wasn't willing to let her stay, but that apparently wasn't the case.

The little old woman studied Beth with an expressionless stare. Beth, for her part, resisted leaning over the counter and screaming, 'Do you want my fucking money or not?'

Beth's day so far had been a royal bitch, and at that moment all she wanted to do—no, *needed* to do—was to find somewhere comfortable and take a nice hot bath. Hell, even though she was hungry, food could wait. She just needed somewhere to lay her head.

'Fine,' Ms. Jacobs said, eventually. 'But you will have to pay upfront. That is non-negotiable.'

'No problem,' Beth replied, setting her bag down on the oak reception desk and pulling out her purse. The reception area was little more than an entrance hall and stairway, but a spacious one. There were doors off to the left and right painted white with thick, detailed architraves. The ceilings were high, and the area was lit by a dangling chandelier and tasteful, wall-mounted lights. The floor was tightly butted pine planks with a polished finish, and the stairs had a plush red carpet. The whole area smelled strongly of incense.

'So how many nights will you be staying?' Ms. Jacobs asked, smiling politely. It was an unnatural smile, however, forced, and Beth noticed stained teeth behind the woman's thin lips.

Beth paused. She hadn't considered that. 'Erm... three nights?'

It was the first number that came into her head. Beth wasn't sure if that was enough time, or even too much time. Regardless, if she was able to help Josh, but overpaid as a result, so be. If she needed more time, then she would likely have to negotiate with Ms. Jacobs again.

'Three nights,' the old woman repeated. 'That will be six hundred pounds.'

Beth paused. Two hundred pounds a night seemed excessive for a room in such a small town, especially one that had no tourism to speak of. Still, Beth knew that she would get nowhere trying to barter, and Ms. Jacobs had likely inflated her prices just because she could. Beth had been too eager by practically begging for the room, playing right into the old woman's hands. So, Beth decided to accept with no argument.

'That's fine,' Beth said, then pulled out her credit card. As the transaction was going through, Ms. Jacobs cast Beth a curious gaze.

'Everything okay?' Beth asked, a little uncomfortable.

'Your accent,' the woman replied. 'Not a local one. You from down South?'

Beth nodded, not feeling the need to lie. 'Yes, I am. That a problem?'

The woman scoffed. 'Of course not. Just don't get many southerners here. Can't imagine what brought you to Netherwell Bay.'

Beth decided to leave that unanswered, and the two remained silent until the card machine started to print out a receipt. Eventually, Ms. Jacobs handed Beth a copy, along with a key.

'Room three. First floor. Take the stairs here.'

'Thanks. What time is breakfast tomorrow?'

Ms. Jacobs shook her head. 'We don't serve it.'

Beth's eyes opened a little wider.

'But it's a bed *and breakfast*,' Beth exclaimed.

The woman just shrugged. 'The Chef isn't working today.'

Six hundred pounds for only three nights, and no breakfast? It was a con. But Beth was desperate, and so she swallowed her annoyance. 'I'll eat elsewhere. Thank you.'

Ms. Jacobs just nodded and again sat at her desk. She picked up the book she had been reading and started to study the pages. Evidently, their interaction was finished.

'Bye then,' Beth said and headed upstairs, her carry-all in hand. She easily found the room on the first floor, and, upon entering, was quite impressed. Not two-hundred-pounds-a-night impressed, but still. It could have been much, much worse.

The room was spacious, with a high, four-poster bed that looked nice and soft. The pillows and quilt had white covers with grey, flowered patterns which matched the pelmet at the head, and valance at the base. The walls had white wallpaper to them, and the carpet was a very light grey, and it felt soft and thick underfoot. Tied-back curtains framed a tall window with Georgian bars across the glass. The view out over the cliff's plateau was as good as Beth had hoped, though it was growing quite dark outside now, which lent the vista an ominous feel.

An old-style television sat on a chest of drawers against the wall opposite the bed. A door beside the drawers led to the en-suite. The bathroom was roomy as well, with a double shower, toilet, and vanity unit with a handwash basin set into it. A large mirror stood above the vanity unit and white tiles covered the walls and floors.

If this place had been situated somewhere else, such as London or another major city, then the two hundred pounds a night would have seemed like a bargain. She started to unpack, hanging the clothes she'd brought with her in the wardrobe and placing her socks and underwear in the top of the chest of drawers. She then sat on her bed with her sandwiches, fruit salad, and one of the bottles of water. The tuna and mayo sandwich was serviceable and was washed down with the lukewarm water. The food filled a hole in her belly, but she endeavoured to have a hearty meal at some point early tomorrow, knowing that she would need fuel to keep her going through what would undoubtedly be a long day.

Beth then used the remote to flick on the television, then scrolled through the channels, though she was disappointed to find the hotel only had the five basic terrestrial channels available. She hoped to find the local evening news, thinking they might run a story about the murders.

The reporter back in town had said she'd learned nothing concrete, so Beth doubted there would be anything worth hearing as yet, unless the police had put out a statement. Sadly, the news wasn't playing, so she had to settle for a gameshow. The host was funny, and it was a bit of mindless entertainment that Beth hoped might quiet her thoughts. She was feeling stressed, and the throngs of an oncoming headache started to drum in her temples.

But her brain wouldn't cooperate. For one, she kept thinking about Josh, and the whole fucked-up situation of the murders in town. No matter how much she tried to convince herself differently, Beth's instinct told her the two were somehow linked. She just prayed that Josh wasn't among the people who were dead.

On top of that, the red wine was calling out to her. When inspecting the bathroom, Beth had noticed a couple of glasses in there to set toothbrushes in. While far from a proper wine glass, they would certainly do the trick, and beat drinking out of the bottle like an alcoholic.

The alcohol might be a bad idea, considering that she wanted to be up early tomorrow in order to get to work proper.

Today had been a bust.

Oh, what the hell. A few drinks couldn't hurt, and could serve to relax her. She retrieved a glass from the bathroom and poured herself a healthy measure.

Beth started to drink as she plotted out the next day's course of action, to make it go better than that day had. She certainly had options.

She could locate the payphone Josh had used, to see if anyone nearby had seen him make the call. There was also the reporter back in town—Karen Porter. If the woman was still around in the morning, it would be worth speaking to her again for an update. And, if not her, perhaps another covering the story could shed more light. Beth was deep in thought as she took yet another drink, surprised that there was now only a little wine left in the glass. She drained it and poured herself another.

That went down a little too easily, she thought, but went ahead with her second glass anyway. Before she knew it, Beth was on her second bottle, and was indeed feeling more relaxed. A warm, familiar sensation enveloped her like a protective blanket. She kicked off her Converse and lay back on the bed. The room around her spun a little, but Beth paid that no mind, instead basking in the sensations overtaking her, making her worries seem a million miles away. She soon drifted off into a drunken sleep, with the half-empty glass of wine still in her hand, perched on her stomach. As her body relaxed, the glass fell, spilling its contents onto her clothes and the white bedsheets beneath. Despite the spill, Beth didn't wake.

12

BETH'S EYES FLUTTERED OPEN, though she dearly didn't want them to.

Her head pounded and her mouth and throat felt desert-dry. Movement, no matter how slight, only made her head feel worse. The blinding lights in the room only added to her newfound misery. Beth felt a sticky sensation across her stomach, and the fabric of her blouse clung to her skin. She suddenly remembered the glass of wine she had been holding, and sat up, her stomach lurching at the motion. Through blurred eyes, she saw that it was still nighttime outside. She also noticed the glass lying by her side on the bed, and a large stain of deep red across her stomach and over the bedsheets.

'Fuck!' she snapped, realising what had happened. Her vision spun and she had to stop from letting the contents of her stomach jump free from her mouth. Grabbing the glass and setting it on the nightstand, Beth then heaved herself from the bed, wavered on her feet for a moment, and then undressed. The bedsheets were ruined, and would no doubt cost her—Ms. Jacobs didn't seem like the type to let it go.

But, in fairness, Beth wouldn't be able to hold that against her. She felt ashamed. With her clothes piled on the floor, Beth then stripped the bedsheets. Her bladder screamed at her, but she held on until the sheets were free. Only then did Beth wobble into the bathroom and relieve herself. Afterward, she made her way to the sink and ran the cold tap, greedily gulping down mouthful after mouthful of refreshing water while she tried to exorcise the dull, metallic taste from her mouth. After switching off the tap, Beth stood upright and looked at herself in the mirror.

She didn't like what stared back at her.

Red, bloodshot eyes that looked tired and sad. Her hair was a mess and her lips were stained purple. She'd seen herself like this far too often after deciding to 'just have one to relax.'

Fucking idiot, Beth chastised herself. *You don't have time for this. You're here for Josh.*

While she would eventually need to deal with the spillage on the bed, Beth's exhausted body screamed at her for more sleep. She could then sort out everything in the morning. For now, she needed rest, and she just prayed that extra sleep would be enough. A hangover was something she could ill afford. So, she padded from the toilet, passing the window as she did, curtains still open. It was then she cast a look outside.

Beth stopped and squinted, trying to focus her vision. Though the light from the room itself reflecting back in the window's glass made it difficult to see through the darkness outside, she could tell something wasn't right.

The stars were visible in the night sky, but many seemed to be blocked out. And, as crazy as it seemed, something outside appeared to be moving. Something massive. Other twinkling stars were then blotted out by the immense bulk that shifted in the night. With no light source outside to illuminate it, and with the light inside the room hampering her vision, Beth was unable to clearly make it out. She then moved quickly to the light-switch in the room and clicked it off, before returning to the window.

The reduction of light pollution really helped, though Beth instantly regretted turning off the light. Her hand instinctively came up to her mouth. She wanted to scream, but the cry became lodged in her throat and she was unable to expel it. Instead, she made a pathetic mewling sound.

That can't be real!

With the additional illumination, Beth was now able to make out a little more of the monstrosity that rose from the sea, held up on many massive legs. The central bulk of it writhed with long, thin tendrils, and Beth could just make out huge, open mouths. There wasn't just one, and they were all wide, as if screaming. Thousands of rolling eyes lined the surface. The monster's face was maddening and nightmarish, and the whole form seemed a mix of the insectile and cephalopodic.

However, Beth could hear no sound from the nightmarish titan. There was only the noise of the waves outside, dulled by the double-glazed window. Despite what her eyes were showing her, Beth had to question if it was actually real. Could something so massive and inhuman actually exist? Surely not. There would be chaos all around. Even in the dead of night, someone else would have spotted it.

Frozen to the spot, Beth could only continue to stare, feeling her grasp on reality slip. But then she noticed that the stars were a little more visible. And the body of the creature was not so clear anymore. It became harder to make out, and Beth was soon less sure that she was actually seeing anything. Soon, no matter how hard she searched, she couldn't see anything at all, only the stars in the night sky and the sea below it. Beth stood for a few moments longer, still frozen with fear, before her body relaxed enough for her to finally move again. She took a tentative step closer to the window, desperate to make sense of what was happening, but she saw nothing.

Absolutely nothing.

She felt tears spill from her cheek and her breathing became rapid. Her skin felt like a thousand pins had punctured it, and a cold sweat broke out. Beth had never suffered a panic attack before, but knew enough about them to realise that was what she was experiencing. She moved quickly over to the bed, almost tripping on the discarded sheets, and sat down. She then rested her elbows on her knees and put her head in her hands.

Breathe, she told herself. But rational thought was not winning out here. Not after what she had seen.

The continued stream of fucked-up things she'd seen weighed on her. Eventually, the panic attack ran its course, lasting twenty minutes before Beth's body eventually started to calm down. Her tight muscles eventually began to ease, and her breathing began to slow. Beth laid back on the bed and her whole body started to tremble. She didn't know what to do, and instinctively pulled the thick duvet across her, wrapping herself up into a bundle and trying to warm her quivering form. Though Beth remembered little about it happening, she shut down, utterly exhausted, and passed out into unconsciousness.

13

THE BLASTING hot water from the showerhead above her felt good on Beth's skin. Her flesh had reddened due to the heat of the water, and the room was filled with thick steam that actually helped clear her head.

Upon waking that morning, Beth had felt disorientated and confused. It had taken a while to remember where she was and, more importantly, what she had seen the previous night.

It was clear after waking that a hangover had taken hold, but it was a lot more subdued than Beth might have expected. The shower was helping bring her back to normality, but she still felt tired, and there was grumbling in her belly that craved food.

But despite all that, her mind was still stuck on the vision from the previous night. That titanic impossibility that towered from the sea. Silent, slowly moving its long, writhing limbs that had been too numerous to count. And that nightmarish face, with multiple mouths and thousands of wide, wild eyes. Beth had never before felt such a profound sense of worthlessness. It was as if she were no more than an ant to the behemoth. Less so. Tiny and insignificant, almost beyond notice. At the time, however, Beth had had a horrible feeling that it was looking right back at her.

But it was morning now, and the daylight brought with it the realisation that what she had seen was flat-out impossible. It couldn't have been real. That left only one answer.

She had imagined it.

Either the alcohol had affected her in ways it hadn't previously, or at the time her mind still hadn't been fully awake. Whatever the reason, Beth was certain she had somehow dreamed it up. It was the only plausible explanation.

Of course, the fact that she'd had two similar experiences yesterday concerned her. She had been wide awake during those, and not under the influence of a significant amount of alcohol.

The implications, therefore, were worrying. If she was seeing things in broad daylight, when fully awake, did that mean there was something wrong with her? Was she mentally ill, or about to suffer a breakdown of some kind?

Beth had never experienced anything like it before in her life, and the thought of her mind unravelling caused an uneasy feeling to weigh down on her. She didn't need this, not when Josh was in trouble. For the life of her, Beth couldn't understand what had brought this on. Sure, she was worried about her brother, and also being jobless was a blow, but would that suddenly bring on something so serious? It didn't feel right.

Ignore it, she told herself. *Just get on with the job at hand.*

It was all she could do, Beth reasoned. So, she shut off the shower and readied herself for the day ahead. The first task was to fill her belly. Then, she needed to get to work. The stained sheets on the floor of the room concerned her, and she knew that the right thing to do would be to report it. If Ms. Jacobs provided a turn-down service, then they would be found anyway. For now, however, she scooped up the sheets and deposited them in the bath. She would deal with that later. Beth then dressed in a fresh pair of jeans, the same Converse as the previous day, a light-blue wool jumper, and a coat. Beth then left her room and headed downstairs, ready to speak with Ms. Jacobs. However, the old woman was not at her station.

Beth checked her watch to see that it was a little before nine a.m. There was a bell on the desk that she could ring, but she thought about the conversation that would likely follow if she grabbed the owner's attention. Ms. Jacobs definitely seemed the type to make a big deal out of a spilt drink. In truth, Beth just couldn't face that right now. Her hunger was actually making her feel nauseous, so she left. She would deal with the old woman and the fallout from her spill later. Beth decided against driving, reasoning that she could reach everywhere in town on foot.

It took her about twenty minutes to reach the centre, and she ended up close to the Trout and Lobster, which was closed. The North East News van was still parked nearby, though no one seemed to be inside at the moment. There were a handful of people standing looking out towards the crime scene on the beach, but nowhere near the numbers that had been present the previous day. There were a couple of other news vans from different stations, but no activity to speak of. Beth looked out to the beach, over towards the cliffs. The police tape was still there, along with a single cruiser parked on the pebbles and a couple of officers. Again, the activity when compared to the previous day was greatly reduced. Beth then looked to the low wall that separated the open area from the pebbled beach. She remembered the sounds of babies crying. Then she remembered the monster standing out at sea.

All in your head.

Beth cautiously approached the wall and peered over it. There was nothing.

Definitely all in your head.

She was both relieved and concerned at the same time. At least those horrible, infantile things on the beach weren't there, and probably never had been. But that definitely raised questions about her mental state.

You're fine, Beth told herself. *Concentrate on the job at hand.*

She then looked around town for somewhere to eat, and eventually found a small cafe. The smell of cooking sausages and bacon was a welcome one and sent her hungry stomach into overdrive. The cafe was a quaint place, with only a couple of other people present. An overweight lady with a kind smile took Beth's order—bacon, eggs, two sausages, baked beans, and toast. The food was out to her in just under ten minutes, and Beth greedily gobbled it all down, polishing it off with a nice cup of fresh, steaming coffee. The food was good, but this coffee was *great*.

Then, she needed to be on the move again. While she could have asked the people in the cafe if they knew Josh, she really wanted to follow up on that phonebox first. With the magic of her mobile phone and Google—though the signal and connection here was poor—Beth was able to actually locate where the payphone was, and cross-checked it against the map application. It was part-way up the main hill coming into town, and according to the app was approximately ten minutes away on foot. The steep incline would be taxing, but the phone was easy to reach. Beth bought a bottle of water from the cafe before leaving, then headed back outside and followed the route to the phonebox.

While hiking up the bank again out of town, Beth took in more of the detail of Netherwell Bay. She admired the stone walls to the front gardens of the townhouses, neatly manicured lawns, and wrought iron gates and railings. There was an expanse of grass and trees to her right that dropped down towards the running river. While the town centre felt packed and crowded with buildings, the road out was more spacious, with welcome expanses of greenery giving the road a more naturalistic feel. It was quite idyllic, and somewhere Beth could imagine people retiring to.

She soon found the phonebox, on the left-hand side of the road, set just against the edge of the footpath. How Josh had managed to make a call on this thing, she would never know. It looked ruined.

It was constructed from a tall aluminium frame which was inset with glass panels to the walls and door. Or, more accurately, it *used* to have glass panels, but most of them had been smashed, and all that was left was jagged shards of glass. The metal frames were bent and twisted, and the whole thing was covered in graffiti. The phone inside was covered in a layer of grime and dirt. If she had just stumbled upon the phonebox without knowing anything else about it, Beth would have just assumed it out of order and left. As it was, she wanted to check. After using her handkerchief to pick up the receiver, Beth brought it close to her. Sure enough, she heard a dial tone. She set the receiver back down and looked around. Her attention was drawn to the townhouse directly adjacent to the phone. The render and roof tiles to the house looked immaculate, as did the front lawn, which was cut and sculpted to perfection. A small hedge to the front of the lawn was cut so neatly that a set-square could be positioned against the edges and would exactly show ninety-degrees. In the living-room window, a figure peered back at Beth.

This person, however, was nothing like the tapping thing she had seen yesterday. They were real, and very much normal. The person looked to be an elderly man, with a thick grey moustache, bald head, and a red face. He did not look happy, and Beth remembered her brief conversation yesterday with someone who had picked up the very phone she now stood before.

It didn't take a genius to realise this was the same person. He quickly came outside to confront Beth.

'Something interesting about that phonebox?' the man asked as he emerged from his front door, walking with a slight limp. He was dressed in burgundy trousers and a cotton jumper with a checked pattern that ran down the middle.

'Not really,' Beth replied defensively. 'Is there a problem with me looking at it?'

'Just wanted to know what you were up to,' he said, walking across his lawn to get closer to Beth. She had him sized up straight away. A curtain twitcher, someone who had to know *everything* that was going on outside of his house, and who would gladly get involved in anybody's business if it meant them leaving him alone. The man's voice was curt in its tone—definitely the same one Beth had spoken to yesterday.

'Just having a look around,' Beth replied. 'And I'd thank you to leave me to it.' She had zero patience for an attitude like his.

'You're the one that called that bloody phone yesterday,

aren't you?' He jabbed an accusatory finger over in her general direction.

'So what if I was?' Beth asked, raising her voice. 'You don't own this phone, or the street it's on. So butt out. Understood?'

The cantankerous old man's face dropped a little, and he paused. She'd clearly surprised him by going on the offensive, and he obviously wasn't used to being spoken back to. He reminded Beth of her old boss in that regard.

'Part of the neighbourhood watch,' he said petulantly, though his voice was a little softer than it had been.

What a fucking surprise, Beth thought. *Of course you're part of the neighbourhood watch. I bet you chase kids off for just standing around doing nothing.*

'Everything alright out here?' another voice said, this one feminine. Someone else stepped from the house, and Beth presumed the lady to be the man's wife. She had hair that was still black and wore it in curls down to her shoulders, and was dressed in a shawl, tan shirt, and cream trousers. The wrinkles on her face indicated her advanced years, but the woman certainly carried herself well, Beth noted.

'Got a snooper out here,' the husband said. 'She was the one calling the phone all day yesterday, disturbing us while we were out doing our gardening. Bit of a nuisance, I think.'

'Oh, stop being silly, George,' the lady said with a dismissive wave of her hand. 'You really do know how to think the worst of people.' The woman flashed Beth a charming smile and joined her husband on their lawn, standing on the other side of the boundary wall. She extended her arm over it. 'My name is Sadie, dear. Sadie Orson. Sorry about my husband.'

Beth smiled and shook Sadie's hand. 'Pleased to meet you, Sadie,' she replied.

'Is there something we can help you with? George said he spoke to a person yesterday who was calling this phone. Are you looking for someone?'

'Actually, I am. Someone called me from it early yesterday morning. I'm looking for them.'

'Josh?'

Beth was stunned into silence. Had the woman just named her brother? Did she know him? After standing open-mouthed for a few moments, Beth eventually gathered herself enough to respond. 'Yes, that's right. He's my brother. You know him?'

'A little,' Sadie said. 'You look a little like him. Sound like him, too.'

'How did you know it was him who called me, though?'

'I saw him, dear. Yesterday.'

Beth scowled at George. 'Yesterday your husband told me he didn't see anyone.'

'He didn't,' Sadie said. 'He was out in town. But I saw Josh making a call out here, which was strange, as I can't remember the last time I saw someone using this phone.'

'Was he okay?' Beth asked, finally feeling hopeful. This was a break. An honest-to-God break.

'He looked a little distressed, I have to say,' Sadie replied. 'Something had shaken him.'

'Where did he go after?'

Sadie shrugged. 'Ran off. Headed farther up the hill. Not sure where after that.'

Beth nodded. It didn't give her a lot to go on. Had he skipped town? Was she here for nothing?

'I have to ask... do you know Josh well?' Beth asked. 'I was just surprised you knew him by name.'

'I wouldn't say *well*,' Sadie answered.

'He's a bloody no-good nuisance,' George cut in. 'Always getting into trouble. He mixed with the wrong crowd.'

Beth clenched her teeth together. She knew her brother wasn't a saint, but hearing this man put Josh down angered her, more so because of who was doing the name-calling.

'That's my brother you're talking about,' Beth shot back. 'And I don't appreciate you talking about him that way.'

'Then leave,' George stated. 'Go on, get!'

Beth surged with anger.

'George!' Sadie snapped. 'There is absolutely no need to talk to this lady like that.'

'Well, I think—'

'I don't care what you think, George,' Sadie said. 'Now, you go inside and calm down.'

'But—'

'No buts! Leave the two of us to talk.'

George looked back at Beth, scowling as he did, but eventually complied with his wife's order and marched back inside. Beth forced herself to calm down. She dearly wanted to give that old fool a piece of her mind, but there were more important things at hand. Sadie somehow *knew* Josh, and could potentially help Beth locate him. So, Beth swallowed her anger. And her pride.

'Thank you,' Beth said. 'I honestly don't want an argument.'

Sadie waved a hand. 'Oh, I know that, dear. I'm good at reading people. You aren't any trouble. You'll... have to forgive my husband. He's old and stubborn and pig-headed, but he has his reasons for being awkward with you.'

'What do you mean?' Beth asked.

'Tell me, dear, is there a reason you are looking for your brother?'

Beth paused. 'I just want to make sure he's okay.'

'So you came to town just to check on him? Does that mean you have no other means to contact him?'

'Well, I...' Beth wasn't sure how to answer. She didn't know if she even wanted to. But she needed to know what Sadie knew, so she decided it was time for the truth. Or, at least, part of the truth. 'In all honesty? I haven't seen him for a number of years. I found out he was here when he called me, but I didn't get chance to speak to him. I came here to see if he was okay.'

'You two estranged?'

'You could say that.'

Sadie nodded her understanding. 'That sounds like Josh, I guess. Don't get me wrong, I don't know him well, but he has been here in town for, oh, it will have been about two years or so now.'

'Two years?' Beth asked. 'I've never known him to stay anywhere that long.'

'Well, I think it is the company he keeps that made him stick around. He has become quite involved with Alicia Kent, a local girl.'

That made more sense to Beth. 'Okay. Any idea where I can find this Alicia?'

'I'm not sure exactly where she lives, but her uncle owns a few places here in town. William Kent is quite a well-connected man. But, I'm afraid to say, he's not someone I'd choose to associate with.'

A picture began to form in Beth's mind. It wasn't a stretch to assume the reason for Josh's panicked call was because he had gotten caught up in something with the wrong crowd. The murders on the beach were forefront in her thinking.

Please, Josh, I hope to God you've not done something stupid.

'Josh isn't a bad person, Sadie,' Beth said, more to convince herself than the old lady before her. 'He really isn't.'

'Well, that may be. But the reason my husband was so keen to get rid of you, and the reason he denied knowing who made that call to you is because the Kents spell trouble. Josh too, unfortunately.'

'What do you mean?'

'Well, I remember when I first noticed your brother in town. I have no idea what brought him here, but he was quite pleasant at first. Spoke to people, said he was just wandering through. But then the Kents got their claws into him. They have a way of doing that to people. And when they do, they don't let go. I haven't seen Josh since yesterday, dear, but if you want some friendly advice, if you are able to find him... pull him out of here. And quickly.'

Beth was certain the woman would have heard about what happened yesterday on the beach—there was no way she wouldn't in a small town like this. Beth wanted to ask Sadie about it, about the murders and if she thought Josh could be involved somehow. But Beth couldn't bring herself to. It would all be pointless speculation anyway. What she needed from Sadie was a next step.

'So, is there anywhere I can find William Kent, then?' Beth asked. 'You said he owns a few places in town.'

Sadie nodded. 'I'm not sure you *want* to find him, dear. But, if you must, I know his family owns the Heritage Centre. Bit of a pointless building in a town like this, if you ask me, but I think it's just a vanity project. Their family has long been a part of the town's history, so that place is really just around to flaunt it. It is usually open, so you might find someone inside who can tell you more. Could be a good place to start, without going to one of their homes.'

'And what would be wrong with going to their homes?'

Sadie smiled, but it was devoid of humour. 'Their estate is protected by a security wall and is a little isolated. The Heritage Centre would be a little more... public. Less could go wrong, if you take my meaning.'

Beth *did* take her meaning, but was shocked at what the woman was implying.

Just what the hell kind of family had Josh gotten caught up with?

'You'll forgive me, Sadie, but this town just gets stranger and stranger.'

'Well,' Sadie replied, 'I don't suppose you are wrong—not that I know any different. I always joke with George that the town was named Netherwell because things here are *never well*.'

Beth chuckled a little. 'I guess the Heritage Centre is somewhere to start. Thank you.'

'It's no problem, my dear. I'd tell you not to go, as I really don't think you should, but I can tell you aren't the type to just let things lie. But be careful. I mean that.'

'I will,' Beth said, still a little stunned.

Sadie nodded. 'Then I'll leave you to it. George needs his breakfast, and if I don't feed him soon, he'll get even *more* cranky, if you can believe it.'

Beth wasn't sure she could believe it.

The two women said their goodbyes, and Sadie went inside, closing the door behind her.

Beth's head was spinning. She'd finally found a lead. The uneasy feeling in her gut when it came to Josh had only soured, and her hopes of finding him safe, or at least not up to his eyes in serious trouble, were fading fast.

She set off towards the Heritage Society, which Beth remembered spotting on her drive the previous day. On the way, she called her friend and former colleague at the newspaper.

Erland Cowell.

She needed a little outside help and felt he could be just the person to lend it.

14

It was a late start for Jim.

He was normally up and out on his walk at the crack of dawn. But today he had slept in, and even now felt exhausted. Much more so than normal on a morning. Even the fresh air didn't do much to rejuvenate him.

He had decided to avoid the beach today, knowing he probably wouldn't be able to get on it anyway. So, instead, he had decided to simply make his way into town and stretch his legs. Jess kept looking up at him as the pair walked down the long bank of Old Town and towards a footbridge that would lead them into the town centre proper.

The dog looked confused, as if she wanted to know why they weren't taking their normal route. She loved the beach in any weather, and Jim felt a little bad knowing she would be disappointed today.

'Sorry, girl,' Jim said. 'We might get back to our normal walk tomorrow.'

Though Jim wasn't certain, as he couldn't be sure if it would be open to the public again by then. In truth, he wasn't sure he even wanted to be here in Netherwell anymore.

He hadn't felt that way since his youth.

But, in the intervening years since that terrible night—when the town had seemed evil—things had improved. Hell, he'd found love with Ada, and they bought their first home here. Even during his tours away with the military, this place was always home.

His life with Ada had been a happy one. Jim was still sad that he'd lost her a few years ago. He'd always felt, selfishly, that he should have gone first. However, he had found a level of comfort and acceptance in staying here to see out his life. Jim was contentedly waiting for the inevitable, when his body could be buried next to Ada's and his soul would be reunited with hers.

But, after yesterday morning, seeing those bodies in Hollows Cove suddenly made him feel like he was in his early twenties again. Barely a man.

Back when the darkness was here last.

Leaving would feel like a betrayal of Ada, who was waiting for him to join her in the local cemetery. Joining her when all was said and done was all he wanted out of whatever life remained.

Or so he thought.

Because if what he dreaded was true, and that evil was indeed back, then he had to re-evaluate things. He was around when the town had gone to hell last time. He knew there were some things worse than death.

15

THE HERITAGE CENTRE was quite the imposing structure, nestled in between the more traditional town buildings of the street. This one, however, was taller, bolder than its neighbours, and though clearly not a church, had a hint of grandeur normally reserved for buildings of worship. Now that Beth stood before it, she could take in more details she had missed when driving past yesterday.

Smooth grey stonework was framed and detailed by quoins on the building's corners. Feature trims of thin, protruding stonework jutted out halfway up the front wall, and the windows all had feature stone surrounds from the sills to the arched heads. All of the external stone was the same colour, but this precise and often intricate detailing helped break up the elevation visually. A central, circular window on the upper floor, with stained glass, topped off the grandiose design. Beth stared at the higher window— and noticed movement beyond. Though it was little more than a few drifting shadows, she thought perhaps someone was on the other side.

The main entrance door, which sat at the top of a couple

of steps, was slightly open. It was black and heavy looking, tying in well with the cast-iron guttering, downpipes, and railings to the building's frontage.

Beth took a breath and moved to the front door, then pushed it open the rest of the way. Though heavy, it moved easily on the hinges, and Beth found herself in a small draft lobby with glazed doors. She pushed her way through those as well and then entered a large room, the perimeter walls of which were all lined with bookcases, glass display cabinets, tables and side tables, study desks, and a variety of pictures and artwork. The bookcases were filled to the brim with leather-bound books and tomes. The display cabinets contained what looked to be old artefacts of varying materials—metals, clays, stone, and fabrics—and the tables had on them hand-drawn maps and handwritten scrolls, all on parchment. Everything in the dusty room seemed old, even the wallpaper, which was two-tone green in light and dark vertical stripes. The floor underfoot was creaky, with dark-stained floorboards. While the walls that surrounded the room were packed with items, the open centre was spacious in contrast, with only a few empty desks and tables to fill the void. At the far side of the room there was a reception counter, and behind that, a closed wooden door with detailed panelling. A young man, who Beth assumed to be in his early twenties, sat at the desk, earphones in, leaning back, eyes closed and mouth open. Beth could hear the faint drone of music from the earphones, along with his nasally snoring. The only other sound was the steady tick-tock of a grandfather clock.

She coughed, loudly, hoping to draw his attention. Either his sleep was too deep, or the headphones were blocking out her efforts. Likely both.

She studied the young man. From this position, and

with his head tilted back, Beth could make out a defined jawline, slight stubble, and bird-like features to his thin face, complete with a pointed nose that dropped close to his top lip. He had black hair worn in a centre parting, though it flopped back given his current head position. He was dressed in an off-white shirt and grey-coloured waistcoat, and Beth could just make out a pair of round, frameless glasses over his eyes. Overall, the man looked an odd mix of smart and scruffy. Given his relatively young age, Beth highly doubted that he was William Kent.

Given the size of the building from the outside, Beth had expected the Heritage Centre to be huge, but it seemed to be just this single room. At least, that was all that looked to be accessible to the public. The door behind the reception desk had a steel sign blazed across it: Keep Out.

So, this was it? A building this big and only one room in use for the public? The space appeared to be all that was on offer to showcase the town's history.

Beth walked slowly over to the reception desk, inspecting some of the pictures, scrolls, maps, and books. The maps, sketched in ink, were simply of the town through the ages, and they grew in size as the years progressed. The original settlement started on only one side of the river, then grew out over to the opposite landmass. The Heritage Centre appeared on a map dated 1867, and was called Kent House. One map had a pretty accurate sketch of the building's frontage. Earlier versions on this spot, however, showed the footprint of a different building, with no other structures surrounding it. Scribbled cursive gave it a name, which Beth could just about read if she squinted. It was difficult to make out, but she was fairly sure it read: 'Molech Church House.'

The books on the shelves were a mixture of titles. Some were expected, such as *Histories of the North East* and

North Yorkshire regions of the U.K. Others were on symbol-ism, some on the study of geometry, and others on the moon, the solar system, early religions in the North of England, and others still had words that were alien to Beth: Canaanite, Ba'al, and others. Most of the books were leather-bound, but there were even simple collections of parchment and papers, bundled together with rope or twine. The objects on show in the display cases seemed to be what Beth would have expected to see from archaeolog-ical digs: old arrow heads, some small plates stained with dirt, and metallic emblems. Interesting, certainly, but fairly common finds throughout the country. Nothing that hadn't been dug up in most towns and cities around country down the years. There were even a few books on the bloodline of the Kent family, it seemed, and Beth was reminded of Sadie's words earlier in relation to the Heritage Centre.

'*I think it's just a vanity project.*'

As fascinating as all of this might have been, it didn't help Beth. She had come here for a reason: to find out more about this Alice Kent, who—it seemed—was Josh's girl-friend. That could be Beth's best chance to finally find her brother.

She coughed again, louder this time. Still no reaction.

'Fuck it,' Beth mumbled to herself and walked over to the reception desk. A thick book lay on the desk's surface, with blue leather covering, the front embossed with gold writing that read, *A History of Mathematics: The Golden Ratio, The Fibonacci Sequence, and Pythagorean Theorem.* Beth couldn't imagine trying to read something so dull. If the steward had been reading this then no wonder he'd fallen asleep. It certainly was a subject that would have sent Beth into an early slumber. She picked up the book, which felt quite heavy in her grasp, lifted it to shoulder height with her arms extended before her, then let go.

The tome dropped and slammed forcefully onto the desk with a thunderous bang. The young man jumped as he snapped from his sleep in shock, almost falling out of his seat. His eyes were wide, and he pulled in a surprised breath.

'What the...' was all the man could mutter as he struggled to get his bearings. Eventually, his confused gaze settled on Beth, who stood with her arms folded, though she had an amused smile on her face.

'Oh, sorry,' he said, composing himself and pulling free his headphones. He brushed his shirt and waistcoat down and then ran a hand through his floppy hair. 'That was unprofessional of me.' His cheeks flushed red.

'It's okay,' Beth said. 'Reading stuff like that,' she nodded to the book she had just dropped, 'would put me to sleep, too.'

'Huh?' The young man looked genuinely confused. Then he looked down to the tome Beth had motioned to. 'Oh, I see.' He gave a laugh that sounded awfully proper and polite. 'I suppose it might seem that way, but it is actually quite fascinating.' He shifted uncomfortably in his seat.

'Pythagorean Theorem? Fascinating? Really?' She chuckled.

The red of his cheeks deepened, and the man cast his gaze away from Beth in embarrassment. 'Yes, well, I guess it is a bit of an acquired taste. But things like that tend to hold my interest.'

'If that's true, how come you were asleep?' Beth asked, still smiling. She could tell the young lad wasn't too comfortable talking to a woman, probably not something he did a lot of. 'Out partying all night last night?'

'Partying?' Again, he seemed genuinely confused.

'Yeah,' Beth said. 'You know, out getting drunk with friends.'

'Oh, gosh no,' he said, looking slightly appalled. 'I'd never... I mean, that kind of thing is not...'

Beth laughed. 'Relax, I'm only teasing.' She held out her hand to him. 'I'm Beth.'

The man looked at her hand like it was a foreign object. Eventually, he took it in a soft and limp grasp. 'Aiden,' he replied with an awkward smile.

'Pleased to meet you, Aiden,' Beth said. 'Sorry if I scared you. It probably was a bit much just to get your attention.'

Aiden shook his head. 'Oh, no, the fault was mine. I shouldn't have been sleeping. My apologies.'

'Don't mention it,' Beth said with an amused chuckle. There was a brief silence, which Aiden apparently felt the need to fill.

'Can I help you with something?'

'Possibly,' Beth said, and then proceeded with the story she had come up with on her walk over from Sadie's house. She didn't know if Aiden was trustworthy, even though he seemed unassuming and socially awkward, and didn't know how much information she would be safe divulging. She had prepared a story in case she had met William Kent here, and she hoped that it could act as a cover to help dig up further information without explicitly mentioning Josh. 'I'm gathering information for a book I'm writing.'

'A book on what? Netherwell Bay?' Aiden asked with a confused frown.

'Not exclusively,' she replied. 'It is going to be a bit of a guide to lesser-known coastal towns across the country. I've not long been in Netherwell Bay, but it is a fascinating little town. Not many places I've visited have their own Heritage

Centre, so when I learned of this place, I thought it would be perfect for my research. What better place to learn about the town and its history? I assume this Centre is open to the public?'

'Erm, it is, I guess. I have to admit, though, we don't really get many people in.'

'Oh, really? Well, in that case, is there any reason to keep it open?'

Aiden took a moment. 'The owner of the centre, who owns the building itself as well as the collections you see here in this room, feels it is important to preserve the town's history. So, this is a kind of labour of love. That works well for me, as it feels a little bit like home for me.' Aiden cast a longing gaze around the room.

'So, you've worked here for a while?' Beth asked.

'Not worked. I volunteer,' Aiden said. 'A little bit of a labour of love for me, too.'

'That's nice,' Beth replied. 'Are you related to the owner yourself?'

Aiden shook his head. 'I'm not.'

'But you are a local? Lived here all your life?'

Aiden nodded, then narrowed his eyes at her. 'This feels a little like an interview.'

Beth laughed. 'Sorry, that's just the reporter in me coming out.'

'You're a reporter?' Aiden asked, his eyes widening a little.

'Well, I used to be,' Beth said. 'But I've been writing books for a few years now. Just eking a living out that way. The royalties aren't great, but it's much more rewarding.'

Aiden nodded. 'I see.' He studied her, and Beth could tell the man was trying to figure her out, weighing up if he believed her or not.

'So...' Beth said. 'Am I okay to use this place for my research?'

'I guess so,' he replied. 'Everything you see in here can be studied and inspected, but we do insist nothing leaves the site. So you will need to do your research here.'

'Cool. That works for me. Is there anything else, or is it just this room? Pretty big building for it all just be condensed into one area.'

Aiden shook his head. 'Just what is in here, I'm afraid. The rest of the building is off limits.'

'No problem,' Beth said. Already her mind was working on a way to subtly drive the conversation towards Alicia Kent. Hopefully she could get Aiden to divulge where that girl lived—if he even knew. Beth, however, didn't get the opportunity, as the front door behind her opened. She turned to see a man enter. His dark, almost soulless eyes immediately landed on Beth.

'Hello, Mr. Kent,' Aiden said. 'I'd like you to meet someone. This is Beth.'

A smile crossed the man's lips. 'Good morning, Beth. How can I help you?'

16

Beth left the question hanging in the air.

Whoever this 'Mr. Kent' was—William or not—he was an imposing figure, standing over six feet tall. At a guess, Beth would have said six-two, maybe more. He looked to be in his fifties, with brushed-back greying hair that was streaked with a few surviving strands of black. The years had started to sag the skin around his thin face a little, and there were distinct ageing lines around his eyes and mouth. However, despite this, he still had traditionally handsome features: a narrow, symmetrical facial shape, high cheek-bones, dark eyes, and a healthy tan, as well as a strong posture, with his shoulders thrust back and chest pushed out. His smile was an easy one, revealing perfect white teeth.

He had an athletic frame, too, indicating that he either worked out, or at least looked after himself. He wore an open blazer with a sky-blue shirt beneath. The buttons were not done all the way up, revealing his chest underneath. His clothing reminded Beth of the way her old boss, Mark, used to dress, only this gentleman seemed to pull the style off with ease.

The man continued to stare at Beth expectantly, but Aiden answered the question he had asked.

'She is in town writing a book,' the young man said. 'Studying coastal towns throughout the country, I believe.'

Mr. Kent raised an eyebrow. 'Is that so? How quaint. Who's your publisher?'

That seemed like a random question, and it threw Beth for a loop. 'I... don't have one as yet. I'm going to shop around when the book is done.'

The man smiled and nodded. 'Is that so? Well, how long have you been in Netherwell? Have you found anything of interest yet?'

'Since yesterday,' Beth replied. 'I'm really just getting started. Though, I am obviously aware of what people are talking about at the minute, and of the police presence on the beach.'

Mr. Kent held his smile. 'Yes, horrible business, that.' His tone, however, was still upbeat and almost jovial, as if the deaths were of little concern or interest.

'Have you heard anything about it?' Beth asked. 'Apparently a number of people have been killed.'

He simply shrugged. 'I believe there has been a statement by the police indicating they are investigating an incident, but they haven't released much more detail than that as yet.' Beth made a mental note to follow up with that, as she hadn't been aware of any statement, although she hadn't checked any of the news websites that morning, either.

'Truly horrible,' Beth said, trying her best to sound sincere.

'Something to include in your book, though, eh? Quite fortunate timing, if you look at it that way.'

'That's not really the angle I'm going for with the book. It's more of a travel piece.'

'Well, we don't get a lot of tourists here,' Mr. Kent said. 'Despite its rich and interesting history, the town seems to be dying. Has been for a number of years now.'

'That's sad,' Beth replied. 'But what is so interesting about the history of Netherwell Bay?' Beth was padding for time, trying to draw the conversation out a little without giving anything away.

'Oh, where to start? It would take me a whole afternoon just to cover the bullet points, I'm afraid,' he said.

'Well... I have the time.'

'I don't, I'm afraid. Apologies, but I really am quite busy, so I'll have to cut this short.'

'No problem,' Beth said. 'Thank you for your time anyway... Mr. Kent, was it?'

He nodded. 'Yes, William Kent.'

It *was* him.

'Pleased to meet you,' Beth said and held out a hand. William simply left it hanging and kept his eyes on hers. Beth slowly and awkwardly withdrew the gesture. 'Would it be okay if I looked around here? Aiden said this centre was open to the public?'

'Ordinarily yes,' William replied. 'But not today. I am going to have to close the Centre.'

'Oh?'

'Yes. Something has come up.'

'Can't Aiden watch the place for you? That's what he was doing anyway.'

William Kent's face clouded in an instant. 'I am in need of Mr. Chambers' assistance. The Heritage Centre will be closed for the rest of the day. Come back another time.' His tone was short and curt. Beth knew immediately that questioning the man had been a mistake.

'Understood,' Beth said, feeling the opportunity of

getting closer to Josh slip away. However, she didn't want to push things too much. 'I'll leave you to it.'

Beth then started to walk from the building, holding her breath as she passed William. For some reason, she half-expected him to reach out and suddenly grab her. He didn't grab her, though he did stare at her, unblinking, until she reached the door.

'Can I ask a quick question?' she said, deciding to push something that had been bugging her. William Kent didn't verbally approve the request, but raised his eyebrows, which Beth took as a sign to proceed. 'A lot of the books on the shelves here,' she motioned to the shelves around the room, 'many of them seem to cover rather odd subjects. Mathematics and geometry and things like that.'

'Yes,' William replied impatiently.

'Well, what is the connection? Why have these kinds of books displayed in a place that is supposed to cover the history of your town?'

William sighed and pinched the bridge of his nose in exasperation. He didn't look amused. 'What does geometry mean to you, Mrs... sorry, I didn't catch your last name?'

Now it was Beth's turn to pause, as she didn't want to reveal her surname to him. If he did indeed know Josh, then it would reveal a link that Beth didn't want known. 'Andrews,' she eventually lied.

Mr. Kent's smile retuned, but it wasn't a nice one. Beth knew she had waited too long with her reply. She quickly added, 'And it's Miss. I'm not married.' She desperately hoped that made her lie more believable.

'Miss Andrews,' William repeated in confirmation. 'So, as I asked, what does the term geometry mean to you?'

It certainly was an odd question. 'The same as it means

to anyone else, I assume,' Beth replied. 'Spaces, shapes, patterns, that kind of thing.'

William shook his head, looking disappointed, even annoyed. 'That is an incredibly simplistic explanation, if you don't mind me saying, Miss Andrews. To be expected, I supposed.'

'What do you mean by that?'

'Precisely what I say. Now, I think we are finished here. If you don't mind...' He then nodded towards the door behind her. Beth didn't give any response and simply turned away. However, it didn't seem that William Kent was quite finished yet. 'Your accent,' he said, just as Beth was reaching for the door. She turned back.

'What of it?'

'Not a local one.'

She was getting tired of hearing that. 'No, it isn't. Is that important?'

William Kent shrugged. 'Not really. Probably just a coincidence.'

'What do you mean?' she asked.

'Nothing much. I just know someone else with a similar twang, is all. And, if I'm honest, you have a look of him.'

Beth felt a chill run up her spine. 'Not sure who you mean,' she said.

'I'm sure you don't. Now, if you don't mind, I must ask you to leave, Miss... *Andrews*.'

17

Beth walked quickly away from the Heritage Centre.

She felt her skin flush with anger and annoyance at how stupid and reckless she'd been. William Kent knew Josh, and now he'd obviously figured out there was a link between Josh and Beth. The older man was clearly smart. While Beth had been trying to play him to gain information, he'd turned that on its head. William had simply returned to his premises, found a strange lady there, and quickly and efficiently sussed her out.

Beth, however, still had nothing.

Well, not quite nothing. She now knew for certain that there was a link between William Kent and Josh. William had made that perfectly obvious with his less-than-veiled insinuation.

The question still remained: if Josh was still alive, then why had he been so scared yesterday? Beth just prayed he hadn't done something that couldn't be undone.

She was unconsciously moving back to the centre of town, lost in her own frantic thoughts, when a conversation between an elderly couple drew her attention.

'You're being ridiculous, Brian,' the lady said. 'Same as you were last night when you woke me up at a stupid hour. It's your medication, I'm telling you.'

'It isn't,' the gentleman said defiantly. 'I know what I saw.'

They had been slowly walking in the opposite direction as Beth, but on the same side of the road, so she was close to them as they passed each other. The words from the old man had caught Beth's attention, and she stopped and watched the old couple shuffle their way past.

They were carrying a few bags between them, and he was wearing a cotton beige coat and flat cap. She was dressed in a blue shawl and ankle-length navy skirt. The man reminded Beth of Droopy the Dog, with a long, tired face.

The old woman saw Beth staring and stopped. 'See?' she said to her husband. 'That young lass there thinks we are crazy.'

'Don't care,' the man said. 'I saw it. I'm telling you, I saw it.' His voice, though defiant, had a certain fearful edge to it.

'Don't mind him, dear,' the old lady said to Beth. 'Don't know how much you heard, but the old fool is just getting confused. He had a bad dream he thinks was real.'

Normally, Beth would have given the bickering pair their own space and not really listened to what had been said. But, given what she had seen since her arrival in town, how could the conversation not spark her interest?

'What was it you think you saw?' Beth asked without really thinking. It was none of her business, of course, but she had asked anyway.

'You don't want to know,' the woman said, shaking her head.

'Out at sea, last night,' the man began, and Beth felt her

heart seize, remembering her own experience. 'There was... something... out there. Can't really explain what. A monstrous thing.' The poor old man seemed to be shaking at his recollection, and Beth—feeling fear rise in herself—could fully understand why. Could it be? Had someone else seen the same thing she had?

'You're a bloody fool,' the woman repeated. 'He had a dream, brought on by his heart tablets. Couldn't tell the difference between what was real and what wasn't. Woke me up at an ungodly hour, clutching his chest and looking white as a sheet. Thought he was having another heart attack, I did.'

'I saw it!' the man insisted.

'Well there was nothing there when I looked,' the woman stated. 'Nothing at all.'

'I saw it,' he repeated, and Beth could hear the pain and confusion in his voice. There was wavering and doubt, and the questioning of his own sanity. It was something Beth had experienced herself recently.

'Do you live up on the cliff, near the Overview Lodge?'

Both sets of eyes went wide.

'Yes,' the man replied, nodding enthusiastically.

'How the devil did you know that?' the woman asked.

Then the man's face dropped in realisation. 'You saw it, too, didn't you.'

Beth didn't reply at first, feeling like a rabbit caught in headlights as both the old woman and her husband stared back at her expectantly. The old man almost looked hopeful. The old woman's face was a picture of confusion. Beth didn't know what to do. If she corroborated the old man's story, then that was admitting that the thing out at sea—the towering, nightmarish behemoth—might have been real.

Her mind wasn't ready to accept that. Also, would it really help the old man?

But, if she denied it, then it might plunge the gentleman back into swirling confusion and self-doubt. Something Beth knew all too well since arriving in Netherwell Bay.

The tapping figure in the window and those infantile abominations on the beach both flicked into her mind.

Beth shook her head. Her decision was made. 'Sorry, I didn't see anything,' she said.

'How did you know where we lived, then?' the woman asked.

'Lucky guess,' Beth said. She suddenly wanted to be away from the two of them. Not through any dislike of them, but because she was struggling to come to terms with the fact someone else had seen the same thing she had. It made her head spin. So, she turned and walked away from the confused couple.

'You *did* see it,' the old man called after her, but Beth ignored him. 'I know you did. I ain't crazy. Something is going on here. Something is wrong.'

Though she didn't reply, Beth couldn't disagree with the man. She then heard her mobile phone start to ring and retrieved it from her pocket, welcoming the distraction.

It was Erland.

18

'HEY,' Beth answered the call. 'What have you got for me?' She tried to keep her voice even and calm, which took effort.

'Well,' Erland replied, 'I still don't know what you're doing all that way up north, but you've landed in the middle of something, that's for sure.'

After speaking with Sadie Orson earlier Beth had called her friend, hoping for a favour: to try and find out anything he could about the recent murders in town. In addition, she asked him to dig up anything he could about the Kent family. It was an open net, one she'd hoped Erland would cast as wide as he could, as quickly as he could. He'd been confused as hell at her request, of course, and had instead wanted to make sure Beth was okay after her sudden departure from the paper. She'd insisted she was fine but said that she really needed his help. Erland was great at what he did, had a lot of contacts, and in the past had proven he could dig up things that most people would miss.

However, that was back home. Netherwell Bay was a long way away, and Erland's connections wouldn't likely extend this far. Still, Beth needed all she could get.

'Go on,' Beth said, keen to hear what her friend had dug up.

'Well, there isn't much to know, but the local police up there have put out an official statement. They say they are investigating an incident at a cave but as yet haven't given any indication as to what that incident might be. So not a lot of help there. But I do know a couple of reporters in the North East, and one of them knows a journalist near Netherwell, just a few towns over. He has a connection within the police force up there. There's a lot of buzz over the story. Problem is, the paper this journalist sub-contracts for can't run anything major yet, as nothing is corroborated.' Beth understood, and actually appreciated the publication's morals and patience, something her old boss didn't have any of. Erland went on, 'But I know that three people were killed. The deaths are being treated as murders, and... well... I don't really know how to say this, Beth. They were fucking ritualistic killings, or something like that. Really savage, as well.'

'Sorry, did you say ritualistic?'

'That's right,' Erland replied. 'Apparently there were some kind of symbols left on the ground. Like what you'd see in a bad horror movie. The bodies, what was left of them, had been left on display. Whoever did this had no intention of hiding the mess.'

'Jesus... any idea on the deceased?'

'Two men and a woman, apparently, but no formal identification. At least, none that has been leaked.'

Beth held her breath. Two men. Could one of them have been Josh?

'I have to ask, Beth. What's going on up there? Seems a bit weird that you travel to the arse-end of nowhere, just to get away from it all, only to end up in the middle of a story that looks like it's set to go nationwide at any second. I'd heard nothing of it till you called, but something like this is going to catch on. How did you end up at ground zero? Is this something you had been following?'

'No,' Beth said. 'I swear. It's just been the craziest coincidence.'

'Jesus,' Erland replied. 'That *is* some coincidence. And such a random place for you to end up, too.' Beth could tell that he didn't really believe everything she was saying. But she was thankful that he didn't pull at that thread any further just yet. 'So, are you going to cover it while you're there?'

'Cover it?'

'The story. Working or not, you're still a reporter, aren't you? And stories like this almost never fall into our laps. Could bring in some good money if you go freelance.'

'I hadn't thought of it,' Beth replied, and she meant it. She had other things to worry about that were much more important to her.

'I find that hard to believe,' Erland replied. She could understand his scepticism, given the work ethic he was used to seeing from her. 'You're always looking for the next big scoop.'

'Not this time. I just wanted to relax and get away from everything.'

Erland was silent for a moment. 'So why follow it up in the first place? Why even call me to look into it?' Another pause. 'Is everything alright up there, Beth? I mean, are you okay?'

'I'm fine,' Beth said, but even as she said the words she didn't really believe them. She doubted they sounded sincere. 'Look, Erland, I just want to know what's going on. That's it. There really is nothing to worry about.'

'Honestly, I'm not sure I believe you. But you know you can count on me if you need to.'

She had to keep from breathing a sigh of relief. Right now, the last thing she wanted was to have to explain herself or get into what was going on here. Erland helping out and even while he knew he was being kept at arm's length meant a lot. 'Thank you,' she said. 'Did you find out anything about the Kent family?'

'A little, but not much. The journalist I know had heard of them and gave me a few tidbits. They certainly don't sound like a well-to-do family, despite the persona they try to convey. He says they've gone hand-in-hand with that town for as long as he can remember, and the rumours are that they have their claws into everything. Nothing happens there without their approval, and they own quite a lot of the property there too. This journalist thinks they have ties to some pretty unsavoury characters, but they keep themselves removed enough to never get drawn in officially. I get the impression they aren't nice people, Beth. Do you think they're involved in these murders somehow? Is that why you wanted more info on them?'

'I don't know yet,' Beth said, honestly. 'Still looking into it. But I've heard them mentioned around here, even met one of them. A guy named William. Did you turn anything up on him?'

'No, sorry. No specific names were mentioned. Also, I couldn't find anything on the girl you asked me to look for, that Alicia Kent. But, with a little more time, I think I might be able to find something. Want me to keep looking?'

'Couldn't hurt,' Beth said.

'You still aren't going to tell me why you want to find her specifically, are you?'

Beth gave a pause before answering. 'Sorry,' was all she said.

'Christ,' Erland sighed in response. 'I really don't like this, Beth.'

'It'll be fine,' she said. 'Anything else about the Kents?'

'The only other things I could find were online, but it's more to do with the town's history. It's a little sketchy, but what I *have* found is more than a little fucking weird.'

That seemed in line with Beth's experience of this place so far, and she was less than surprised. 'Okay, what have you found?'

'Well, there have been a few... how do I put this... events over the years. In the early eighteen hundreds, the population of the town severely dropped. There isn't too much detail, but what I've found suggests that a lot of people disappeared. No other explanation is given, just that it was sudden and unexplained. There have been a few murders down the line as well, and many were—get this—occult or ritualistic in nature. Ring any bells?'

'Shit,' Beth said. 'So the town has a history of things like what happened here yesterday?'

'It would seem so. Again, the details on these records are sketchy. To be honest, you're probably in the best place to learn more, if you want to. Is there a library in town? They would likely have records that are more detailed than what I've managed to pull up online.'

'I have a place in mind,' Beth replied.

'Good. There was a similar thing happened a little over fifty years ago, too. Nineteen sixty-eight. A spate of disappearances, I'm guessing, as the population that year dropped quite a bit again. I couldn't find anything to explain it. The only thing I found was from the Online Newspaper Archive. There was a small story in a North Yorkshire paper, which mentioned Netherwell. A trio of killings that apparently had occult symbology present. That was in sixty-eight as well, around the same time as the disappearances. But other than that, it was like everything surrounding the events was scrubbed clean.'

'Three killings? So, what, history is repeating itself?'

'I have no idea,' Erland replied. 'Like I said, the information isn't very detailed. But there are records of the Kents being associated with the town stretching back as far as I could find. If you give me a little more time, I know I could uncover more, but I wanted to let you know what I'd found so far. Especially those past killings that seem to echo the ones from yesterday. I found that very fucking strange.'

'Me too,' Beth agreed. 'No way that it's a coincidence.'

'Indeed. Which is why I'm more than a little concerned you've ended up in the middle of it all. Can't you just pick another place to relax in? Leave Netherwell Bay behind?'

'I'll consider it,' Beth lied.

'So, that's a *no*, then?' Beth didn't reply so Erland carried on, 'Just tell me what's going on, Beth. Maybe I can help.'

Part of her dearly wanted to tell Erland everything. The thought of confiding in a friend that would listen and understand was alluring, and for a moment she forgot why she was so reluctant to tell him. But then she remembered: Beth had no idea what it was that Josh had done. She also didn't even know if he was still alive. If it was really bad, then Beth knew the more people involved, the more difficult it would be to try and smooth things over. Keeping everyone out of the loop seemed the safest option. And, in truth, putting her trust and faith in people did not come easily to Beth.

'You're already helping, Erland,' Beth said.

He sighed. 'Fine. Want me to keep digging?'

'If you don't mind, and it doesn't get you in trouble at work.'

'That's no problem,' Erland said. 'Mark doesn't even know what I do most of the time anyway. Speaking of which, you didn't tell me what happened between the two of you, and why you ended up quitting?'

Beth's gaze suddenly fell on someone up ahead. Someone she *definitely* needed to talk to. 'I'll tell you everything, Elrand, and soon. But right now, I need to go.'

'Fine,' Erland said, sounding anything but. Beth felt bad, and it seemed like she was taking advantage of their friendship a little, but at the moment, especially considering the situation she was in, she didn't feel like she had a choice.

'Thank you, Erland. I really do appreciate all of this. When I'm back, we will catch up, and then I promise I'll tell you everything.' Beth ended the call, not sure herself if she intended to keep the promise she had just made. Her eyes were focused on a man she'd spotted walking towards her along the street, with his black Border Collie in tow.

19

'Jim!' Beth shouted, drawing looks of surprise from the townspeople around her, as well as from Jim himself. Soon, however, the confused frown on the old man's face fell away and a quick look of recognition took its place. Then, the frown returned.

'You again?' he asked, as Beth jogged over to him. 'Thought I made myself clear to you yesterday.'

She nodded. 'You did. And I'm sorry.' She realised that a little honesty might help grease the wheels of information. All Beth had to go on was her gut, and she felt confident Jim was a good person at heart. 'Look, you were right yesterday. I wasn't being entirely truthful with you.'

'Is that right?' Jim asked, still eyeing her suspiciously.

'Yes. And, again, I'm sorry. But the truth is, I'm here looking for someone. I don't know what's happened to them, and all I know is they were here the last time we spoke. I'm terrified that this person could have been one of the people you found dead over in that cave. Please, Jim, I'm begging you, can you help me? I just want to know a little more about what you saw. If I give you a description of the man

I'm looking for, maybe you can tell me if any of the people you found dead match that description?'

Beth realised that her eyes were watering. She was starting to feel overwhelmed. Just saying the words out loud —that she was scared and needed help—acted as a kind of release, and the pent-up frustrations and worries started to wash over her like a tidal wave. These tears weren't an act. She wasn't trying to dupe Jim into pitying her and talking, but Beth was well into her second day here now, and she had turned up precisely nothing. Indeed, even if Josh had been alive when she'd arrived, he might still be dead now. If that were true, she would have failed him.

She saw Jim's stern features soften.

'Who are you looking for?' he asked.

'My brother,' she told him as her voice started to crack. 'I got a voicemail from him yesterday. I haven't seen him in years, but he sounded scared. I mean really scared. Said he was here in Netherwell Bay. I'd never even heard of this place before. But I can't find him, and I'm worried something has happened. Please, Jim, I'm sorry I wasn't completely honest with you, but I wasn't sure what else to do. I don't know what Josh has gotten mixed up in and I didn't want to get him into any more trouble.'

'Your brother is Josh Davis?' the old man asked, not sounding surprised at the connection.

'Yes!' Beth exclaimed.

'I figured that might have been the case,' he said. 'You look a little like him. Talk the same as well.'

There it was again. Why were these people so fixated on Beth's accent? Did it just reinforce that she was an outsider and not welcome here?

'Do you know Josh?' Beth asked, keeping focused on what she needed to do.

'A little,' Jim said. 'Saw him around town every now and again. Didn't mix with him, though. I don't particularly like the company he keeps. Never have.'

'The Kents?' Beth asked.

Jim raised his eyebrows in surprise but nodded his confirmation. 'That's right. You heard of them?'

'A little,' Beth admitted. 'Heard nothing good about them, though. Even met one... wasn't a fan.'

'Sounds right. They are a bloody sickness in this town. Always have been.'

'Please, Jim, do you know if my brother is still alive? Was he one of the bodies you found?'

Jim looked to the ground. 'Horrible sight that, you know. Seeing those poor people. The state they were left in... it was sickening. I recognised one of the faces, a girl, but the other two I can't say I knew.' He looked back up to her, his eyes a little wet. 'No, I don't believe Josh was one of them.'

Both of her legs wobbled slightly, and Beth had to fight to keep from bursting into floods of tears. She felt instantly lighter, like an unbearable load was lifted. It was disorientating. Of course, this didn't mean everything was going to be okay. Beth still had to find Josh, and even if he hadn't been one of the three murdered out on the beach, something could still have happened. However, she allowed herself to feel the slightest bit of hope.

'Thank you,' she said, and her voice cracked a little as she spoke. 'Do you know where I can find Josh? Do you know where he lives?'

Jim shook his head. 'No, can't say I do. Sorry.'

'I heard he was seeing a woman, one of the Kents...'

'Alicia,' Jim confirmed.

'Yes. Do you know where she lives, then? Perhaps I can start there.'

'Probably with the rest of the Kents,' Jim said. 'They own a few houses up on the outskirts of town. Fancy ones. Not on the beaten path, though. You have to know where you are going to find them.'

Beth's eyes widened. She felt like in the space of only a few minutes of talking with Jim she had made more progress than from the rest of her time here combined. Hell, if she had just been honest with him from the start she might already have Josh back safe and sound.

'Can you show me?'

'You might want to re-consider,' Jim said. 'It's a private estate that's walled in. Not something you can just walk into. I don't think hiking up there and demanding to see your brother would do you much good.'

'I have to try,' Beth said. 'If Josh is here there has to be a way I can get to him.'

Jim shrugged. 'Sorry, I don't know what to tell you. Not a lot of help in that regard, I'm afraid. He used to be fond of a drink, so you could try the Trout and Lobster again, or the Ship Inn. They're the main pubs in town. Might get lucky and find him there.'

It was an option, but a woolly one, and not one that gave Beth any kind of certainty. Perhaps a last resort, then. After the recent revelations, Beth felt like she was finally gaining some momentum. If Jim wasn't going to tell her where to look, then surely it wouldn't be too hard to find out where the Kents lived, private property or not.

'However, I still think you should leave town. You seem like a nice person. Believe me, you don't want to get caught up in what's coming.'

The comment certainly struck Beth as odd. 'What do you mean? What is coming?'

'Evil,' was his reply. 'Something from a long time ago. The killings on the beach? It's just the start.'

A sudden chorus of screams caused Beth to jump. She looked beyond Jim, farther up the street, to see a group of women scamper away from a small alleyway that cut through between two buildings. The women were yelling in fright as they eventually stopped and looked back.

'What's that about?' Jim asked, looking back as well. Beth felt her heart rate accelerate a little. She wasn't sure why, but her first thought was that perhaps another body had been found.

'No idea, but maybe we should find out,' Beth said, and started to walk up towards the group of three women. They seemed panicked and one was almost hysterical. Beth felt Jim by her side as the two approached the group. Others drifted towards the terrified women as well, concerned, asking if the ladies were okay. Beth got close enough to hear the reply.

'There's something down that path!' one woman said, a lithe forty-something with lots of makeup, styled dark hair, black trousers, high heels, and an expensive-looking wool coat. Despite the makeup, Beth could see that her skin had grown pale. The other two women, both of a similar age to the first, were dressed a little more casually, both wearing jeans, one in sports shoes and the other in loafers, and both with coats that looked significantly less expensive than the first woman's.

'What is it?' a bystander asked. Beth and Jim settled in with those who had gathered round the women, one of whom had put her shaking hands over her head.

'I don't know,' the smartly dressed woman said. 'It was... a...'

'A monster!' another of the women cut in.

Beth felt the combined mood of those gathered shift from worry, to confusion, and then to disbelief. She saw a few of those surrounding the panicked women look at each other, casting suspicious glances and smirks. Clearly, they didn't believe a word of it. Perhaps even thought it a joke.

But Beth wasn't so quick to discount the story. 'What did it look like?' she asked them.

The woman who had made the claim turned her eyes to Beth. She had a cherubic face and hair cut into a messy bob. She quickly realised Beth was asking a serious question, and gave a small look of relief. 'I don't know,' the woman said, and looked back to the small alleyway between the buildings. She stepped farther away from it. Beth did notice, however, that a few people up ahead—unaware of what was going on—strolled blissfully past this cut and didn't seem perturbed in the slightest.

'It was horrible,' the first woman said. 'It seemed to be coming out of the fucking walls. All twisted and fucked-up. Kind of like a person, but with this bulbous, misshapen head, like a giant wart.'

'And its head was covered with little eyes,' the woman who had her hands on her head said in a scared whisper. 'These little white sack things that all turned to look at us.'

'And the noise it made...' the second woman, with the bob, added.

Beth heard a few sniggers from the people who were crowded round. They clearly didn't believe the fantastical tale. And, Beth would have agreed with them, had she not experienced some strange things herself. She started to walk towards the narrow alleyway in question, but felt Jim gently grab her arm.

'Where are you going?' he asked.

'It's fine,' Beth replied, confident that it was. One thing

that all three of her visions—if that was the right word—
had in common was that they were very brief. Once they
were seen, the horrific abominations quickly vanished. And,
up until she had overheard the old couple talking a little
earlier, Beth had been convinced these things were all in her
head, witnessed by her and her alone.

Apparently not.

She pulled her arm free and moved to the gap. The
buildings either side had brickwork with a worn and weathered buff finish, and the mortar joints were set back deeply,
giving both structures an aged look that seemed in keeping
with the rest of the town. The width of the alleyway, roughly
a couple of feet, was just enough to fit a person through. The
ground was paved in cobbles that looked to have already
seen their best days, and despite it being daytime, the thoroughfare was quite dark, given the tall buildings either side
blocked out a lot of natural light. It reminded Beth of the
small nooks and alleyways that Victorian London was
famous for. Even with people around her, it seemed like an
ominous little short cut.

But, one thing was certain... there was no monster here.

'Nothing,' Jim said, appearing beside her.

'It would seem not.'

'Maybe they got confused. Saw a shadow or something.'

'It was a pretty detailed description for a shadow.'

'Then maybe they're nuts?'

'All three of them?'

'Could be. Or maybe they're just looking for attention.'

What Jim was saying made sense and was the way a
rational mind should be thinking. Before yesterday, Beth
would have agreed with him. However, there was something
in Jim's tone—a hint of doubt—that seemed like he was
saying the words without really believing them.

'Maybe,' Beth replied, still looking down the alleyway. 'Maybe not.'

As she turned, she could see Jim looking at her. His expression seemed... odd. 'You drink tea or coffee?' he asked.

Beth frowned and tilted her head to the side a little. It was an odd question, straight out of the blue. 'Coffee,' she replied.

Jim nodded. 'I know a quiet place where we can get a drink. Come on, there's a few things you should know about Netherwell Bay.'

The old man turned and set off. His dog, faithful as ever, trotted along beside him.

Beth paused. She had no idea what it was Jim wanted to tell her, and part of her dearly wanted to know. But she still felt an urgent need to get to Josh as quickly as she could, and this seemed like it was going to be a distraction.

'You coming?' Jim asked without looking back.

Given Beth had nowhere to search next—other than trying to find this private Kent estate—was there really a viable alternative to Jim's offer right now? Something very weird was going on in this town, and Beth *knew* that Josh was somehow caught up in it all. If knowledge was power, as her father always said, then Beth needed more of it. And Jim had certainly been a help so far.

'Yeah,' she said. 'I'm coming.'

20

THE CAFE WAS EVEN SMALLER than the one Beth had visited earlier that morning for breakfast. The seating area was a single space that was no bigger than the living room of her apartment. Bare brick walls were decorated with mounted fish and old photos of boats on the sea. Unlike the gaudy aesthetic in the Trout and Lobster pub, it all seemed fitting and refined, as if everything had a place. The ceiling was exposed oak boarding, and single-bulb lights hung down on black wiring, creating a partial, but intentional, industrial feel. It meshed well with the traditional brickwork wall and wooden plank flooring. There were only four tables inside, all small and round, each only able to seat three people. There was a single counter to the rear, with a glass case that displayed cakes and pastries. Behind the counter was a large coffee machine. A lady with greying blonde hair pulled back in a ponytail, sat behind the counter, reading a magazine. Beth and Jim ordered coffees—which Jim had bought, at his insistence—and Jim requested a bowl of water for Jess. They then found a seat, and the Border Collie took a few gulping mouthfuls of the water. Satisfied, she then lay on the ground at Jim's feet.

Other than the lady serving, Beth and Jim—and the dog —were the only ones present. Jim took a long, deliberate mouthful from his steaming drink. Beth sat waiting for him to begin his story. She had her hands cupped around her own hot mug, enjoying the warmth that radiated into her palms. Jim eventually looked up.

'Have to say,' he began, 'I was surprised you listened to what those ladies back there were yelling about. You didn't dismiss it outright, as I might have expected.'

'Should I have?' Beth asked.

Jim shrugged. 'Most people would. Sounded pretty far-fetched.'

'Maybe,' Beth agreed. 'But despite what you said, I got the feeling you weren't disregarding them, either. Why is that?'

'You first,' Jim said. 'If you would be so kind as to indulge me. It's just, you don't strike me as the type of lady to believe in... you know, monsters and such.'

'I guess I don't, really,' Beth said. 'But, if I'm being honest, this trip to Netherwell Bay has me doubting myself.'

'Any reason?'

'Other than turning up to find that three people have been brutally murdered?' Beth asked.

Jim nodded. 'Yes.'

Beth knew he was trying to get her to admit to something, and she had a feeling he wouldn't judge her when she did.

'Well, I've seen a few weird things here myself since arriving,' she told him, hoping that would be enough.

'Things like what those women described?'

'Kind of,' Beth confirmed. *Don't ask me to give you any*

detail, she prayed. *I don't think I could say it out loud without sounding crazy.*

Thankfully, that seemed enough for Jim. 'In all honesty, I've had an experience myself. But it was a long time ago. Back when I was young.'

It was Beth's turn to ask the question now. 'An experience like what those women described?'

Jim nodded, and repeated Beth's answer. 'Kind of.'

He then took another slow mouthful of coffee, leaving her stunned—even if she had half-expected that answer.

Just what the hell is going on?

'Okay, Jim, what is it you want to tell me? I'm feeling a little overwhelmed here and I need answers.'

'What I have to tell you won't give you any answers, I'm afraid,' he told her. 'You'll just wind up with more questions. And it also won't do anything to make you feel any less overwhelmed. But I figure I'll tell you anyway, if only to get you the hell out of this town. Cos truth be told, I'm going to be leaving soon, as well.'

'What? Where are you going to go?' Beth asked, confused.

'No idea,' he replied. 'But I think I know what's coming. Seen it before... kind of, and I know I don't want to see it again. Ever.'

'Okay, Jim, spill it. What is it you want to tell me?'

Jim leaned forward and rested his elbows on the table between them, cupping his hands around his mug just as Beth had. He stared into the liquid inside, getting lost in his thoughts.

'Happened a little over fifty years ago,' he began.

21

1968

This was madness. A fucking nightmare come to life. And it seemed to be happening all over town.

It had all started with the bodies they'd found in Hollows Cove. Dismembered, they'd said. All chopped up. Displayed in a sickening state. Symbols on the ground, too —weird occult things. Jim hadn't heard exactly what they were, hadn't seen the bodies, but in his head he was imagining one of those devil-worshipping pentagrams or something. The cut-up bodies had been sacrifices, people said. But no one knew what they had been sacrificed to.

Jim would have maybe expected something like this down in London—he'd heard everyone was crazy there. After all, that place had given birth to Jack the Ripper. But here, this far up north?

He'd been surprised when a friend had told him of the murders. Jim and his friend had even ventured to the beach to look at the police cars and officers. Everything was closed off, however, and they weren't allowed to get very close.

It had rocked the town, and was so close to his

favourite place: the clifftops above. The houses up there next to the hotel were lovely. He could imagine retiring into one of them someday with a good woman. There, they could live out their days with a great view over the sea.

Perhaps Ada could be that lady.

Of course, he'd need to get up the nerve to ask her out first.

But everything in town was starting to change now, and those bodies in the cave were just the start of the madness. Over the past day, things had been getting stranger and stranger. People reported seeing... impossible things. Horrible things. 'Like a nightmare made real,' one person had told Jim.

The town was whipped into a frenzy. Some of the older generation made mumblings that this savagery was not new to Netherwell. Then, it escalated.

More death.

Another three bodies were found in similar circumstances to the first ones: mutilated with occult symbols left on the ground surrounding them. Jim had been told about the fresh bodies, found up on the cliff top he loved so much, only a few hours ago.

Everyone seemed to be in a state of panic, searching for loved ones who had simply... vanished. Men, women, and children. Gone.

No trace left behind.

Police swarmed the streets as people called out for their missing family and friends.

Then, the screaming started. People running through the streets, calling, shouting, begging for the missing people to show themselves. Others were seemingly running from... something. A frenzy built.

And Jim was outside, on the streets, in the middle of it all.

The air seemed charged. People ran past and he heard snippets of wild conversations, where people babbled about seeing monstrous things. Screams came from near and far. Then, he heard something that made his blood run cold.

A sound. A rumble. Like a distant, powerful thunder, but seemingly made by a living thing coming out from sea. Jim's throat dried up and everyone around him stopped dead as they looked out to the massive body of water.

'What the fuck is that?' someone uttered. Jim squinted his eyes and peered into a night that seemed somehow... unnatural. The thing was massive and blocked out the very stars in the sky. Then it moved.

A nightmare come to life.

Jim instinctually started to sprint in the opposite direction, even before his mind fully realised what he was doing. He just had to get away from whatever that thing was. Another rumble. Then, more screaming. As Jim ran, he was knocked to the floor by two men who passed him. Feet thundered close to him, threatening to trample him underfoot—Jim could only lie on his front and bring his hands over his head for protection. Thankfully, the people leapt over him. Nearly all of them were shrieking in panic, but apparently they had the wherewithal to avoid a downed person. As he lay prone, Jim turned his head to the left, and he looked to the line of buildings ahead. There was an alleyway directly in his line of sight.

What he saw there made his heart seize. A woman was fighting against a thing that should not have been real.

It was huge, over ten feet tall, and had, as far as Jim could tell, grey skin. Its lower half was humanoid in form, but the bulky creature could not be mistaken for a person.

From the waist up, the hulking thing became something else completely. The entity of its broad chest was taken up by a huge opening, a salivating mouth with black gums behind. The gums were lined with what looked to be thousands of small needles. Not quite teeth, as they were far too thin, and they moved and bristled like fur.

What made the sight even more terrifying was that the poor woman fighting against this monster had her lower half engulfed in the terrible mouth. She was being held up off the ground, squirming, as the stabbing needles pierced her flesh and the black gums gnawed at her. The woman's screams were blood curdling, and red liquid erupted from her nose and mouth each time the horrific beast chomped down. Still, the woman continued her desperate fight and struggles. The creature had no defined head or shoulders, and no arms at all. Above the mouth was simply a pulsating, tumour-like mass of flesh that dripped and oozed a black liquid. Within the tumorous clump were scores of eyes, all of different shapes and sizes. Some were small orbs, others were larger, wider, with wild pupils that stared manically in all directions.

The terrified woman then saw Jim.

The expression on her face was one he knew he would always remember. Pure terror mixed with an unbelieving bewilderment. She knew she was about to die, yet her mind could not accept what was happening. The monster's upper half lifted her higher, and then it tilted back, like an animal straightening out its neck before it devoured a large piece of meat. The woman rose up with it, her exposed upper half now vertical. The mouth opened wider and gulped.

She dropped to her shoulders. The gums clamped down again, hard.

The woman screamed, little more than gurgles now, as

blood bubbled from her mouth. Beyond the chaos around him, Jim was certain he could hear the cracking of her bones when the mouth compressed even more around the struggling woman. Her terrified eyes stayed on Jim as she was pulled down a little farther, and the gums pressed down onto her head. Jim heard a crack. One of her eyeballs popped free and dangled on an optic nerve as the woman's cranium was crushed and her brains exploded from her shattered skull. The creature took a final gulp, like a snake sucking down a mouse, and the poor woman disappeared into the bulk of the monster.

Jim forced himself to his feet and sprinted forward, pushing his way through the throng of people that all ran in panic as well. Up ahead, the heaving crowed seemed to veer to the left as one, and their terrified screams increased. Through the mass of people before him, Jim managed to see what everyone was trying to keep away from: a pack of short but disfigured abominations that had a man pinned down.

The short, squat attackers were clearly demonic, yet also humanoid, and their naked bodies were a mottled grey with thick black veins visible beneath the skin. Pudgy bellies and baby-like rolls of fat were at odds with the long and razor-sharp talons at the ends of their arms. The creatures stood about three feet high and their mouths were long and open in a permanent cry—stretching down and attaching to their chests. There were no teeth inside of their mouths, only a black, glistening membrane that was lined with clusters of moving barnacle-like growths.

The poor man pinned down by these surprisingly powerful demons was having his skin peeled from his body. He cried and wailed in agonising pain as the sharp talons gripped his flesh and pulled it away from his body in long strips. The long chunks were then dangled over the permanently open mouths of the creatures before being dropped inside and swallowed. The man's torture had clearly been going on for at least a little while, as much of his skin had been torn away, exposing the raw and tender meat and tendons beneath. He lay in a pool of his own blood and fought frantically, but was simply overwhelmed. One creature waddled round to his front and, in one quick motion, ripped off his jaw, before depositing it whole inside of its own mouth.

Jim forced himself forward, managing to find enough space to break into another sprint. He didn't stop running until he hit the edge of town, certain he was losing his mind.

None of that could have happened, he told himself. *It couldn't have.* He was just going crazy, that was all. He'd much prefer going crazy to the alternative.

The next day was like a dream. He forced himself back into town to see what had gone on. It seemed safe, at least for the moment. No screaming. No monsters to see. Just lost people unable to make sense of what had happened the night before.

Scores of people were reported missing over the days that followed. None of the missing were ever found. People talked about what they had seen that night, but over time, the stories became less frequent.

Jim asked out Ada only a week after the night of madness. She was a woman he'd admired from afar. In person, she turned out to be everything he could have hoped for, and more. He quickly fell in love.

But she couldn't leave town.

She had a responsibility to care for her ailing mother. And Jim couldn't leave Ada behind. The two were married within a few years of meeting. They bought their first house together. And, even when Jim left on tour with the military,

Netherwell Bay was always the home he thought of. Because that's where Ada was waiting.

Even after her mother died, Ada and Jim didn't leave town. They had built a life there. The night of the disappearances had moved further and further into the past. Nothing like it ever happened again throughout the years they lived together. Some say it hadn't happened at all. Many excuses had been given back in the day, of course. Mass hysteria. Shared psychosis. A poisoning of the local water supply that acted as a hallucinogenic. Even mass suicide, where many of the townsfolk had supposedly thrown themselves into the sea.

And after all the time that had passed, Jim himself started to doubt his memory of that night. Any other explanation, no matter how wild and fanciful, would have made more sense to him than what his eyes had shown him that night.

The years continued to roll on. Netherwell Bay was the only home Jim had ever known, and Ada was there with him. They lived a happy life together and he became certain that nothing like what had happened during that horrible night would ever happen again.

It was a legend, relegated to the annals of time.

And then, over fifty years later, he'd stumbled upon the remains of three people in Hollows Cove. Slaughtered and sacrificed. The terrible but fading memories of that night over fifty years ago had come flooding back.

22

Beth sat in stunned silence at what she'd just heard. She had no clue what to say in response. A thousand questions seemed to be tumbling through her mind, but none were clear or focused enough to be able to ask. It was all simply a mass of confused noise.

'I... don't believe it,' was all she could say. Though, it wasn't quite a statement of fact. She *could* believe it, if even only a little, considering what she had experienced herself.

Jim let out a humourless chuckle. 'Quite the tale, huh?'

'And you stuck around here for all those years after?' Beth asked.

Jim nodded. 'Had to. My Ada was here, and I could never leave her. And, as the years went on, that horrible night started to seem like... I dunno... a dream, maybe? Nothing like it ever happened again. Though there were always stories from people of my generation, a lot of us doubted ourselves. The officials who came to investigate obviously didn't want to hear what we told them. Said the disappearances could have been linked to mass suicide or something. Said the people had likely been in a cult. Not that any bodies were found. And the stories were explained away. Something in the water that caused hallucinations and mass panic. As the years go by, you kind of start to believe it, at least on some level. It's a more comforting thought. Ada and I... we were happy here. For a lot of years. I honestly thought all that... whatever it was, was in the past. Until yesterday, when I saw those bodies.'

'And now you think it's happening again?'

'Possibly. Back then there were rumours and stories of weird symbols in the cave. Cult-like stuff, you know? Well, that's exactly what I saw yesterday. On the ground, beneath the bodies. There were circles, with odd markings in them. Weird shapes—though I didn't stick around to take much notice. Knew I needed to get the hell out of there.'

'Jesus,' Beth exclaimed. She didn't know what else to say, and finally took a drink of her own coffee. Surprisingly, it was delicious, as the one that morning had been as well: a good mix of acidity, sweetness, and bitterness. Netherwell Bay might be fucked up, but it apparently knew good coffee. 'Can you try and remember what you saw in that cave, Jim? Please? I have a feeling it might be important.'

Jim shifted uncomfortably in his seat. 'Jesus, it ain't something I really want to remember. For one, the bodies were all chopped up. Well, maybe that isn't right. Pulled apart is closer to the truth.' He took a breath. 'Didn't exactly seem like clean cuts at those bloody stumps. There were trails of... flesh... and things.'

Beth noticed his cheeks pale. She knew talking about the scene had to be hard on him.

'I'm really sorry you had to see it, Jim,' Beth said, and reached out to put a reassuring hand on his. 'And I know this is difficult.

'How could it help you, though?' Jim asked. 'It was just a sickening mess.'

'You'd be surprised at what small details can sometimes lead to, and what they can give away.'

Jim's brow furrowed and his eyes narrowed. 'You a copper or something?'

Beth laughed and shook her head. 'Journalist. At least, I used to be. So, can you think of anything specific there that you saw? Maybe something odd that stood out?'

He cast her a withering look. 'Lady, it was *all* odd. It all stood out.'

'Okay, okay, I get that. But beyond that. I mean, can you think of anything beyond the obvious?'

Jim shrugged. 'Not really. The heads had been decapitated. And,' he closed his eyes tightly as he remembered, 'I think each of them were put inside of some circle on the ground. Also, whatever sick bastard had done this, they had left a string of... guts? Intestines? I don't know, but there was a red, fleshy string that ran from one circle to the other.'

'Connecting them?' Beth asked.

Jim nodded, opening his eyes. 'Yeah. All of them were connected to the others. The heads and circles seemed to be set equally apart, too, so they formed kind of a triangle. The point of it faced towards the back of the cave. Towards land, away from the sea. Not sure if that makes a difference?'

'I have no idea,' Beth said. 'But my father always told me that knowledge was power. Over the years, I've learned he was right.'

'I hope that's true. Not that we have a lot to go on.'

'Anything else?' Beth asked, not wanting Jim to slow down. Jim sighed, but closed his eyes again.

'The whole cave was a mess, I can tell you that. Body parts strewn around. Didn't seem to be any order to that.

Guts and meat everywhere. I saw limbs. It seemed so... savage. The heads and those circles, though? They seemed to have a purpose. The rest was just carnage.'

Something clicked in Beth's mind. 'You mentioned before that one of the deceased was a girl? Was it someone you recognised?'

Jim opened his eyes. 'Aye, that's right. I didn't know her, exactly, but had seen her around. Quiet thing. Odd. Always had this intense stare about her, like everyone she looked at was beneath her. I never associated with her—don't think we ever spoke. I think her name was Marie, but I couldn't tell you her last name.'

'Was she one of the Kents, perhaps?'

Jim shrugged. 'Couldn't tell you one way or the other. I know what people say about small towns, that everyone knows everyone else. You might know faces, sure, but there are still over a thousand people living here and in the surrounding area. Do you know a thousand people by name?'

Beth shook her head.

'I don't know if she was related to the Kents or not. Couldn't say. She was just someone I saw around town every now and then. I didn't interact with her.'

'And the two men who had been killed? You said you didn't recognise them.'

'That's right,' Jim said. 'Though it took me a moment to realise who the girl was, to be honest. If you'll forgive me, these heads... they weren't just like a preserved mannequin head or something. They had been left on the ground for a long while, so the blood had drained. And the eyes had been gouged out, as well. Those decapitated heads were a mess. But, even so, if I had seen those men before, then it ain't clicking in my brain. And believe me, as much as I don't want to, I've tried to place them. The police asked me the same thing. I really don't think there is anything else I can tell you.'

Beth sat back. She had been so focused on finding out the details Jim knew, hoping it could help in her search, she had forgotten—or ignored—that three poor people were actually dead. It was the comment about the eyes that hit her: that they had been gouged out.

Jim had been right before when he had called it savage.

'Okay,' Beth said. 'I'm sorry I made you relive that, but thank you.'

'Not sure it will be much use,' Jim replied. 'You'll understand now why I advised you to get out of here as quickly as possible. If history really is repeating itself, you're going to want no part of it.'

'I hear you, but—'

'Josh,' Jim said, finishing Beth's sentence.

'Yeah, Josh.'

'Well, you best be quick about finding him.' Jim drained the last of his coffee.

'You leaving town, then?' Beth asked.

'I am—as soon as we finish here, in fact. Have no idea where I'm gonna go yet. Just take the bus out of here and get a hotel or something for a few days. Follow the news. See what happens. Might be safe to come back eventually, and I can sort out a permanent move then.'

'So... you're just running away?' Beth asked. She couldn't help herself. It wasn't her place to judge, but, apparently her subconscious had done so anyway. She immediately regretted it, however, as Jim's expression turned furious.

'Excuse me?' he asked, raising his voice. 'Did you hear what I just told you?'

'I did,' Beth said, taking on a more diplomatic tone. 'And I'm sorry, that came out wrong. I didn't mean it like that.'

Jim rose to his feet. 'You do as you please,' he said, through gritted teeth. 'But, young lady, I've seen a lot in my lifetime. Whether you believe it or not, it takes a lot to scare me. What's coming here, scares me. I have no issue admitting that. Staying here to face what's coming don't make you brave. It makes you a damn fool.'

He then put on his coat.

'Jim, wait,' Beth said, getting to her feet as well. 'Can you at least tell me—'

'I've told you enough!' he snapped. 'Best of luck to you.'

Shit, shit, shit.

Beth quickly grabbed her coat, ready to follow him. She felt like Jim could still help her, even if it was just to tell her the location of the Kent's private estate. But as she finished gathering her things and stood, she noticed that Jim had frozen in place.

Standing directly outside, with a dark smile, was Pete. A few of his friends were with him, and they were all wearing the same evil grin. Pete gave Beth a wave, then beckoned them towards him with his finger.

'Someone wants to see you, little lady,' he shouted through the door. 'You best not keep them waiting.'

'Not interested,' Beth shouted back.

'We'll see if there is a back door out of here,' Jim said, keeping his voice low and his eyes focused ahead. 'Don't listen to this yob. Don't go anywhere with him, either.'

Beth had no intention of going with him, but she also didn't like the idea of having to go out through a back door, running away like a coward. Jim turned to the lady behind the counter. 'Patricia, is there a way out back there?' he asked, nodding to a door behind her. 'Don't really feel like dealing with these idiots outside, to be honest.'

The lady looked up from her magazine, then rolled her eyes after noticing Pete and his friends standing beyond the door. 'That fella? He's a bloody nuisance. Still goes on like he's a teenager. Someone should tell him he's almost bloody forty. Come on back here, Jim. I'll take you through the kitchen. Does Pete have a bone to pick with you or something?'

'It would seem so,' Jim said. 'Come on, Jess,' he added, and started to walk towards the counter with his dog following behind. The bell above the entrance door sounded and the door opened. Pete—and only Pete—stepped inside. He was wearing jeans, Doc Marten boots, a white t-shirt that did little to hide his belly, but no coat. Considering it wasn't exactly warm outside, Beth assumed this was done as a statement. *Cold don't bother me, none. Cos I'm tough.* Either that, or his bulk insulated him enough to ward off the chill.

'Where are you two off to?' he asked, wearing a smug grin Beth just wanted to scratch clean off his face.

'Away from you,' Beth replied.

'Why?' Pete asked, bringing a hand up to his chest, feigning hurt. 'I've only come to deliver a message. Something you will want to hear.'

'I very much doubt that,' Beth said, turning away from him. 'I don't care who wants to talk to me, I'm not interested.'

'Shame,' Pete said, with a shrug. 'I'll tell Josh not to expect you, then.'

23

'Josh?' Beth asked, quickly turning back around. The self-satisfied grin on Pete's face only intensified.

'That's right,' he said.

'Where is he?' Beth demanded, not trying to hide the sudden anger that hit her. 'Tell me!'

Pete held up his hands defensively and laughed. 'Take it easy, sweetheart. He's close by. Come with me and we'll go see him.'

'Beth,' Jim said, resting a hand on her arm. 'Don't go with him.'

'You shut your mouth, you old fucker!' Pete spat. His grin vanished in an instant and he bared his teeth in a snarl. 'Ain't got nothing to do with you.'

'Both of you stop!' Patricia shouted from behind Beth. 'I'll not have any trouble in here. Pete, go away. I'll call the police if you keep pushing things. You know I'm serious.'

Pete turned his raging eyes to the cafe's owner. After he stared daggers for a few moments, a smirk returned. 'I'm not doing anything to warrant that, Pat,' he said. 'This lady and I are just talking. I'm passing on a message, is all.'

'Of course you are,' Patricia said, her voice dripping with sarcasm. 'And shouting at Jim in the process?'

'He needs to keep his nose out of things that don't concern him,' Pete said, glaring at Jim.

'Just go away,' Patricia shot back. 'Take your mates outside with you, too. Pubs will be opening soon. Go, get drunk, and keep out of everybody's way.'

'Not today,' Pete replied. 'Got business to take care of.' He turned back to Beth. 'Now, do you want to come and see Josh, or not?'

'Where is he?' Beth asked again.

Pete stepped aside and motioned towards the front door. 'I'll take you.'

'Not a chance,' Jim said, answering for her.

But Beth wasn't as quick to dismiss the offer. She wasn't an idiot, of course, and knew that the whole thing smelled fishy as hell. But it was *something*.

'Tell me where we are going first,' Beth insisted. 'Then I'll come.'

'Can't do that, I'm afraid.'

'Then she ain't going,' Jim said. He tugged at Beth's arm, which finally got her attention. 'Don't be a fool. You know nothing good can come from this. That man and his friends can't be trusted. They're just errand boys for the Kents.'

'Fuck you!' Pete shouted. 'I'm more than a fucking errand boy!'

Jim ignored him. 'Don't let the need to find your brother land you in danger.'

He was right, of course, Beth didn't doubt that. But she was hoping to keep Pete talking and get him to let something slip.

'Come on,' Jim said, pulling her away. Beth allowed herself to follow, but felt her stomach drop. She was *so* close.

'He's gonna be sad to learn you didn't want to see him,' Pete said mockingly. 'So, I guess you might as well just fuck off home, then, leave Josh to his life here, where he's happy.'

'It's a trick,' Jim whispered as they walked through the hatch in the counter. 'He's goading you.'

'I know,' Beth said. Pete wasn't a smart man, and Beth was sure he was quite incapable of fooling her. Still, Josh was close, and Pete knew where he was.

Patricia pushed open a door behind the counter, revealing a kitchen behind. It wasn't a commercially sized one, more like something that would be seen in a modest house, with wooden panelling on the units, as opposed to the metallic finish Beth normally associated with restaurant kitchens. This only gave further onus to the small, homely operation Patricia was running. At the back of the kitchen was another door, this one an external one. It was metal, with a push-bar across its middle.

'Through there,' Patricia said, pointing. Beth, Jim, and Jess quickly made their way through the kitchen to the door beyond. Beth didn't like it. She hated that Pete had managed to make her turn tail and flee. She needed to know what he knew, and this felt like an opportunity slipping away. Jim was right, of course. It was a fucking trap, and Josh was the bait.

Jim pushed the door open, quickly, and they all emerged into a narrow backstreet. Before them was a bare brick boundary wall—complete with curled barbed wire at the top. Patricia closed the door behind them, and Beth heard it click shut.

'Which way?' Beth asked, looking left and right. A few bins and piles of rubbish lined the backstreet separating two rows of buildings, each backing on to it. Then Beth saw a group of three figures step into view from her left from around the corner at the very end of the street.

To her right, Beth saw more people emerge, and recognised some from the bar yesterday. They had been among Pete's group. She felt her stomach drop.

'Oh for fuck's sake,' Jim said. A low grumble emitted from Jess. 'What do you want?' Jim called out to them. The street was isolated and unoccupied, save for Beth, Jim, Jess, and the thugs pinning them in. No one answered Jim's question. Eventually, from the right, Pete came jogging into view, joining his friends. He was panting and red in the face.

'You fuckers made me run,' he said, struggling for breath. 'Not the way I like to get my exercise.' He then made a show of cracking his knuckles, and he began to advance, followed by his gang. The three to Beth's left started to walk towards them as well.

Pete laughed. 'No one can help you out here,' he said. Jim turned and knocked on the door they had just escaped through, banging as hard as he could. Then, Pete broke into a sprint, and the rest of his pack followed suit. 'That bitch won't help you,' he shouted. 'I gave her a good warning before leaving. She's fucking sitting on the floor crying her eyes out right now. Her attitude was nothing a good slap couldn't sort out.'

As much as Beth was afraid of the gang, that comment caused pang of anger to flare up within her. Pete really was the worst kind of scum.

The slapping feet of the advancing attackers echoed around the small alleyway as the men quickly closed the distance.

Beth wasn't going to make this easy for them.

She put a hand into her pocket and grabbed her keys in

a fist—the jagged, metal edge protruded through two fingers. Jim dropped his stick to the ground.

'Won't you need that?' Beth asked, nodding to the walking stick on the ground.

'Better with these,' he said, bringing up his fists. 'Learned a little boxing in the army.'

Jess' growls turned into angry barks. Beth took a breath and readied herself to fight.

24

AT THE HEAD of the pack, one man in particular seemed to be making a beeline for Beth. She cowered a little, hoping to lull the attacker into a false sense of security.

Come on, then, you fucker.

As soon as the man got close to her, Beth brought out the hand that held her keys and forced the metal edge forward, cutting through the cheek of the shocked thug. There was a little resistance from the flesh at first, then it gave way and split apart. Beth felt a spurt of warm liquid streak across her hand from the wound, and the man went down screaming. Another, who pushed his way past the first, grabbed her by the throat, and Beth quickly brought a knee up as hard as she could into his groin. He let out a sharp squeal, his eyes went wide, and his grip on her neck slackened.

Beth then brought the palm of her hand up into his nose, forcing his head back. Bone and cartilage crunched beneath her driving hand.

But two others were quickly on her, and in the moment

before Beth was tackled to the ground, she caught a glimpse of how Jim and Jess were handling themselves.

Jim had one fella down, and the old man's knuckles were streaked with blood. He held a boxer's stance, fists up to his face, eyes focused and determined. The man he faced looked weary, evidently surprised that Jim was no pushover. Jess had a man down on the ground and her mouth was clamped over his arm. She violently tugged it this way and that.

'Get fucking off me!' he cried out.

Then Jess took a savage kick to the gut from Pete, who had now entered the fray proper. The poor dog yelped and was forced backwards. The two men pressed down on Beth, pinning her to the floor. She then saw Pete joining in the fight against Jim, and with two-on-one, the odds were too much. Though Jim connected with a stiff left jab to the face of the first man, who Pete had thrown forward, he was then left exposed as Pete leapt in and thrust a thick arm around the older man's neck. Pete then pushed his weight forward, down on to Jim, pulling the chokehold tight. Jim spluttered, coughed, and wheezed, but continued to fight back. The first man, who had taken the punch, swung a kick that connected with Jim's ribs. The power of the blow, and the weight pushing down from behind, forced Jim to the floor. The two attackers then started to kick at Jim, who could only hold his arms over his head to try and protect himself from the blows.

Jess was soon involved again, however, barking and snarling. She grabbed onto the first man's leg, and he cried out in pain. Beth saw Pete pull free a blade.

No!

The knife was just a Swiss-Army one, but the edge appeared sharp. Jim looked up to see Pete advance on the dog. Beth held her breath, not wanting to watch what was coming. Pete raised the knife.

'No!' yelled Jim, and quickly pushed himself up and stumbled forward into Pete. Jim grabbed the man round the waist and tried to force him back. Pete dropped the knife.

'Jess, run!' the old man yelled, but the dog remained focused in its attack. Another man was up now, however— the one Beth had kneed in the groin. He swung a kick and the poor dog took another nasty blow, sending it rolling to the ground.

'We need to go,' the man said to Pete as he stepped in to help deliver punches to Jim's head. The old man fell again.

'Get them all in the van now!' Pete snarled. 'Make it quick.'

Jim was hauled to his feet and dragged away by two of them. Beth felt her arms pinned painfully behind her back, and she was pulled up from the ground as well. The two were dragged forward, and Beth saw a nondescript white van skid to a stop at the end of the street. The side door slid open.

I'm actually being fucking kidnapped! Beth thought.

She saw Pete run up to Jess and plant more kicks into the poor dog, who yelped at each blow. When satisfied, the thug quickly caught up with the others. Jess, however, again got to her feet and started to growl. She was obviously not done yet. But, as much as Beth and Jim struggled against their captors, there were just too many of them. Beth and Jim were soon thrown into the van, and the group of attackers jumped in as well. They wrestled Beth and Jim to the floor and tied their hands behind their backs. Pete was last inside, and he turned to see Jim's brave companion come sprinting down the street, ready for more.

But it was too late. Pete slid the door shut.

'Move!' he yelled to the driver. The van lurched forward and they were off.

25

THE DRIVE WAS A SHORT ONE.

With Beth and Jim beaten and tied up, they could only lie on the floor of the van, rolling around slightly as the vehicle moved quickly, arcing around corners and wobbling while it rolled over uneven ground. Some of the thugs had taken the opportunity to spit at their two prisoners, cursing them as well. The one with the gash on his face—from Beth's keys—constantly antagonised her, calling Beth a bitch and a cunt.

As battered and pained as Beth was, she at least took heart in the knowledge she and Jim had given the thugs a run for their money.

Ultimately, however, they had still been taken, and Beth had no idea where they were headed. She tried to keep track in her head of the amount of time that was passing, counting slowly to get a rough idea of the trip's duration. The van came to a stop and shut off its engine after about five minutes of driving, according to Beth's estimate. She suspected that meant they were still in the town centre somewhere. Or at least close to it.

Pete leaned in close. 'Not that anyone would hear you, but if you start screaming when we pull you out of here, I'm gonna have my boys cut the old man's throat. Understand?'

Beth didn't blink or look away; she simply held Pete's gaze. She could tell in his voice that the pitiful excuse for a man didn't have it in him to carry through with the threat. But she wasn't going to push him on it, as she doubted her screaming for help would do any good anyway. Plus, Beth didn't want to give Pete the satisfaction of seeing her scared and begging.

'I'll take your silence as a yes,' he said, then turned to his men. 'Get them inside, quickly.'

Beth and Jim were then pulled from the van. They found themselves in a small, enclosed area. A high stone wall encompassed them, running well above head height. Automated iron gates were closing behind them with a screech. Beth looked up at the building before them, which was clearly the rear of the structure. With its grey and smooth stone blockwork, arched window heads, and stone detailing to the corners, Beth knew it to be the Heritage Centre. A place she had left only a few hours before. The back elevation of the building was similar to the front, only the windows were more numerous. There was also a metal external escape stair that hugged the wall and ran down from a flat section of roof up above.

'Josh is in there?' Beth asked.

'No questions. You had your chance to come quietly.'

Beth shrugged. 'To be honest, I thought that cutting up your friend's face there,' she pointed to the one with the gash in his cheek, 'and putting that one down,' now she motioned to the one she had dropped with a knee to the groin, 'would be more fun.'

'That a fact?' Pete asked with an amused smile. The two

men she'd pointed at bristled with anger and embarrassment. 'Gotta say, lady, I kind of like you. Liked the look of you when I first saw you, too. But let's be clear: you try anything now, and *I'll* be the one to knock you down.'

Beth didn't respond, simply glared at Pete again.

She and Jim were then led towards a sizeable double-leaf access door. It was tall and wide, made of solid black metal, and was likely used for large deliveries, Beth assumed. One leaf of the door was pushed slowly open a little from within, and Aiden walked out. He looked down at the ground, clearly uncomfortable, and fidgeted with his hands. Initially, Beth hadn't been sure what to make of the young lad. She'd wanted to like him, and had hoped he wasn't tied too strongly to the Kents. That hope was now quashed.

'You are to take them inside,' Aiden said softly to Pete.

'You kicked my dog,' Jim suddenly said. He was glaring at Pete now, with fury in his eyes.

'I would have killed it, too, if I'd gotten the chance,' Pete replied with a scowl. 'Still might, you know. I could go back and find it. Gut it. Put the thing down.'

'You'll pay for hurting her,' Jim said. 'I always had you down as a thug, but nothing like this. You're going to be sorry. Mark my words, boy. I'm gonna make sure of it.'

There was an eerie certainty in Jim's voice. A gritty determination that surprised Beth. And, judging by how Pete's eyes widened in shock, it seemed to have caught him off guard as well.

'Enough chit-chat. Take them in,' Pete commanded to his group.

Beth and Jim were led forward, and Beth glared at Aiden as she passed him. The young man would not look back.

They entered the building and Beth saw that they were

in a large storage area with a high concrete ceiling and bare concrete walls and floor. It felt cold, and the space was filled with metal shelving units. Boxes and crates of God-knows-what sat on the shelves. Another set of double doors was at the end of the large space, and it appeared to be their destination. The group walked through the doors and into an open stairwell area, which was quite the contrast to the storage room they had just been in.

The floor underfoot was stone marble tiles, light in colour with swirls of dark grey embedded within. The walls had dark oak panelling up to the midpoint, and rich red wallpaper above. The ceilings were high, and multiple dark oak doors were set into the walls. Beth guessed that one of them probably led to the Heritage display area she had been in earlier. The stairs were carpeted a deep red, similar to the walls, and had dark wooden balustrades and handrails. At the top of these stairs, a group of people stood, gazing down.

William Kent was at the head of this gathering.

Beth had no idea who the other people were. They all looked of an older generation, and were dressed well in elegant clothing: dark suits, ball gowns, and evening dresses, which was odd, given the time of day. Even William had changed clothes into something a little more formal. Among their number, however, Beth noticed one girl who was notably younger than the rest. She was dressed in a black, shoulder-less dress, and her blonde hair was pinned back into an elegant knot at the nape of her neck. She wore sparkling earrings that dangled down to her shoulders, and her face had high cheekbones lightly layered with flawless makeup. On top of that, her eyes were a striking blue.

The girl was stunning.

'Hello again,' William said from his position at the top of the stairs. 'Beth, was it?'

'You do realise you've kidnapped me, don't you?' Beth asked. 'That is a criminal offence.'

William just chuckled. 'I saw the resemblance straight away,' he said. 'You talk just like him, too. In fact, talk a little much. Must be a family trait.'

'Where is my brother?' Beth snapped.

William ignored the question and went on, 'I had to be sure, of course. Couldn't just take you there and then. Have to be careful, you know? So, I showed Josh some camera footage of you when you waltzed in here earlier, bold as brass. He didn't say anything, but the worry on his face told me everything I needed to know. He had originally told me he didn't have any family left. Quite the liar, your brother, isn't he?'

'What have you done with him?' Beth asked, raising her voice. 'Tell me where his is!'

William just turned to Jim instead. 'Shame you've gotten caught up in all of this, isn't it?'

'You behind those killings on the beach?' Jim asked, raising his head defiantly. 'You murdered those poor people?'

William chuckled. 'You have no idea what is going on, Jim.'

'I know enough to realise things are going to go to hell, just like they did fifty years ago.'

'Well, I suppose you could say things are going to go to hell, Jim. That's certainly one way to look at it. We have a different view, of course, but you are welcome to yours. But no, this isn't like last time. This is something much more... divine. Bring them up,' he called out. Beth wasn't sure who he had shouted to. Even Pete and his goons looked around confused, unsure if they were to follow that instruction.

However, the group at the head of the stairs then parted

and four men came stomping down. They looked to be in their twenties or early thirties, and the men all had shaved heads and almost blank expressions. All were dressed in dark combat trousers and tight black jumpers. They didn't seem to be mere street thugs, like Pete and his friends, and had a terrible intensity about them.

Both Beth and Jim were quickly grabbed. Beth's arms were forced behind her back with much more force than anything Pete's gang had managed to exert. The way they snapped her into position was quick and efficient, and she cried out in pain.

'Pete,' William said, 'you and your friends are finished for the day. Run along.'

Pete looked a little confused, almost hurt at being cast aside. But he didn't argue. 'Yes, Mr. Kent,' he replied obediently.

'Errand boy,' Beth said to him with a sneer. 'Run along, little puppy, your master is finished with you now.'

She saw Pete clench his jaw and step forward, but one of the men restraining Jim simply looked up to Pete with a stern gaze. The shaven-headed man slowly shook his head, eyes serious and jaw set. Pete backed off.

'Let's go, lads,' he said to his friends, and they all slowly filtered out the way they had come in.

'Aiden,' William called down, 'see them out. Then you can busy yourself with scripture.'

'Thank you,' Aiden said, and an excited grin broke over his face. The young man then hurried along to complete his task. Beth and Jim were forced up the stairs and up to the waiting group, who moved further aside to let them pass.

'Take them to see him. I'll be along shortly.'

Beth and Jim were then hauled down the corridor to their left. The floor was carpeted as the stairs had been, and the walls were covered in that same red wallpaper from the stairwell downstairs. Many pictures were hung along the wall, dominating the vertical planes. Beth stared at the paintings as she was dragged past, but could scarcely understand what she was seeing. It wasn't traditional art, but rather horrific images that had clearly been painted by a troubled mind.

One was of a hellish landscape, with mountains of black and perfectly cylindrical towers that touched a star-filled sky. Creatures of magnificent size could be seen roaming on the edges of the titanic mountains, but the centre of the piece was the sky itself. The stars there swirled together to a point, forming a great eye that looked down over everything. Amazingly, the title of the picture, embossed on a brass nameplate at the bottom of the frame, was *Heaven*. The artist's name was beneath: Aldrich Kent.

Then there was a depiction of a room, walls papered similarly to the walls of the corridor Beth was in. In this picture, four bodies hung from the ceiling by their necks. The corpses' bottom halves were gone, and their insides hung to the floor. Their arms were bound behind their backs, their throats had been cut, and the eyes were empty sockets. The hanging bodies were spaced equally apart, like the vertical corners of a cube. Beneath them, on a wooden floor, a white outline of a square had been drawn, and the corners lined up with the bodies above. This square was filled with cryptic marks and symbols. Sat centrally to the shape, and hungrily devouring a pile of heaped meat, was a strange figure. It was almost human, and sat cross legged in a pile of gore. It was multi-armed, and its head, with a low-hanging mouth, had multiple eyes over the cranium, like that of a fly. This was called *Ascension Begins*.

One painting displayed a sickening scene on a beach,

with people gathered round at night. They were robed in plain, simple cloaks. Beth actually let out a small gasp as she saw a pile of infants—*babies*—that were heaped on the stony ground. Three mounds of bodies were spaced out equally, like points on a triangle. The tip pointed inland, away from the sea behind. One child was held aloft—its face locked in an eternal cry—by one of the robed figures. The title of this piece was *Ritual of Moloch*.

Another showed the interior of a cave, and the sea beyond it. The cave, however, was a bloody mess, with three skulls sat in white circles. These circles all had markings within them: an inner ring, and also symbols that were alien to Beth. The skulls were connected by chalk lines, and it did not take Beth more than an instant to recall the scene Jim had described. Worse still, she saw a giant, monstrous figure half hidden by the dense fog above the sea and just breaking through the mist. It had many legs, as well as curling tentacles that punctured the fog. Any face it had was hidden, but Beth recognised its form. It was titled *The Harbinger Comes*.

The artist of all the pieces was Aldrich Kent. The pictures were dated, and all were from the early eighteen hundreds.

There were other paintings lining this wall as well, all as grotesque and as nightmarish as the last.

Eventually, Beth and the others stopped outside of a door, midway down the hallway. It was just as the others were: dark oak panelling. One of the men pushed the door open and forced Beth and Jim inside.

The room was, for the most part, empty. The floorboards were old and stained. The wallpaper, too, was worn, and some of it was hanging loose. It was a room that appeared to have received no care or attention in a long time.

A window sat on the far wall, tall and narrow, and a thin strip of daylight—the only light source in the room—shone in through it.

Two men were sat central to the room, each facing forward, and both bound to their respective chairs. They were naked and bloody and had burlap sacks covering their heads. One of them groaned.

It was the man on the left who drew Beth's gaze, however. Even without seeing his face, she knew instantly who it was.

26

THE MEN that were holding Beth released her, and she ran forward towards her brother.

There were multiple cuts and lacerations on Josh, and blood ran freely from each. However, even though she wasn't medically trained, her initial, panicked conclusion was that they were all surface level. His body was also covered with a layer of sweat and grime, and the hairs on his chest were matted down. She quickly pulled the burlap sack free of his head and, for the first time in a long while, looked down at her brother's face.

Tears erupted from her and she started to sob.

It was him, without question. Even after so long, Beth recognised the strong jaw line covered with black stubble. His greasy hair was slicked back, messy and wild, and it fell to his shoulders. Josh also had their father's thin nose. And, even though he looked terrible—with a swollen and beaten face—his blue eyes locked onto hers, and Beth saw a wave of realisation wash over him. She cupped his face delicately with her palms.

He coughed, then wheezed out a word. 'B... Beth?'

'Yeah, it's me, Josh.'

'You came?'

Beth nodded, tears still running from her eyes. 'I did.'

He shook his head and started to cry as well. 'You shouldn't have. You made a mistake. Go. Please. Run.'

'But you called me,' she said.

'I know,' he replied. 'I shouldn't have. Get out of here, Beth.'

'She isn't running anywhere, Josh,' a voice said. Beth swivelled her head to see William Kent step into the room. 'She's staying right here. You three will be needed tonight.'

'No,' Josh said, pain evident in his voice. 'Let her go, please. Just let my sister go. You don't need her for any of this.'

William, flanked by the four men in black, shook his head. 'Afraid not, Josh. You *know* that isn't true.'

'What the fuck are you talking about?' Beth snapped. 'What the fuck is going on?'

'Please,' Josh said again, fighting against his bonds. 'I'm begging you.'

'Too late for that,' William said. 'You made your choice, and now you will live and die by it. You should have done what was instructed of you. Instead, you ran—even hurt a number of our brethren in the process. What? Did you think you'd stop what was coming? Stupid, Josh. Naïve. You were destined for something truly magnificent, boy. Your role would have changed things forever. You could have brought about permanent change and opened the door to the Gods, but you threw all that back at us. For what? A misguided sense of right and wrong?'

'I'm sorry!' Josh cried. 'Let me make it right.'

'Oh, that will happen,' William said with a sinister chuckle. 'It will *all* be made right. The ritual will be completed. Then—and only then—when your blood is spilled and flesh is torn and the doorway is open... then you will have made it right, Josh.'

'Beth,' Josh said, turning his wild, wet eyes to her. 'You need to get away. I don't care how. You need to escape. I shouldn't have brought you here. I shouldn't have called.'

'But you did, Josh,' William said. 'The blame for all of this lies with you for your betrayal. You could have been one of us, you could have seen true paradise, but you threw it away. And you should know, Josh, that we aren't the forgiving type.'

William then walked over to the other restrained man in the room, whose body was shaking. The burlap sack was quickly yanked free and the man's face was revealed. He was young, in his early twenties, and had dark hair and wide, terrified eyes. A length of duct-tape covered his mouth.

'For example, take Kyle here,' William said, and ruffled the man's damp hair. 'He had the chance to stop you that night, Josh. Do you remember? When you tried to run, Kyle here actually showed a little initiative and stepped out in front of you to stop you. However, when you held up your knife, Kyle failed. Despite us giving an order to attack and stop you, Kyle put his own well-being before the needs of the group. He showed fear and stepped aside. If Kyle had simply stood his ground, I think we would have caught you. But he failed, and he let you escape. That is something we cannot forgive.'

The young man started to thrash around in his chair, fighting against his bonds. Tears started to fall, and though his cries were muffled by the tape, Beth knew he was begging for mercy. William retrieved his phone and stepped back a little, holding it up and pointing it at Kyle.

'Kyle, my boy, you know what your punishment will be. I

will record your death so that the others can see the price of failure and cowardice. And it will also show our guests here just how serious we are.' He then turned his head to the group of four men who were with him. 'Proceed.'

One of the men stepped forward, and a disturbing smile grew over his face. It was the first show of emotion Beth had seen from the zealots. The man stopped just before Kyle, reached behind his back, and pulled something free from the waistband of his trousers. Beth let out a gasp when she saw the size of the Bowie knife. The blade was huge and looked horribly sharp. Kyle started to thrash with renewed vigour.

'Stop,' Beth pleaded.

'There is no stopping any of this, my dear. Something you would do well to keep in mind.'

The three other men stepped in front of Beth and Jim, blocking them off from Kyle. Not that Beth would have tried.

William chuckled, then turned to the man with the knife. 'Have fun, Brother Sutton. And make the boy *feel* it.'

Brother Sutton's smile increased, but his gaze was a manic one. To Beth, it seemed like there was no humanity behind his eyes, only darkness.

The knife was brought up, and the tip pressed into Kyle's cheek. Sutton made a quick swipe sideways, nicking the skin and drawing blood. Kyle yanked his head back and squirmed in pain. The knife was then pressed into the young man's chest. Another nick.

And again.

'Let him go,' Beth said to William, but the older man just ignored her and instead concentrated on recording.

Brother Sutton took hold of Kyle's head and forced it to the left. He then grabbed Kyle's ear with one hand, while he used the knife in his other to begin cutting. Beth winced as

Kyle's muffled screaming intensified. Blood flowed down the side of his face. Brother Sutton worked furiously, with violent sawing motions, and hacked at the ear, forced the blade through cartilage. Eventually, the ear came free, and he dropped it to the floor. Once Kyle's head was released, he shook it frantically and continued crying out behind the tape in absolute agony. Beth saw a glimpse of the raw and exposed flesh where the ear had just been.

Brother Sutton then grabbed the chair Kyle was bound to and spun the man around so that his tied hands were facing William. Sutton took hold of the index finger on Kyle's left hand, and the tip of the knife was moved beneath the fingernail. Sutton thrust the blade forward.

Kyle exploded in a fit of writhing muffled screaming, but it was useless. Sutton took his time in pushing the large blade deeper beneath the nail, and started to twist the knife as well. Most of the fingernail was forced away from the bed, and dangled uselessly as blood dripped from the finger.

The process was then repeated on three other nails. After this, Sutton grabbed the small finger on Kyle's right hand. But he didn't use the knife this time. Instead, he just quickly snapped it back, breaking the digit completely. Beth heard the crack. Her body tensed and she started to sob, unable to cope with the violence.

'Very good, Brother Sutton,' William said above Kyle's moans of pain. 'But I don't think this young man has learned his lesson just yet. I think we need to step things up a little.'

Sutton nodded, then turned Kyle back around to face everyone. The large man wrapped an arm around Kyle's head to keep it still, then again brought up the knife.

This time to Kyle's right eye.

The blade was forced in beneath the eyeball, cutting

through the skin of the lower lid as it moved. Sutton was slow and deliberate, wiggling the knife as he pushed it in deeper. The tape over Kyle's mouth came free at one side, and his horrible screams of agony were allowed to bellow out unhindered. Kyle desperately tied to pull his head away, but Sutton was far too strong.

The knife was pushed farther in, but was too big and cumbersome for any kind of delicacy, and only succeeded in cutting into and partially mashing-up the eyeball. With a twist, the mangled eye was popped free and dangled down on a fleshy cord.

William chuckled at the sickening torture. 'Oh, Kyle, if you could only see what you look like.'

Sutton then smiled and took hold of the ruined eye. He lifted it and twisted it around, so it was pointing back at Kyle.

'There you go,' he said in deep voice.

William and the other three men all erupted in laughter. The sight of such violence had Beth on the cusp of vomiting, but the sheer *joy* these people were getting from the pain and suffering only made things harder to deal with.

'Just kill him,' Beth said. 'Put him out of his misery.'

'Not a chance,' William said. 'Keep going, Brother Sutton.'

And like an obedient dog, Brother Sutton got to work cutting off Kyle's lips.

The top was first, which was stretched out before the sharp blade messily cut through the flesh, leaving a small jagged flap just above the now exposed teeth and gums. The bottom lip was then taken. Blood smeared Kyle's disfigured face, which was then relieved of its nose. Next, Sutton got to work scalping poor Kyle, whose screams and cries continued to get higher and more intense. With the younger man's hair pulled back in Sutton's grip, the cultist used the sharp edge of his knife to hack and saw at the skin as he yanked it free. A large section of skin and hair was cut loose, revealing an expanse of bone wet with blood.

With each feature lost, Kyle's head looked more like a twisted skull than that of a living human. His one good eye flittered around in utter panic and anguish.

'Okay,' William finally said. 'I think we can draw this to a close. But make it good, would you, Brother Sutton?'

Sutton nodded, then thrust the knife deep into the gut of Kyle in a quick and savage motion. Kyle drew in a gasp of breath, then Sutton forced the knife upwards, cutting the young man's stomach open as Kyle screamed. Brother Sutton then dropped the knife and, with both hands, forced the newly created wound open, pushing the two sides apart and letting guts and glistening-red intestines spill to the floor. A pile of gore lay at Kyle's feet as his single eye rolled back into his head.

'You fucking monsters!' Beth screamed. 'You're a bunch of fucking animals!'

'No,' William said, shaking his head. 'What we are, is *devoted*.'

'I don't see much of a difference,' Beth shot back.

William just chuckled again and put his phone away. 'That might have seemed savage to you, my dear, but that is only because you are blind to the truth. Soon you will learn. This base, animalistic savagery is *needed*. It is to be both understood and embraced if we are to ascend.'

Beth's head was spinning. The insanity was all too much. 'I don't understand what you're talking about! What the fuck is going on, here?!'

'I can show you,' William said. He then addressed the men under his command. 'Follow me with the girl. The other one,' he pointed at Jim, 'leave here. Tie him up with this traitor.'

'Let me go!' Jim commanded as two of the men grabbed him. There was fear in his voice. Beth fought, but she was quickly overpowered by the other two men—one of whom was Sutton. Beth was then dragged out of the room and away from her brother.

'Beth, I'm sorry!' Josh cried out just before the door between them slammed shut.

27

BETH WAS LED across the hallway by the two guards, one either side of her. She struggled against them, but they were both too powerful, and were able to keep her held with what seemed like minimal effort. The journey was a short one, into a room opposite. William Kent stood inside, still wearing that infuriating grin.

This room was larger than the last, and in pristine condition. There was no peeling of the wallpaper or stains on the floor like the one that Josh—and now Jim—were held in.

But despite its size, it seemed cramped, considering the number of things that were crammed inside. Like the public area Beth had visited earlier, the large room also served as a display area, with bookcases, glass cases, chests, and cabinets. Two large windows would have let in a healthily amount of natural light, except wooden shutters were pulled closed over them. The ceiling and wall lights gave the only luminance to the area.

Beth was in no mood for research or investigation, however—she just wanted to get Josh and Jim away from this madness. 'What the fuck do you want from me?' Beth asked William Kent through gritted teeth.

'I'm actually going to bestow on you a huge honour,' William said. 'Despite what I said to your brother, you may yet have a way out of this. He *was* destined for something, but no longer. Perhaps you are more worthy.'

'Worthy of what?' Beth asked, exasperated. But he avoided the question and moved on to something else.

'Those people who were with me back on the landing? They are very important people.'

'More Kents?' Beth assumed.

'Some,' William said. 'But certainly not all. Many of them are here to witness what we are going to accomplish.'

'I'm going to go out on a limb and guess you people are behind the murders out at the cliffs? And that, somehow, you—or those that came before you—were responsible for the same thing fifty years ago. Am I right?'

William smiled as he paced between the bookcases, hands behind his back, like a teacher calmly walking between seated students. 'You are on the right track, certainly.'

'And you are going to do something again tonight. Three more people need to die.'

'Impressive,' William said. 'And how did you find that out?'

'I asked around and put things together,' Beth said. 'Honestly, it wasn't difficult.'

'You are resourceful, I'll give you that.'

'What I don't get, though, is the endgame. I mean, what is the point of the killings? And this talk of paradise? Are you guys a cult?'

She saw him bristle, and he quickly turned to face her. 'I don't like that word.'

'Like it or not, it's accurate. That's all you people are. A bunch of sadistic and idiotic sheep who believe in fairytales.'

William's scowl darkened. 'You'd do well to stop insulting me and my brethren,' he said. 'You asked why we have killed? Well, I'm not sure you can handle the answer. Regardless, I'm curious. Hence why you are here, and not tied up in the other room.'

Beth didn't really want to listen. As much as she tried to remain calm and think clearly, it was all she could do not to lose her shit and start screaming.

Instead, Beth felt she could perhaps buy for time. 'So, what is it?' Beth asked. 'Because let me tell you, I've seen some pretty fucked-up things since I've been here in your town. Not least what you just did to one of your own.'

This drew his attention. 'What have you seen?' he asked. 'Ignoring what just happened in the other room, of course.'

Fuck it, Beth thought, and went for broke. She had a feeling the things she was about to describe were not going to be a shock to him. 'Where to start? Almost as soon as I arrived, I saw something in an upstairs window of a house. A weird, deformed human, with bandages around its head. It just kept knocking on the glass, trying to get my attention. I looked away, and then it was gone.'

'Go on,' William said with an enthused smile.

'And yesterday, on the beach, I heard babies crying. When I looked, there were these small... things. Squirming deformities that were crying out. Again, they disappeared the second I looked away.'

'Exquisite,' William exclaimed in an approving tone. 'Did you know there were child sacrifices on that beach in this town, many years ago? It was one of the first incarnations of the Ritual of Moloch. Sacrifices to the Canaanite

God. I believe what you saw on the beach were the souls of the sacrificed, changed to a pure, chaotic image.'

Beth didn't even know where to start with what he said.

'Moloch? Canaanite?' she asked.

William laughed. 'Forgive me, I get a little carried away at times. The Canaanites were an ancient civilisation. But, I believe, some of their practices were based on truths that they just did not understand. Moloch was the name given to one of their greatest, darkest Gods. A God of sacrifice. Though we do not know how, exactly, we believe that they found a way to commune with the Great Old Ones. The beings that reside in that *other place*. The Ritual of Moloch is part of that. It has informed our religion through the centuries. Indeed, it is my belief that we actually descended from a sect of Canaanites that were cast out.'

Beth shook her head. 'You aren't making things any clearer.' She tried not to sound sarcastic, as she didn't want to anger him again. Instead, she wanted to keep him talking as her hands worked at the bonds that held her wrists. She tried to keep her movements subtle and undetectable, but was finding it difficult to get free of the thin rope.

'I suppose not,' William said, and chuckled again. 'So, is that all you have seen?'

'No. The hotel I'm staying at looks out over the sea. Last night, I saw something out on the water. Something I can't explain. It was huge. Monstrous. I'm not even sure I could properly describe it.'

William clapped his hands together excitedly. 'Oh, you have seen such wonders! The things I could tell you about that great being would astonish you. Tell me, how did it make you feel, gazing upon that divine entity?'

Beth didn't like the way the man revered what was clearly a monster, but she answered truthfully anyway.

'Insignificant,' she said, remembering the feelings clearly. 'Worthless. Like I'd lost my understanding of how things really are.'

'Exactly!' William said. 'That is how it should be. What you have been witnessing are shadows, or rather, echoes, cast by that other plane of existence. We are very close to it now, thanks to the Ritual of Moloch.'

'That was Moloch? The thing out at sea? That was what those Canaanite people worshipped?'

William shrugged. 'Possibly. Perhaps not. But it is one such entity. Though, I'm not certain it is a true Great One. We consider it, rather, a harbinger: a sign that the ritual is working. And it is truly magnificent to behold. The Order has been aware of this other place for centuries, and it is the foundation of our religion. It is our obsession.'

'It sounds like hell,' Beth said.

'That is what this world has conditioned you to think,' William said. 'But this world is *wrong*. Its eyes are fused shut, and humanity rolls around in ignorance like a blind worm. But *our* eyes are open. We have seen the truth. We have seen true majesty and glimpsed unimaginable existences. That is what we aim to ascend to.'

'So, fifty years ago when all those people disappeared, that was the last time you performed this ritual?'

'It was,' William said. 'However, it is not something that can just be done at will. It needs many pieces to fall into place. The sacrifices are one element. Then there is the location of where the ritual is carried out, as well as preparing the seals on which the sacrifices are completed. And the time when all of this happens has to be when the two realities are at their closest. *Then* the door can be opened.'

'Closest?'

'Yes. Just like our planet, things rotate and shift. Our

solar system, hell our *galaxy*, is never stagnant. So it is with other realities, other planes of existence.'

Beth had to stop from shaking her head in disbelief. The things he was saying wouldn't have sounded out of place in an insane asylum—and yet, Beth couldn't deny what *she* had seen.

'And what happened to the people in town after you opened the door last time?'

'Well, in the past, we have only ever been able to open the door a crack. We have used the limited opportunity to offer what some of those Great Old Ones hunger for: the lives and souls of the living from our world. People were taken that night and served up to higher beings.'

'And then the door closes again,' Beth stated.

William nodded. 'That is how it has always been. Our knowledge was not great enough to keep it open any longer. Though we are still searching for other doors as well.'

'Other doors?'

'Yes,' William said, nodding quickly. 'You see, our world touches a specific location in this other plane, one that exists in a pure state. A chaotic state. What we think of as normality is just an accident, born out of a mutation from the real, original existence. And, though we think our universe is vast—and some believe this world's God is omnipotent and all powerful—we are actually barely noticed by the real Gods of existence. That is how insignificant we are. You have felt that insignificance, haven't you, Beth? Because our world is so close to the other, there are points on our Earth that touch it. At times, the lines can blur. Things can, and have, come through. What the Order is trying to do is simply facilitate that. Create doorways. Here in Netherwell, we believe we now have a way to ensure a grand and huge doorway is opened permanently. This time, the ritual will have a significant difference. This world will never be the same.'

He started to wander between the shelves again, running his hand along the spines of the books on display while gazing at them longingly. 'You know, the artefacts and tomes in this room are priceless.' he said. 'Worth more than money could ever buy.'

'And the things downstairs, on display to the public?' Beth asked.

William shrugged. 'Surface-level trinkets. There for the local bottom feeders to look at, if they so wish. It allows us to keep tabs on people in this town, to see if any pick up on the clues, and show an aptitude for true knowledge. It helps us grow our ranks.'

'So, what is different about the ritual this time? How will you keep the door open?'

Frustratingly, the rope that held her wrists was not getting any looser. William turned around. 'You can stop trying to escape,' he said, causing her to pause. 'I'm not sure if you could make it any more obvious, but I assure you, the rope will not give.' Beth didn't know what to do besides squirm under his scowl, like a pupil getting scolded by a teacher. 'And as to your question about what's different? You will see. But, suffice it to say...' He then approached a cabinet, lifted the lid on a box file, and pulled out an old folder. He threw it down on a table close to Beth. 'Our sect here in Netherwell has been blessed. It is a being, technically born from the Order, via our research, which has returned to show us the way. A being we weren't sure even existed, just hinted at in the mumblings of an interred patient, one that was kept in one of our asylums many years ago.'

Beth looked down at the folder. The title was printed in

the typewritten font, in faded ink. It read: Statements from Adrian James. The Arlington Asylum Incident. 1954.

'Is that supposed to mean something?'

'Do you recognise that name?' William asked. Beth studied the folder again. *Adrian James.* It wasn't a name she was familiar with. She shook her head. 'No. Am I supposed to know it? Nineteen-fifty-four was a long time ago.'

'Indeed,' William said. 'I was just curious.'

'Well, I've never heard of that man.'

'Okay. I accept that. In all honesty, I didn't think you would have.'

'One of your Order?' Beth asked.

'No,' William said, shaking his head with a chuckle. 'Not at all. But his story would interest you. Would you like to hear it?'

'Honestly? This is all a bit much to take in. So why don't you just tell me why you brought me in here? Why tell me all of this if you just plan on using me and my brother as sacrifices?'

'Because *you* might yet have another choice,' William said. 'Josh's fate was sealed the moment he turned his back on the Order. And, in truth, I am pleased. He didn't deserve the honour of what was to come. He wasn't fit to be the one. And Jim? Wrong place at the wrong time. Normally, we need to keep the sacrifices internal and of our own number, so we can control things. As the years went by, it became harder and harder to keep external forces—the police, the town—in the dark. We needed to avoid discovery. But this time, things will be different. We do not need to worry about any of that once the final sacrifices take place.'

'How come I have a choice? What's so special about me?'

William smiled and his eyes narrowed. 'You will find out,' he said. 'I'm not sure if it is fate or blind luck that brought your brother, and now you, to us. But for now, there is someone you must meet. He will assess if you are worthy of the honour. I do hope you are, as I'd hate for it to pass back to your worthless brother.'

'Just tell me what the fuck is going on!' Beth shouted, utterly frustrated with the lack of answers. She then heard a side door to the room open. Slow, heavy, and deliberate footsteps made their way towards the group, but the approaching figure was hidden by the bookshelves that packed the room. Beth saw William Kent draw in a sharp breath, and he actually dropped to his knees before bowing his head to the floor. The two guards either side of Beth dropped too and pulled her to her knees with them. She had no idea who was coming, but the three men in the room with her were visibly scared by whoever approached.

Then, the figure emerged, dressed in a fitted black gown with a high collar similar to what a clergyman might wear, but without any white tab. Beth looked up to the face of the figure and saw immediately that it was not human. Not quite.

She screamed at what she saw.

28

THE MAN—IF that was the right word—that stood before Beth looked like some kind of dark fucking priest. And he was a terrifying sight to behold.

Perhaps it had been a man once, as it was of human form and height, but its skin was not like that of the living. It was pale, almost grey, with distinct lines of scar tissue, like the flesh of a corpse. The scarring was most severe on the top of the bald head, as well as its withered lips, as if these areas had been regrown with thick and imperfect fibrous tissues.

The creature moved with a slow grace, its posture straight, almost regal. Beth couldn't see its hands, as they were clasped behind its back. But the thing Beth noticed most of all were the eyes: completely white, with no pupils or irises. Still, Beth could feel this dark priest's gaze as it slowly approached her. With its simple robes, high collar, and slow and deliberate movements, the being had a certain aura to it.

'What... what are you?' Beth managed to stutter out.

The thing tilted its head to the side. *'I am your salvation.*

If you are worthy.' The voice had an ethereal, almost echoey quality to it. It was deep and ominous—and certainly not human

Beth stared back at the thing before her, but noticed that no one else was. William and the two guards had their heads down to the floor. They clearly revered whatever the hell this was.

But, as scared as Beth was, she would not bow so easily. She quickly shook her body and arms, managing to pull free of the grasp of both guards, and she jumped up to her feet. The two men reached up for her, but the pale-skinned being raised a hand, and they stopped, then resumed their bowed position.

'*You stand up to me, wretch?*' it asked.

Beth was shaking. And under the gaze of the priest she felt similar sensations to what she had the previous night, when looking upon that monster that rose up out of the sea —helplessness and insignificance. But the dark priest was no giant, no nightmarish titan touching the sky. It was horrible to look at, of course, but even so she couldn't understand why it made her feel as that gigantic creature from the previous night had.

Beth clenched her jaw and spoke through gritted teeth. 'You're damn right I do.'

The thing laughed. A deep, resonant, baritone sound. Then, it held two fingers up on its pale hand—the index and middle—before quickly pointing them down.

Beth dropped to the floor.

Her body slumped against her will, knees bent, and head lowered, forced into a bowing position. Despite straining against it, she could not move at all.

'*Only if I allow it,*' the entity said. '*You would do well to remember that.*'

'Let me go,' Beth said, fighting against the invisible force that held her. Then her body was pulled upright to a standing position, before being lifted off the floor completely with her feet dangling above the ground, and her body locked rigid. Looking ahead, Beth saw the Dark Priest take a step towards her, its hand and two fingers again held up.

Panic and terror surged through her. How could this be possible? How could anything, even if it were not human, control her like this? That feeling of helplessness—of complete loss of power and agency—only intensified.

'You are nothing but an object. A clay for me to mould. But you could yet serve a purpose. There is a way to give your existence true meaning.'

'I don't want any part of it,' Beth said as tears started to well up in her eyes.

'That choice is not yours to make. You will help me open the doorway to my home. Your body will become a vessel. Through me, you will birth a child, and we will draw the eternal gaze of Vao so that the door will remain open. Then your pathetic mistake of a reality will be devoured by the chaos from which it escaped.'

Beth still worked to move even an inch of her body, but it was futile. The only freedom she had was the ability to talk and breathe, to blink and to sob—micro-movements rather than the grander gestures of moving limbs. Perhaps the power of this thing did not run down so deep as to be able to affect the more minute details, and it felt more like a puppet master holding the strings of the extremities. It was still terrifying.

'I don't know what the fuck you're talking about,' Beth snarled.

The thing stepped forward now, holding its face inches

from hers. All Beth could smell was a pungent, sulphuric odour.

'*You don't need to,*' it said. Then, it turned to William, who was still bowed and not making eye contact. '*She is the one. Make the preparations. Tonight is the night.*'

'It will be done,' William said, fear in his voice.

'*Ensure it is. This time I will be present to make sure nothing goes wrong. The last time I left you in charge, the boy escaped.*'

'Again, I apologise,' William stated, still not looking up. 'However, that is what brought us the girl.'

'*And that luck is the only reason you still live.*'

Then, the pale, disfigured entity moved from the room, going back the way it came with that same slow and regal walk. Beth heard the door close behind it.

She then dropped to the floor, released from the invisible hold. The guards immediately rose up and once again took hold of her. Beth offered little resistance. What she had just witnessed sent her mind into a spiral. It was scarcely comprehendible.

'You see,' William said, who now stood and was walking over to her. 'We are on the verge of something amazing here. And you will have a special role to play.'

'Why me?!' Beth screamed.

Kent shrugged. 'Because of your blood. Our Master has tried to sire a child before, but those attempts have been... unsuccessful. It will be different this time because of you. You should have been one of us from the beginning, Beth.'

'Fuck you,' she shot back through gritted teeth.

You should have been one of us? What the fuck did that even mean? The whole thing was maddening.

'I won't let you,' Beth added.

'Like our Master said,' William replied, 'you don't have a choice.'

29

It was close to midnight now, and Beth had finally been reunited with Josh. Jim was present, too, and Beth once again found herself in the back of a van and seated on the floor.

William Kent and others were positioned on wooden benching along the inner walls of the vehicle. Jim was silent, and Beth worried for him. He looked close to breaking. She was shoulder to shoulder with him, and also a miserable-looking Josh.

'I'm so sorry,' he said softly. 'I shouldn't have dragged you into this mess.'

Beth took a moment to reply. 'You can always ask me for help, Josh, I'm your sister. But I'm not going to lie, this is a fucking doozy.'

He cracked a small smile, which despite the situation made her feel a little warm inside. 'Yeah,' he agreed, hanging his head.

'So what the hell happened? How did you get caught up in all of this?' Beth quickly cast a look back to William, now dressed in a red silk robe that had intricate black stitched patterns to the cuffs and base. To Beth, it looked ridiculous. William stared back at them, watching with a grin, but seemed happy enough to let them chat. Anything they had to say to each other was obviously irrelevant now.

Josh took a deep breath but kept his eyes on the floor of the van. He had been covered up now, thankfully no longer naked, but was dressed only in a simple black t-shirt, some jogging bottoms, and a pair of trainers that looked old and tattered. God knows where they had been dug up from. 'A girl,' Josh replied. 'I came into this town a while ago. Wandered in after moving on from the last place, where work had dried up. I was making my way farther and farther north. Don't really know why. Ended up coming out to the sea. I had half an idea of just chucking myself in the sea.'

'Josh!' Beth exclaimed.

His cheeks reddened a little, but his solemn expression didn't change. 'Sorry, Sis, I'm just being honest. Not the first time I've had thoughts like that. But... it didn't happen. Spent a few days here. Got to like it. Even met a girl. She didn't seem interested, at first, which only made me keener. It gave me something to focus on, something to chase. I won her over... or so I thought. She brought me into the Order.'

'You joined a cult for a *girl*?' Beth asked, lowering her voice even more so that only her brother could hear.

'Yeah. Kind of. At first it was just to please Alicia, and I thought it would just be like the Masons or something, you know? But then... I saw things, Beth. Things that freaked me out. But they also got me curious. Opened my eyes to what is real, what is really out there in the void beyond what we know. Problem is, when you see shit like that, or even just catch a glimpse of it, you can't close your eyes again.'

'You could have run,' Beth said.

'Thought about it, but they made me feel special here.

Kept telling me I was destined for something amazing. That my blood and lineage was special.' Beth cocked an eyebrow at that, confused, but Josh went on, 'Alicia seemed to love me for it even more. But then the time came when they pushed me to do something evil. They wanted me to kill for them. Murder someone, in a cave on the beach, just to start all this madness.'

She held her breath, then asked the question she had been dreading. 'Did... did you do it?'

He turned to look at her, and in his eyes, Beth saw hurt. Josh didn't answer the question, however. Instead, William stepped in.

'He didn't.'

Beth felt relief wash over her.

'He took a stab at me, though,' William went on. 'And a few more of our brethren. Cut one of them very badly, then ran out of the cave and into the night. We didn't find him until the next day. And then, lo and behold, you show up, Beth. Someone carrying the same blood and lineage. So, we no longer need your brother, and he can instead pay for what he's done.'

'Fuck you,' Beth said, and spat at him.

William leaned closer to her and stared intently. '*Fuck* me?' He laughed. 'Sorry to say, I don't *fuck* anymore. It is beyond mundane when you have seen and experienced what I have. You'll see soon enough.'

Beth wanted to reach out and claw the arrogant prick's eyes out. She wanted to cause pain to this entitled parasite who thought that he and those like him had the right to shape the world. But she couldn't—she was still restrained, and she was still outnumbered. Instead, Beth asked him a question, one that had been building.

'What is it about our lineage? I mean, I'm pretty sure you

have the wrong people here. My dad was a journalist and my mother... well, she believed in God, but not the type of God that you people seem to believe in. There is no way she was part of this. So, you need to rethink, because whatever you're planning isn't going to work. You have the wrong people.'

William shook his head, as if addressing a foolish child. 'Trust me, my dear, we are not wrong. When our Master met Josh, it sensed what was in the boy and in his blood immediately. And, while it's true that your mother is in no way special'—Beth bristled. Who was *he* to say she wasn't special?—'your father is a little different, though he would never have been aware of it. Tell me, did you know your grandparents? From your father's side, I mean.'

Beth shook her head, but a horrible realisation started to creep up in her. 'No,' she said softly. 'Dad was raised in an orphanage.'

'Indeed. And do you know how he got there? In fact, let's go back. Do you remember that file I showed you earlier? It had a name on it. Adrian James.'

Beth nodded. 'I remember.'

'Well, Adrian James was your grandfather. A prisoner of the Order, at a facility that no longer exists. It was there that our Master was born into this world, not that we knew it at the time. We considered the whole thing a failure. Adrian James was the only survivor of what happened there, thanks to a terrible tragedy that he caused. We were so close to greatness. However, during his time there, Adrian was infused with a certain... substance. The blood of the things we worship. After he was relocated following the incident, we had him breed.'

'You had him *breed*? You make him sound like a fucking dog!'

William shrugged. 'He was little more. But yes, my fore-bearers wanted to see what would happen if he sired a child.'

'And he went along with it?'

'Not willingly. But we have ways of getting what we want, as you will see. We didn't need him to *commit* the act, we just needed some of his swimmers, if you take my meaning. A member of the Order, thought to be trusted, was impregnated. It stuck. We were keen to see what the child would become. Human or... something else. But we never got the chance. The mother was unwilling to give up the child. *Our* child. She hid the offspring when it was ours to own. Even though we found her, she never did give up the baby's location. Additionally, your grandfather ensured we could not try again, as the fool found a way to take his own life. We thought the whole thing lost. Not that it mattered—we had other avenues to explore. This town was one of them. Then, years ago, the Master returned to us, made us aware of his presence. Something to celebrate, considering we had thought Arlington Asylum to be a complete failure. And then, another miracle. Josh here wandered right into our midst. The Master sensed what was inside him, in his blood, and we were able to figure everything out from there—who he was and where he had come from. Josh swore blindly he was an only child, however, and that both parents were dead. He plays fast and loose with the truth, that one, doesn't he?'

William kicked out at Josh angrily. Josh took the blow, but he didn't raise his head.

'Leave him alone!' Beth snapped. 'Or I'll rip out your throat.'

William threw his head back and chuckled. 'I do like the fight in you, Beth. And I'm glad you found us. Another miracle from the failure of Arlington. Great things are upon us. It's as if it were all meant to be.'

'*None* of this was meant to be,' Beth said. 'It's horrific. And you people are blind.'

'Oh no,' William said with a sneer. 'That's the point, dear Beth. Our eyes are open. Yours will be too.'

'We're here,' a voice called out from the front.

Beth turned to Josh and saw tears streaming down his dirtied face. 'I'm sorry,' was all he said as the three of them were pulled from the van.

30

THE GRASS beneath Beth's feet came up to her ankles. She felt the night air rush around her and could hear the crashing waves of the sea. Looking around, she saw that they were on a grassy plain, and in the distance behind them she could spot the back of a row of small houses. A larger building stood on the end of these dwellings. Beth knew it to be the Overview Lodge. Turning the other direction, she saw the ground simply stop up ahead, and beyond that drop, the sea met the dark of the night sky on the horizon.

They were on the cliff top, above Hollows Cove.

The vehicle she had just been forced out of cut off its engine, and another three vans rolled unevenly across the grassy earth behind, their engines humming and growling. They stopped as well, then other people spilled out, all dressed in hooded robes.

She thought again at how angry William had gotten when Beth had insinuated he was part of a cult. *What the fuck else would you call this?*

Most of the robes were simple and dark, made of a thick

and itchy-looking material. Some, however, were much more grandiose, such as William's, which was silk red. William was the only person to have his hood down. Beth guessed that the others dressed in red robes were the same people she had seen back at the Heritage Centre.

The Dark Priest was present as well.

'*Prepare the seal,*' it commanded, and those in the dark robes immediately came to life in a buzz of activity. Shovels were pulled from the vans and the grassy earth was dug up. It took close to an hour, but a large, circular section of the ground was scraped away, leaving an area of exposed clay and soil, which was flattened out as much as possible with the flat faces of the spades.

Beth looked to the edge of the cliff and peered into the dark, wondering if the police were still down on the beach below. If so, perhaps they would hear what was going on up here, and come to investigate? The zealots who toiled were not particularly loud, but still it was a hope. However, there was every chance the police were now long gone. Beth turned to the houses behind them. Perhaps someone would wake and look out to the sea and notice what was going on. Surely four vans parked on a clifftop and a group of strangers in robes digging into the ground would be enough reason to call in the authorities?

Though what if the police *did* come? Could they really stop what was happening?

If it was just William and his followers, then they likely could. But with that dark entity here—the Dark Priest who strolled around with his arms behind his back while watching on like a general—would the police even have a chance? Beth's body had been manipulated by that thing like a puppet on a string without even being touched. She had no clue what else it was capable of.

Once the area was free of grass and topsoil, the lower members of the Order then set to work on their next task. Bottles of red liquid—blood, Beth could tell—were then brought from one of the vans. There were also many vials retrieved that contained something quite different: a dark, viscous substance that sloshed around within clear glass containers.

'Careful with that,' William snapped. 'It is a gift from our Master.' He then looked over the pale monster with a look that sought approval.

Snivelling dog, Beth thought to herself. The Dark Priest continued to stroll around and watch the lower members of the Order work, but did not respond to William—or even acknowledge his comment. The cult members then began to mark out symbols on the exposed ground in white chalk, delicately working from an image sketched on an old and crumpled piece of parchment. Three large circles were drawn, with concentric rings within each. Other markings were added: shapes and symbols that Beth had never seen before. The three circles were spaced equally apart, in the form of a triangle, with the one forming the tip pointing inland. Lines were drawn between each of the rings, and, finally chalk was poured around the circular perimeter, encapsulating everything.

'Occult bullshit,' Beth said, looking over at William. 'It means nothing, you know. You're just a wannabe Alistair Crowley. He was bat-shit crazy too.'

She felt a sudden blow as William slapped her hard across the cheek. The temporary pain of the strike, however, was overcome by an anger that surged up. 'You shouldn't comment on things you know nothing about, bitch.'

Beth had no way to strike back at him. However, she sure as shit could antagonise him. 'Those are just patterns.

Stupid shapes and gibberish. Utter bullshit.' She might have believed that to be true, once, but given what she'd seen...

Still, if she could upset William, then it was a thread worth pulling. She had already seen he was quick to lose his temper when questioned. And, in doing so, he could perhaps be pushed into doing something stupid that might create an opportunity for her.

Of course, it might just push him to kill all three of them instead. But then, would that be any different to what they had planned already?

'This seal is far more than that,' William said, clearly enjoying the sound of his own voice. 'I asked you once before what you thought about geometry. You were just as simplistic back then. It is a shame that, after all you've experienced, you cannot open your mind enough to see the bigger picture. Mankind has not grasped the true nature of reality. Of how it works, what bore it, and what brought it about in the first place. The space around us that we take for granted is a façade. These 'stupid shapes and gibberish' are important. They are an equation. No, *a language*. A language of things far greater than us. We try to use this language, spoken with flesh and blood, to commune with a place of chaos. We are only capable of basic communication, in truth, but it is a first step. Enough to open the gateway. And now, with the Master's blood added to our words, along with his wisdom, we speak ever more clearly. We will open the door. And when you birth a new Great One, the Great Vao— the Madness of Eternity—will gaze upon us. That gaze will connect the worlds and keep the door open. Netherwell Bay will become a permanent gateway to paradise.'

'As I said,' Beth replied defiantly, 'Bat-shit crazy.'

Another slap. Beth only smiled, enjoying the anger and frustration she was causing him.

'*Enough!*' the Dark Priest said in a loud, ethereal voice. William stepped back quickly and held his head low.

Beth stared at the thing that scared William so. 'I won't go along with this,' she said. 'Whatever you had planned for me and my brother, I won't let you—'

Beth was quickly forced to her knees, again with a simple hand gesture from the entity. She strained against the invisible force, but it was no use. Beth could still talk, however, just as she had been able to before.

'You can throw me around all you want, but I still won't fall in line.'

'*You do not have a choice,*' the Dark Priest stated as it turned its focus on to the working minions.

'We'll see,' Beth said. 'I don't care what you want me to do. I don't care how much you hurt me. I won't comply.'

The entity did not answer. It just continued to watch as the dark-robed figures worked. First, the cultists poured red blood over the chalk outlines, careful not to spill a drop. As this was being done, others worked behind them, pouring the dark, thicker liquid over the original blood. Beth could see the blood of the entity ooze over the chalk, which had soaked red from the initial liquid.

Eventually, everything was complete.

The Dark Priest looked over its followers. '*It is time to complete the ritual.*'

A man was then dragged from one of the vans, naked save for the burlap sack over his head. He fought and mumbled in defiance, but was forced into one of the circles and held down in a kneeling position. His hands, like Beth, Josh, and Jim's, were restrained behind his back. The hood was removed and a terrified young man, not even in his thirties, was revealed. A filthy gag stopped him from crying out.

'Don't resist, Martin,' William said. 'This is an honour.'

But the young man didn't appear to see it that way. He shook his head and looked pleadingly at William.

Whatever this organisation was, it obviously cared little for its members. Or, at least, those who were of a lower rank. They were simply lambs to the slaughter, to be used—and even sacrificed—as needed.

'Bring the others,' William said. Then, to Beth's horror, Josh and Jim were hauled to their feet.

'Wait!' Beth screamed. 'Wait, no, not them!'

'You don't have a voice here,' William said. 'Think yourself lucky you aren't joining them.'

But Beth ignored him. She did not want to talk to the monkey. She wanted to persuade the organ grinder.

'I'll comply!' she shouted to the entity that now turned to look at her. 'If you let them go and use someone else, then I won't fight you.'

'*You cannot fight me anyway,*' it replied, but started to walk closer to her.

'Maybe not. But whatever it is that you need me to do, or need to do to me, I'll let it happen.'

The Dark Priest cocked its head to the side and smiled. 'What I need from you... is to drink my lifeblood. Then, to devour my heart.'

Beth's mouth fell open. 'Are you... are you fucking serious?' She wasn't sure what she'd expected, perhaps having this thing force itself onto her, especially given the sickening talk of birthing some new entity. But this? Her stomach lurched. 'How would that work?'

'Don't question the Master's wisdom,' William admonished.

'Well someone should. Doesn't it know how the human body works? How would that get me—'

'Silence,' William hissed. 'What will happen to you is

not something you can understand. You are not going to be carrying a child. It will not grow in your womb. Why do you think we were planning to use your brother before we found you? We are perfectly aware how the human body works, girl.'

'It wouldn't surprise me if you didn't,' Beth replied. The entity just watched on, actually smiling, seemingly amused at the exchange. In that moment, it seemed like a parent watching two bickering children.

William shook his head. 'Your sex doesn't matter. Not with this. Only your lineage and your blood. It will help you survive the imbedding process where others have not. At least, I dearly hope so. It would be a shame to see what happened to the others happen to you. It was not pleasant.'

'And why do you think it *will* work?' Beth asked. But it was the entity that replied.

'*Because I have communed with my creator. The blood is the key to everything. And our blood is part of your make-up. The Old Blood is part of who you are.*'

Beth looked again to Josh and Jim. Both appeared terrified, held down within those circles drawn in blood. She focused on her baby brother, the one she had come here to protect. She felt helpless.

Then, she thought of her exchange with the dark entity back at the Heritage Centre, and how it mirrored what was happening now. It could control her wider movements, but she was still able to talk. And if it expected her—and her stomach lurched at the thought—to eat a fucking heart, she doubted it could control her movements enough to make that happen.

Perhaps she had a bargaining chip after all.

'Then let Jim and my brother go. Replace them. Don't sacrifice them and I'll comply. I'll do what you need me to.

Eat your fucking heart and drink your blood. But if they die, then I won't swallow a drop.'

William shook his head and went to speak, but the entity simply held up its hand to silence him. It stepped closer to her. '*No tricks.*'

'No tricks,' Beth confirmed. 'I swear.'

'*Very well,*' the Dark Priest said with a smile. Beth suddenly had a horrible feeling that she had just been played.

31

AT THE COMMAND of the dark entity, Josh and Jim were pulled free of the circles. The cultists who moved the pair away were careful not to disturb the carefully drawn markings, just as they had done when putting Josh and Jim into position in the first place.

'But Master, we need sacrifices to complete the ritual,' William said.

'*Replace them,*' it stated simply.

'With who?'

'*I do not care who the lambs are. Replace them. Unless you wish to give your own life?*' The entity gave an evil sneer and William's eyes went wide. He looked around, panicked, and his focus fell on two robed figures close to him.

'Seize them!' William screamed to the cultists, pointing at the two who stood near. 'Quickly!'

The pair started to back away, and one lifted their hands up in protest. 'No!' a female voice said. But they were quickly apprehended by others—who were clearly relieved at having not been picked. 'Uncle, no!' The hoods were pulled down and Beth saw that one of the unfortunate choices was the blonde woman Beth had seen amongst the older people back at the Heritage Centre. The beautiful girl with bright blue eyes. Even now, though her hair was pulled back in a basic ponytail and her pretty eyes were wide in terror, she would still be considered extremely attractive.

'Alicia,' Beth heard Josh utter.

Beth had expected Alicia to be an Elder, like her uncle, given she was standing shoulder to shoulder with the others earlier today. It seemed she wasn't at that level as yet, given the dull, thick robe she was wearing.

'Wait!' William said, and his look of panic worsened.

'William!' a voice called. Two other robed figures, these dressed in the silky red of the Elders, pulled down their hoods and stepped forward. 'That's my daughter,' the man said. He looked like an older version of William. 'She's your niece! What the hell are you thinking?'

'Wait!' William repeated. 'I've... I've made a mistake. Not her. Someone else.'

Beth had only ever seen this man either cool and collected, or overtaken by sudden, violent impulses. She had never really seen him flustered like this. She liked it. It brought her a kind of vindictive pleasure to watch him floundering.

'Then stop it!' the man shouted. 'Let her go!'

'*Silence!*' the entity bellowed, so loudly and angrily that it sounded like a clap of thunder. Everyone instantly cowered. '*The choice is made. Move the two chosen ones into position, lest you will all be torn apart.*'

William looked back at the man Beth assumed to be his brother. The look in William's eyes was one of complete helplessness.

'No,' the brother said, but even then, the lower cult members were moving the screaming pair.

'I'm... I'm sorry,' William said in a soft, pathetic voice. He looked pale and lost. Tears welled up in his eyes.

'Daddy!' Alicia cried as she was stripped of her robe and underclothing. Her hands were tied behind her back, as were the hands of the man who joined her. They were both forced into a kneeling position in their own circle, joining the first victim within the seal.

'Alicia!' her father cried, and he ran forward. Then, he stopped. Or, more accurately, he froze. He looked to be straining, though he could not move at all.

'*Wretch,*' the dark entity said, with a hand raised, holding him in place. '*You do not defy me.*'

The man started to scream in agony as the priest chuckled. It was a horrible and cruel laugh.

The entity made another gesture, and the clothing of the man, including the robe, was torn free. Now the cause of the pain was obvious, and Beth had to resist the urge to gag.

Gasps and murmurs from all those gathered were drowned out by the man's terrible wails. His wife stood by, helpless, hands over her mouth as tears streamed down her face contorted into a horrified mask.

The man was separating.

His arms and legs were being pulled from the central torso, and the flesh at the joints began to split like the skin of a cooked chicken leg as it was pulled free. Blood soon oozed from the openings. The man's head, too, began to rise up, neck elongating.

His arms and legs soon came free, held only by glistening stretches of stringy tendons. The bones popped from the joints and blood now spurted from the open wounds. The flesh of the neck split, allowing crimson liquid within to run down his torso. The dark entity continued to laugh while everyone around continued to wail and cry in horror.

The man's screams rose higher in pitch and volume as his spine cracked and broke. His head lifted more, separating, and the last pieces of flesh that connected it—neck muscle, vocal cords, pumping veins—all soon split and snapped. His final scream became a sickening, high-pitched squeal. The man's jaw worked independently for a few moments as the life in his eyes died away. Then, all the separated parts dropped to the floor in a bloody heap.

People were crying and whimpering, including William. Moments ago, Beth would have loved to see the man in such a broken state, but now she could do nothing but sob and cower herself. She then cast a glance at the Dark Priest, who in turn looked over its subjects. A new fear rose up in Beth. The savagery, malevolence, and utter lack of care showed just what it thought of those that so revered it. Beth's body started to shake, though she was still held in place by the Dark Priest. It cast a look at her, sneered, then gazed back out over its followers.

'*Now,*' it said. '*Will there be any more dissent?*'

While no one responded verbally, a few—William among them—shook their heads vehemently.

'*Then let us proceed.*'

32

JOSH COULD ONLY WATCH, held in place by his former brethren, his hands still tied behind his back. Nothing could stop the Master now. The ritual would be completed and the door would open.

And, because of his failure, his sister was now in the middle of it all. All because he'd been so weak.

Weak to have fallen for beauty and little else. Weak because he hadn't fled from these people when he knew he should have. Weak, because instead of handling this himself, he'd run to the only person in this world he trusted to keep him safe. Instead of fixing his own mess, he'd brought his sister right into the middle of it.

His one show of courage and defiance had only come when he was ordered to kill. It took that for him to defy the Elders, and he'd used the knife given to him as a weapon to defend himself. Josh had run and managed to escape from the clutches of these people, albeit briefly. Now, however, it had proven to be a pointless escape.

As Alicia screamed, the three people holding the sacrifices stepped back at the command of the Master. Josh expected Alicia to flee, but none of them moved, though they all appeared to be fighting and straining against some unknown and unseeable force.

With the chosen ones in position, and unable to escape, three other people stepped forward from the crowd, each carrying a blade. They positioned themselves behind the victims. A chanting rose up from the Order, though it was far from enthused. Alicia continued to cry.

'Mum,' she sobbed.

Her mother was in tears, but she continued the chanting with the others. Alicia was alone now, her fate sealed. Josh felt horrible for her, despite the woman she had turned out to be. Alicia's eyes fell on him, and Josh was reminded of the female sacrifice in the cave two nights ago. That pleading stare was the same. And Josh knew that Alicia, too, would have happily swapped places to save herself. Hell, when he had been kneeling in that circle, Alicia had remained silent.

Still, he had loved her—if not the real her, then certainly the version that was present to him. That meant something to him. But there was nothing he could do.

The three sacrifices in the circles had their heads pulled back by their executioners, exposing the throats. Josh held his breath.

In unison, the blades sliced over the exposed windpipes. The flesh was parted and blood bubbled free. Each of the victims' eyes went wide in horror. Their breathing became rapid and uneven, panicked, and the blood flowed quicker. Alicia's eyes held pure and unadulterated terror within them. Blood bubbled and spluttered from her mouth. The victim's chests pumped as they struggled to catch their breath. The emotionless executioners—and the dark entity —held all three in place, so they could do nothing but feel the act of dying. Their blood spilled down their naked bodies and began to soak into the earth beneath them. Eventually, the struggled gurgles and wheezing stopped. Alicia went first, growing still a few seconds before the others. They were then released, and the bodies of the dead slumped to the floor as their life-force continued to spill to the ground.

Into the seal.

'*Excellent,*' the entity said. '*I can feel it begin. Now, the desecration. Be quick!*'

Several members quickly ran to the parked vans, emerging with all manner of instruments: saws, cleavers, large knives. And the brethren then got to work. Desecration was the correct term for what was done to the bodies. The members of the Order cut and tore and pulled and hacked, imbuing chaos into the order of the human form. Insides were pulled outside, and stringy intensities were laid over the lines that connected the circular symbols. The heads of the corpses were removed and laid central to these circles, but only after their eyes had been messily gouged out. Body parts were strewn across the clay and soil canvas, creating a terrible work of art. When it was complete, the workers who had carried out such an awful task simply stepped back.

Everything grew silent. Even the sobs of Alicia's mother fell away and everyone waited with bated breath. Had it worked? Or had all of this death been for naught? Had Alicia, the woman he had once loved, been pulled apart merely for a misguided belief?

Then... Josh felt it.

The air itself seemed to charge with electricity, and a wave of static burst from the site of the sacrifices, hitting him like a wall and blowing past him. Goosebumps lined Josh's skin and the hairs on his arms stood on end. The salty smell of the sea seemed to fade away, overtaken by a stronger, sulphuric scent. Even the sound of the waves started to morph and twist and slowly fade away. The same thing happened to the stars in the sky, and the moon—they just faded from view, blurring away into the dark. Josh felt terror like he'd never known before.

It was happening. The door was opening. The Ritual of Moloch was reaching completion, and it would drag them all into hell.

The entity held up its arms to a sky that was now changing.

'*It has begun,*' it declared. '*The merging is nigh.*'

33

BETH FELT the hold on her release, and she was able to climb to her feet. She immediately ran over to Josh and Jim, then hugged her brother.

No one stopped her.

Everyone was too enthralled by the changes around them as two worlds fused together. The vista around them started to change, pushing out from the symbols and markings the three desecrated bodies lay on.

A booming sound echoed from the direction of the sea. Beth spun and saw something start to rise up from the water. Something massive.

Monstrous. Impossible.

Indeed, the seawater, once black in the night, began to change as well, and Beth could detect a faint red hue to it. The waves—instead of crashing and rolling—slowly settled, save for the large bubbles that started to emerge and pop on the surface, as if the whole ocean was boiling. The great, multi-legged creature continued to rise up. Swirling, tentacle-like appendages sprung from the legs, as well as from the horrifying central mass that housed titanic, gaping mouths as well as thousands of eyes of all sizes that rolled and glared wildly. The monstrosity was a mess of forms all meshed together. It towered towards a sky that changed above it.

Old stars blinked out, new ones taking their place, these ones pulsating and even moving through the cosmic expanse. The gargantuan beast bellowed again, a noise so loud that everyone on the clifftop—save the dark entity—ducked and covered their ears.

Cries of terror arose from the cult members, terrified of what they were seeing. But the transformation around them was not yet complete. Immense black mountains swam into view on the horizon behind them, beyond the town's limits. And on the enormous mountains on the horizon, hulking beasts and insectile monsters scattered and roamed about their surface. The creatures were big enough to be seen even from this distance.

Vast towers speared up into the air, perfectly cylindrical, and they rose even higher than the mountains. The pillars were black as well, but they had odd hues of light within them that moved and pulsed. Perhaps the most terrifying thing of all, however, was the way the stars above pulled together into one mammoth cluster, swirling about each other to form a familiar shape. That of a great and cosmic eye, one that looked down over everything.

Beth had to turn her head away, as just looking up at the eye made her feel like she would go mad. For the brief moment her eyes fell upon it, she felt a tapping inside of her head that was both constant and maddening. Strange voices echoed a language she could not understand. While most cast their gaze quickly away from it, some of the cult members continued to look up, enthralled and unable to look away.

Beyond the loud bellow of the great thing out in the boiling ocean, other screams, roars, chitters, and wails sounded: a monstrous cacophony from things that remained unseen. Whatever alien lands now lay beyond the outskirts of town seemed to be teeming with life.

While the sky above was dark, there were distinct red hues to the cosmic skyline, and whatever they were cast a red hue down over the realm Beth now found herself in, which gave it a distinct and hellish feel.

'What is this madness?' an Elder called, dropping her hood and looking around in terror. She had her grey hair pulled back, and her face was sullen and gaunt. She was terrified.

Then, the woman exploded.

Guts, shredded skin, and her insides coated those around her, covering them in a wet layer of glistening red gore.

'It is *home*,' the Dark Priest replied, longingly, as it lowered its hand. It looked around the clifftop, searching for something. Then it walked forward to a certain point away from the rest of them, farther inland. As he strode, Beth was certain she could hear faint cries of panic coming from back in town.

Dear God... has everyone been pulled into this nightmare?

Then, the entity stopped and looked at the ground. It closed its eyes, and slow smile crept over its lips. '*Here*,' it said. '*I feel you.*' It then turned around and locked eyes with Beth. '*Have you wondered why this place was so important? And why now is the time? The space this town shares with my true home is one where my creator lies. Ashklaar.*' It then turned around and held its arms high into the air before it. '*Come, Mother. Focus your strength. I am here for you.*'

Beth had no idea who, or what, the entity was talking to.

As far as she could see, there was just an empty space. It remained so for a number of minutes. But then, things changed. There was a rumbling and shaking underfoot, as if an earthquake was taking place. Before Beth's eyes, a huge portion of the land cracked and then fell into a void. The members of the Order screamed and backed away. Beth saw the view in the distance start to fade, or rather it became blocked. A great thing ebbed into view, pushing its way into existence. The cylindrical object, whose base sat within the newly created opening in the ground, slowly became whole and rose up to an impossible height in the sky. Within its glassy, black surface, pockets of red light swirled within, merging with writhing shadows. Looking at this red light and the moving shapes, Beth quickly became entranced, and it was only the voice of the entity that broke her concentration. Then she noticed something else. Other things swam into view as well, things that were stuck on the great surface of this column. Living things. Human and horrifying monstrosities alike. They wailed and cried and shrieked in pain, all without skin, and the exposed flesh red and blackened. The poor souls were melted and fused into the pillar.

'Mother. We have come. We will sire you another child. An equal to you. This new life will draw the gaze of Vao, who sees all new life.'

The entity turned back to the rest of them, who all cowered, terrified at what they were seeing. *'Steel yourselves,'* the entity said. *'We are far from finished.'* It then pointed at Beth. *'We had a bargain. It is time for me to collect.'*

'Go to hell!' Beth shouted, but was quickly pulled through the air towards the Dark Priest, who held out its arms to her. She could do nothing as her body came to a stop directly before it and hovered slightly off the ground.

'Hell is only a word. One your ancestors attributed to a place

they only glimpsed. It is a home that I was denied. A place that will swallow your world whole. Hell is your home now, girl.'

The Dark Priest grabbed her by the throat. Then it brought the wrist of its other arm up to its teeth. Beth winced as the thing bit down and tore a chunk of pale flesh free. Thick, dark liquid quickly pooled up from the wound and spilled from it, slopping to the ground. The wrist was extended over to Beth and the entity squeezed the hand around her throat tightly. She cried out in pain, then quickly gagged as the liquid from the wrist ran down into her open mouth. As much as Beth tried to cough out what was entering her throat, there was too much of it, and she swallowed involuntarily.

The taste was horrific—sour and bitter to a degree that overwhelmed her. More and more of the vile fluid flowed into her mouth as the Dark Priest continued to put pressure on her neck, and Beth had to keep swallowing to stop from choking. When it was finally satisfied, the entity released her, and Beth was dropped to the floor, heaving and spluttering.

'If you purge that from your body, then I will tear your brother apart.'

At its words, Beth forced herself to bring her gagging under control, which was no easy task.

'We still have more to do,' the Dark Priest said to her. *'Your body is not yet ready.'*

Beth knew what that meant. The deal had been clear. Drink the blood and then eat the heart. Beth's stomach lurched again.

'William,' the entity called. Dutifully, the terrified man ran over. His eyes were wide with horror, like a man in so far over his head that drowning would be a mercy. *'We must continue. Do not waver. What was promised will be delivered.'* It then laid a hand on his shoulder, in the only show of affection Beth had seen from the being. '*You will ascend.*'

William still looked like a scared child, but he nodded quickly. 'Of course.'

'*Good. I will be weakened for a short time, but we need to be strong and make sure the birthing is completed. The doorway cannot be allowed to close, and the girl cannot be allowed to die.*'

'I understand,' William said. 'I won't fail you.'

'*See to it that you do not.*'

Beth then watched as the entity pulled open its robe to its chest and held up a hand, palm facing upwards. The entity started to grimace in pain—actual pain—something else Beth hadn't seen previously. Then, a section of its chest cavity burst open, the ribs breaking apart.

A black, beating heart, misshapen to the point of looking more like a tumour, sloshed from the opening, arteries splitting and snapping as it did. The heart drifted over and settled in the palm of the entity. Beth noticed that the being actually seemed to be panting now, whereas previously, she couldn't even recall noticing it breathe.

'Will you survive?' William asked, sounding concerned. The Dark Priest nodded.

'*It will... reform... but will take... time.*' Its voice, previously deep and powerful, was now strained. The entity looked down to Beth. '*Now... complete... the bargain.*'

Beth slowly stood to her feet and looked in disgust at the black, pulsating mass. She then looked the being in the eye, ready to tell it to go fuck itself. She sensed its weakness and aimed to act on that. But William spoke instead, shouting out an order to his followers, 'If she does not comply, cut Josh's throat.'

Josh was quickly apprehended by four cultists. A blade was brought up to his neck.

'Wait!' Beth screamed. The Dark Priest grinned at her as black blood dripped from its mouth.

Fuck.

She had no doubt William meant what he said. By complying, she would likely be unleashing hell onto her world, but she could not bear to see her brother killed.

She took a breath and picked up the beating heart secreting the same vile blood she had tasted only minutes earlier. The organ was cold and slimy to the touch.

'*Very good, child,*' the entity wheezed. Beth brought the heart to her face with a shaking hand. The odour was horrific, not like anything she had ever encountered before. Beth opened her mouth, moved the heart towards it, then paused for a moment. She desperately hoped something would happen to stop this... but nothing did.

She bit down.

A foul taste filled her mouth as she struggled to tear a bite from the tough muscle.

Beth held her nerve, wanting more than anything to gag, and eventually ripped a lump free. Chewing was like torture, as the rubbery mass resisted in her mouth. Eventually, she was able to break it down and swallow, and felt chunks of meat fall into her gut.

'*Keep... going,*' the entity demanded.

With tears in her eyes, Beth did, and slowly worked her way through the revolting task. She bit and chewed, again and again, swallowing every mouthful until the last of it was in her belly. She felt beyond nauseous, and it was a constant struggle to fight back her gag reflex. The disgusting organ had tasted of rotten and spoiled meat.

'It's done,' Beth said, coughing and gasping. 'Leave my brother alone.'

But the being leaned closer to her. '*Not quite. Still one*

thing remains.' Then its hand shot out again, quicker than she could have expected, and grabbed Beth by the throat. She fought against it as the Dark Priest dragged her towards the titanic, cylindrical tower—the thing the entity had called 'Mother.'

She kicked and lashed out against the weakened Dark Priest, but William was quickly by its side to help, and he held tightly on to her arms. Against her will, Beth was forced over to the vast surface of the tower. She saw red light and moving shadows within.

'We have merely... primed your body,' the entity said. *'But to truly birth a Great One, you need to have the essence of one inside of you.'*

Beth's face was then forced closer to the dark and alien structure, where she felt an intense cold emanate from it. She then screamed as something wormed its way free of the previously solid form, sliding out like it had punctured the surface of water. It wriggled and writhed and looked positively alive—a black tendril with tiny, skittering legs to its underside. Beth screamed in horror, and the appendage quickly jammed itself into her open mouth. She closed her eyes, helpless, as something was secreted into her. Not a liquid, but a solid form. Whatever it was, it moved, and she detected small legs on her tongue. The thing then quickly crawled and pushed its way down her throat, despite her best efforts to clamp her gullet shut. Beth then felt the living thing move around in her stomach, and the tendril quickly pulled out from her mouth. She was again released, and bent double, falling to her knees before heaving and retching. But, no matter how hard she tried, Beth was not able force herself to vomit. She felt the Dark Priest kneel next to her and bring its face close to hers.

'Now, it is done,' the entity said.

Then, a horrific screeching noise drew all of their attention. Up ahead, from the direction of the houses and the Overview Lodge, a horde of creatures came skittering across the ground towards them. From a distance, Beth could make out elongated forms pressed to the floor with grey, wrinkly bodies—about the length of a person—and long, thin legs, like a disgusting meld of spider and worm. Large, gaping mouths filled the circumference of the creature's faces.

'*Protect her,*' the entity said, pointing to Beth. The Dark Priest then stood to its full height and clenched its fists. Beth ran, sprinting back over to Josh and Jim, still coughing and wheezing. She collided with Josh and hugged him tightly.

'What the fuck are we going to do?' Josh asked.

Beth turned to see the entity hold up its arm. With one motion, it scattered several of the approaching beasts. But not enough. In its weakened state, Beth was not certain it could hold off the swarming creatures on its own.

Beth quickly moved Josh and Jim to the rear of the cult members—who all huddled closely together—and ushered the two of them back. 'We escape,' she whispered to Josh. 'Get ready.'

34

As the skittering creatures closed in, Josh noticed that they swarmed away from the dark entity. It fought them off with sweeping arcs of its arms, scattering the monsters to the ground. The things did not seem to be targeting the entity, Josh realised, but the other members of the cult.

Josh felt Beth drag him away, and Josh and Jim ran alongside her as she led them to the left, roughly ninety degrees from the incoming attackers. Josh quickly figured out Beth's plan, hoping that whatever carnage was going to take place between these monsters and the cult would give them a chance to slip away.

The small group sprinted as hard as they could away from the clash. Josh looked back over his shoulder and saw the crawling nightmares spill into the huddled mass of the Order. The monsters leapt with frightening speed and accuracy, landing on screaming targets and forcing them to the floor. The sharp points of their thin legs pierced flesh. Round mouths at the end of the maggot-like bodies opened, but the creatures did not bite down. Instead, a sickly yellow goo escaped, dropping onto the screaming victims. The air soon filled with the smell of cooking meat as the shrieking intensified. Josh saw that the fallen were trying to scrape the thick fluid off themselves, but in doing so only succeeded in pulling away their own melted skin and flesh, leaving melted meat and fat—as well as exposed bone—beneath. *Then* the creatures started to feed in earnest, chewing and chomping and slurping on the dissolving matter.

It was horrific, and the thought of succumbing to a similar fate pushed Josh on.

'I... I can't keep up,' Jim said, wheezing. He was starting to fall behind, and if not for Beth pulling him along with her, he may have even dropped to the ground.

'Keep going,' Beth ordered. 'We're nearly there.'

The line of houses ahead was getting closer, and that meant the road beyond was as well. None of the creatures had paused to give chase, and the entity seemed occupied expending whatever energy it had in dealing with the savage attackers. The Dark Priest was able to sweep many of the giant bug-like things away, and caused others to explode in a shower of sickly yellow goo, but it was down on one knee, clearly struggling. Some of the Order were wielding the weapons they'd used to dismember Alicia and the other two sacrifices, and were actually putting up a fight, but their numbers had thinned.

Josh saw the entity, still down on one knee, look over to them. It shouted something to the rest of the Order, but Josh could not make out what. Despite the suddenness of the attack, Josh could see that his former brethren—mostly thanks to the entity—were going to survive.

'We need to keep going,' Josh said. 'They're going to come after us. William and that *thing* won't let us escape. They need you, Beth.'

'Then don't stop!' Beth stressed. 'Keep running.'

Josh's lungs burned and his limbs ached. He hated to think how Jim was handling the physical strain. Eventually, the group of three burst through the line of houses, passing between two bungalows, and emerged on to the road in front.

It was carnage. People in the road were fighting off other monstrosities and being pulled apart in the process.

'Keep going!' Beth commanded. 'Back into town.'

They set off running again, descending deeper into hell.

35

THE BODIES of the dead surrounded William Kent. Many brethren had been lost. Alicia, and his brother, had been snuffed out by the Master.

Was it all worth it?

It had to be, he reasoned. Especially now, given what had been sacrificed. William had come too far, given too much, for it not to be, and therefore had to put faith in the teachings. He'd been given command of this sect following the death of his father, and the Order had high hopes for what he could achieve. Especially given the arrival of the entity—the thing that had become his Master. Or at least, so it thought.

But the knowledge and insight it brought to the Order was undoubtedly invaluable, and it could yet help to create a permanent doorway. However, William's orders—given by Ainsworth himself, one of the higher Elders—were to also watch this being, as it was not fully trusted.

The truce between the Master and the religion he served had always been an uneasy one.

But what could he possibly do against such a thing with such unimaginable power?

William had managed to avoid the onslaught, and he'd only watched as his compatriots fell around him, killed in horrific fashion. Their bodies were now just a melted and devoured mess on the ground. The immense black pillar stood high, and the titanic creature out in the boiling sea, the harbinger, continued its bellowing roars.

While the Master looked like it may have been overrun at one point, it had managed to save most of the brethren. However, now it looked absolutely exhausted.

The girl still had to be retrieved. She was needed to make the connection between realities permanent, and that was still William's priority. Both his and the entity's aims were in line in that regard. But then what? William knew the Master had no intention of helping his people achieve ascension. It would hold them down. So, perhaps there was a way to keep the door open and somehow end the entity. Then they could directly commune with the old beings that existed in this world.

But for now, William had to follow and obey.

'*Get the girl*,' the Master commanded from its kneeling position on the ground. It was struggling severely. '*Make sure she does not die.*'

'I won't fail you,' William said, knowing he had no choice—for now. But he sensed an opportunely could soon come to rid himself and the Order of the festering problem fast outliving its usefulness. He turned to his remaining kin.

'Retrieve the girl!' he said, giving his best rallying cry. The Elders would offer little in combat, of course, but the lower pledges were younger, fitter, and stronger. They would carry out their duties and protect those of more worth and importance—or they would die trying.

As they readied themselves to leave, he noticed that a handful of the Order were just standing and looking up at the sky. Or, more specifically, to that great eye. William made sure he did not look directly at it again. The brief time he had, he'd felt a strange draw, and odd voices started to whisper in his head. The souls who gazed to the heavens were mumbling and scratching at their skin. William had noticed a number of his brethren doing that before the attack, and these few must have survived by blind luck.

'Hey!' William snapped at them. 'Move!'

'*They are lost,*' the Master said. '*Their minds have been broken. They are no good to you now.*'

William wanted to walk over to each one and strike them for daring to disobey, but he knew there were more important things at hand. So, he led the rest of the group away from their slumped-over Master, and past the terrifying form of the cylindric Old One that towered above them. First, they would get the girl. Then, they would kill the two men that accompanied her. Lastly, he would command his followers to then cast the Master out into the boiling sea. If the lower members were able to act quickly enough, William hoped that the Master would not be able to withstand them all.

36

'THESE MONSTERS MUST BE COMING in from outside of the town,' Jim said, panting frantically. The old man's face was beet-red, and his brow and cheeks glistened with sweat. Beth agreed with his assessment. The town itself still seemed intact, as normal, but the landscape beyond it had changed to an alien world. They had obviously punched through into this otherworld, replacing what was there before it.

The group of three, after escaping the cliff top, had weaved their way down the hill and towards the town centre, avoiding the chaos around them. They had then ducked into a narrow alleyway at the bottom of the bank, hoping for a brief respite. On the way down, Beth had watched people die, attacked by creatures beyond comprehension.

One young man was pinned down by a winged creature that feasted on his eyes with a long, needle-like mouth. The poor man screamed and writhed as Beth heard a loud suckling sound from the needle. Another man was pulling himself along the ground, his legs gone—only bloody stumps trailed behind. A huge, fast-moving mollusc-looking creature with a translucent body and thick, wriggling hairs along its base quickly moved over to him and parked itself atop his body. The man was lost from view and his screams suddenly cut off. Beth gagged as she saw the internal watery mass of the creature start to fill with thick crimson chunks and pluming red swirls of blood.

Some of the monstrosities even fought and killed each other, giving Beth an indication of the savage nature of this new world.

She leaned against the brickwork behind her and drew in rapid breaths. She was shaking with a mixture of adrenaline and fear.

For the last six hours, Beth had been acting on impulse. And, since coming to this nightmarish realm, that impulse had been running on overdrive. Her mind reeled.

She was living an impossibility. It had occurred to her that perhaps she was actually someplace else. Maybe she was in a looney bin, arms strapped together, muttering to herself in a padded room as her mind created horrible fantasies for her to live out.

It would be preferable to what was actually going on, however—potentially the end of her whole world. By protecting her brother, she could have doomed them all— every man, woman, and child in existence—to a living hell.

The thought overwhelmed her, and she had a sudden urge to break down and cry.

It was perhaps the least of her worries that a demonic creature could soon catch them and feast on their entrails.

But, if something caught *her*, at least, would that be such a bad thing? It would be one way—perhaps the *only* way— to foil the Order's plans.

'Josh,' she said, softly. Both her brother and Jim turned

their attention to her, even as the screams and roars of chaos echoed around them. 'I need you to do something.'

'What?' he asked.

She smiled, knowing what she was about to say would need some convincing. 'I... need to die.'

Josh's eyes went wide. 'What? What the fuck are you talking about, Sis?'

'I can feel something changing in me,' she said. And it was true. Since their escape from the cult up on the clifftop, Beth had felt decidedly... off. She could feel something churn and writhe in her gut. But it was more than that. A feeling that she couldn't describe ran out from her stomach to every extremity. 'What happened up there, what they did to me... it's going to work, Josh. Whatever their sick fucking plan is, it's going to work. But only if I'm still alive.'

Josh shook his head vehemently. 'No. No way, Sis. There isn't a chance in hell I'm going to let you die. Not after all you've done for me. Forget it.'

She smiled and caressed his cheek. 'There isn't any other way.'

But he took hold of both her hands and stared at her with an intensity and seriousness she had never seen from him before. 'We'll find one. *I'll* find one. We'll get that thing out of you and get back home. Away from this place. And we'll leave that fucking cult and its leader behind. They can live here in their paradise.'

'Josh—'

'No, Sis!' he stated firmly. 'Don't talk like that. Because if you aren't here, then I sure as shit can't make it. Ever since I found Mum's body, all I've ever felt is lost and alone. That whole time I had you by my side, yet I didn't even look. I'm not going to let you die for me. It isn't happening.'

Beth wanted to argue with him further but could see

that he wouldn't be swayed. She loved him for it, and it broke her heart that it took the end of the world for them to open up to each other.

'Listen to the lad, Beth,' Jim added. His cheeks were still red, but thankfully his breathing had slowed. Beth was worried that they were pushing him towards a heart attack with all the running they'd needed to do. She hadn't heard him talk in a while, so was grateful he was showing a little more life and awareness. 'Don't be giving up now. Not yet.'

Beth nodded, still not convinced, but as she went to take a step forward, her legs gave out and she dropped to the ground.

'Beth!' Josh exclaimed, and both he and Jim knelt down to help her up.

'I'm fine,' Beth lied. Truth was, her legs had simply lost all strength and could no longer hold her. The effects had been momentary, but shocking. On top of that, she felt nauseous. What's worse, it felt... permanent. 'I'm fine,' she said again as she got back to her feet. Her legs were steady again, at least for now.

'We need to find a way to stop all this,' Josh said.

'Yeah,' Jim agreed, 'Close that damn door they are all chirping on about. But how the hell do we do that?'

'Aiden!' Beth exclaimed, feeling a surge of inspiration. If everyone in town had been pulled through into this nightmare, then surely he had as well. And, while Beth didn't exactly trust him, he seemed studious enough know about the cult's practices and rituals.

'The boy who tends the Heritage Centre?' Josh asked.

'Is he part of the cult?' Beth asked.

Josh nodded. 'He was William's gopher, basically. But he knew his stuff. Forever had his nose in a book or in some scripture.'

'I didn't see him up on the cliff,' Beth said. 'Unless his face was hidden.'

'I'd bet he is still at the Centre. He lives there.'

'So, we go speak to this lad,' Jim said, 'and convince him to tell us how to put all this right?'

'It's as good a plan as any, don't you think?' Josh asked. Both Beth and Jim nodded their approval.

'Let's go,' Beth said, getting to her feet. It was a plan... for now. But she knew that if the feeling within her continued to grow, she would have no other choice but to end things.

She just hoped she could get her brother and Jim back home before that happened.

BETH KNEW the journey back to the Heritage Centre would be an arduous one. Given the carnage they had seen on their brief sprint down from the clifftop, the longer path ahead meant there was a very real risk of being caught and ripped apart.

But they had no other choice, so the three of them steeled themselves, ready to run from the relative safety of the thruway. Before they had chance to move, however, Beth felt a shadow pass over them. She looked up.

'Run!' she cried as the form of a horrific creature descended. A thick, grey, wrinkly body filled the space between buildings, and it was pulled along on thin, tentacle-like appendages that stuck to the brickwork walls. White hairs which moved independently covered the body and legs in sporadic patches. At the head of the monster was a large, gaping, and fleshy opening that dripped with a clear liquid. The edges of the hungry mouth were lined with multiple, thick cilia-like protrusions, similar to the teeth of a Venus flytrap. The flesh inside the vertical mouth was pink and lined with fine hairs and small, sharp teeth. It came quickly down at them.

Josh and Jim, both reacting to Beth's instruction, followed her gaze up and also shrieked after seeing what was coming for them. All three bolted from the alleyway, and Beth felt one of the writhing protrusions from the mouth brush against her just before the trio broke through into the street. The small group, now exposed, could do nothing but run.

'Help!' someone called from behind. Still sprinting, Beth glanced back over her shoulder, and saw a young man running down the hill towards them, bloodied and hobbling. 'Wait for me,' he called. But Beth had already seen his mistake. The man was limping as quickly as he could, but his path took him straight past the opening Beth had just escaped from. She had no chance to yell for him to stop before the man, completely unaware, moved before the huge monstrosity.

He was not as lucky as Beth had been.

The fleshy wisps around the monster's mouth quickly extended and wrapped around him, snaring his body like the pedipalps of a spider holding a fly. The man screamed as he was quickly hoisted up and pulled into the fleshy opening. It started to suck him inside and his shrieks hit terrible new heights. Blood dripped from the mouth of the monster as the man was consumed completely, and the crawling nightmare then sloped back into the shadows, appearing content to lie in wait again.

With people dying around them—and the streets running with blood—Beth, Josh, and Jim sprinted over the footbridge, which was thankfully unobstructed. However, as Beth looked down to the running river below, she could see the water was infused with red, and bubbles were starting to pop on the surface.

She felt horribly exposed, especially given they were unarmed. Jim was struggling again, and his face was turning a horrible shade of red. He'd always walked with a stick, so this must have been agony for him. Jim kept trailing behind, and both Beth and Josh repeatedly had to grab him and pull him along with them again, but his breathing was becoming horribly heavy and wheezy.

They arrived in the large open area close to the Trout and Lobster, without much in the way of conflict, after successfully managing to avoid any creatures, all of which had been otherwise engaged in killing other townsfolk. The Heritage Centre was farther up the main road ahead, but the open space where they now stood was host to a wide array of creatures. Through all of the horrible noises around the group, Beth could hear familiar cries of children from beyond the low separating wall. And the small abominations she had seen yesterday now came climbing over that wall as their circular, sucking mouths puckered at the air.

Other things moved closer to them. Tall and gangly figures—with rotted and bloated flesh, alien heads with pulsating brains exposed—moved in. These things had no jaw, only a thin tongue that was pointed at the end and dangled from the roof of a mouth laden with fangs.

Another monster pulled its trailing, slug-like body forward on long arms that kept the front of its body upright. Movement seemed like a strenuous exercise for it, given it looked close to ten metres long. The chest of the vertical upper half was open, revealing a moving cavity lined with tendrils that wriggled like fingers. The pit within was hollow, and the back was lined with masses of fleshy eyes. The head

of the creature was taken up by an irregular-shaped mouth—
a circle stretched at an odd angle—and masses of wriggling
tentacles that swayed and curled on top of the cranium. The
slow-moving horror managed to snare and scoop up a fleeing
girl with a massive talon, and it stuffed her inside of the open
chest cavity. The walls of the torso then slowly closed behind
the woman, cutting her off completely. Whatever was
happening to her inside caused the creature to throw its head
back and start to shudder, an almost pleasurable reaction.

There was also a group of three monsters that all moved
together. They were formed from globs of glistening red
meat and black flesh. The base of the creatures were little
more than masses of gore that spread out on the ground,
each opening like the bottom of a gown. Thin bodies
emerged from these piles of mush, standing about eight feet
tall. These bodies bloomed open at the head into a bulbous
mass of congealed flesh, reminding Beth of a massive, dripping brain, one that was lined with roving eyes. At the lower
edges of this sickening and brain-like ball of meat, two long
protrusions hung down, glistening arms that curled and
moved. The trio of horrors—pulled along the ground by
successive contractions of their bases the same way a snail
pulls itself across the ground—were slowly moving towards
Beth and the others.

'I'm sorry, Jim,' Beth said, as the old man struggled with
breath. 'But we need to get moving again.'

She was confident they could outpace the three
approaching threats, but if anything faster came after them
it would be game over. Especially for Jim.

The group took off again, moving past the three masses
of flesh that closed in, and Beth heard them emit a low and
unsettling moan. Suddenly, something came bounding over
from their left, leaping out from an open doorway.

This is it, Beth thought. *That thing is too quick!*

But Beth then heard a bark. The three quickly turned to see Jess, running towards them. Beth realised that the hound had come running from the same cafe she and Jim had been in earlier that day. Behind the dog, the cafe's owner Patricia came sprinting over as well.

'What the fuck is going on?' she asked, bewildered and terrified. Tears were streaming down her face.

'I'm not sure,' Beth said, being less than honest—though did it really matter? 'But there might be a way to stop it. We need to get to the Heritage Centre.'

Jess was making a fuss of Jim, jumping up at him, and the old man tried his best to pet and comfort the dog, but he was still struggling for breath. 'Good girl,' he said, though it was a strained effort.

A small tremor underfoot drew Beth's attention. After a moment, there was another, and another. They were barely noticeable at first, but growing slightly stronger each time.

'What the fuck is that?' Josh asked.

Beth shook her head. 'I don't want to know. Let's keep going.' A numbness was starting to permeate through her body, and she had to fight not to vomit.

'You okay?' Patricia asked her. 'You look... sick.'

'She's fine,' Josh snapped. 'Let's move.'

The group—now joined by Jess and Patricia—ran again, but did not get far, as yet another call stopped them. Turning, Beth saw a group of people come fleeing from the Trout and Lobster behind them.

It was Pete and his cronies. With them was the young barman who had served her in the pub.

'Shit,' she spat. 'This is the last thing we need. Another fight.'

However, the group that ran towards them looked every bit as terrified as Patricia. 'Wait!' Pete cried out.

Beth wanted to tell them all to leave them alone and to fend for themselves. Though if Pete and his group were wanting help, she knew there could perhaps be safety in numbers.

'What the fuck is going on?' Pete asked, parroting Patricia's initial question.

'Fuck off!' Jim shouted. Beth understood his reaction, but she had already noticed that the group were armed with knives, stool legs, bats, and other weapons they must have pillaged from somewhere.

'Fuck you, old man!' Pete snapped, bringing up his knife.

'Stop!' Beth cut in, knowing there was no time for this dick-swinging. 'If you want to come with us, fine, but we need to get to the Heritage Centre. There may be a way to stop this.'

'Stop what?' Pete asked. 'I don't understand.'

'The people that caused this are the same ones you run around after,' Jim said, finally getting control of his breathing. 'So this is your fault too, lad.'

'My fault?' Pete's eyes were wide. 'I had nothing to do with it.'

'Enough!' Beth shouted. 'We need to move. Come with us and help us stop this, or stay here. It's up to you.'

She turned and ran, not waiting for an answer, still feeling those tremors underfoot grow and grow. Thankfully, everyone ran with her, including Pete and his group. Beth knew that while they might have more protection in a larger group, it also made them a bigger target.

Every creature and monster that was in the street was now advancing on the newly formed group: the masses of gore and meat. The thing that pulled its slug-body along the ground—chest cavity now open again and lined with red chunks of flesh. The tall, gangly figures. And even other horrors that had converged on the area.

However, only the gangly humanoids with exposed and pulsating brains could gather up enough speed to close in on the group quickly. Given the height of the creatures—which looked to be over seven-feet—their strides quickly ate up the ground.

The Heritage Centre was not too far away, but Beth knew they would not make it in time. The four pursuers, giving out angry shrieks, waded into the crowd, swinging their long arms in an arc. The talons at the end of their arms cut into several of the group. One man's head was lopped completely off, his body running a few steps as the exposed neck-stump gushed out blood before he fell. Poor Patricia was grabbed and hoisted up by the throat. She squirmed and screamed, but the long and razor-sharp fingers of the demon's other hand thrust into her gut. The talon was then quickly pulled upward, ripping open Patricia's front and spraying blood everywhere, allowing her insides to slop out to the floor. Her intestines flopped free as well, dangling down like long red strings of spaghetti. The beast dropped her to the ground. She still struggled slightly, wheezing and gurgling in the last throes of death. Her attacker raised a foot and stomped down. Patricia's head exploded beneath it, like a popped water balloon.

And the poor bar-boy who had served Beth her drink was caught as well, with two of the tall attackers violently pulling at his body.

'Help!' he screamed, moments before his left arm was twisted free of its joint. One of the monsters standing behind him jammed its claw into his back and ripped his snapped spine free, pulling it up until his head detached and dangled from the long line of bone, mouth open in a death-scream.

'Fight back!' Pete ordered, not that he needed to. The remaining men had little choice and fought against the attackers in a vain attempt to survive. During the melee, Beth, Josh, and Jim were able to run towards the Heritage Centre door, leaving everyone else behind.

'Fuckers!' Beth heard Pete yell. He broke free and ran towards them, leaving his friends to die.

Beth rammed her shoulder into the door ahead and, thankfully, it burst open. She stumbled inside, along with her brother, Jim, and Jess. Beth then quickly turned to push the door closed, but Pete was right there. 'You left us!' he shouted as he forced his way in.

'Close the fucking door!' Josh screamed and pushed Pete aside just as one of the monsters came bounding over. Josh slammed the door shut and thrust the large, sliding lock on the inside of the door into place.

Pete grabbed Beth by the throat. 'You bitch!' he seethed. 'You left us to die!' But his grip released as Jim clobbered him with a swift right-hand blow. Pete quickly dropped to his knees and held the side of his head. Jim then stood over him, hands up in a fighting position.

'Nothing more than you deserved,' Jim said. He then launched a kick into Pete's chest and a sickening thud could be heard over Pete's cry of pain. Jess was then quickly onto Pete as well, clamping her jaws onto his leg. Pete screamed and tried to push himself up, however Jim delivered another kick to his head. Beth cringed at the sound of the impact, and Pete fell to the floor, sprawled out and unmoving, clearly unconscious.

'I told you you'd be sorry for kicking my dog, boy,' Jim snarled. He then commanded Jess to release. The door that separated them from the outside world thudded and rattled as the monsters beyond pounded against it.

'That might not hold for very long,' Josh said. 'We need to keep moving.'

Beth guided them into the public area of the Heritage Centre, where she had first met Aiden. It was empty now, however, so she then led the group through the door behind the reception counter, and out into the open stairwell.

'Aiden!' Beth shouted. 'Aiden, come out.'

She hoped to God the young man was still here and hadn't been eaten alive by something. The tremors she had been feeling were growing more and more potent, increasing in frequency.

Boom, boom, boom.

'Something big is coming,' Jim said. Beth agreed, but didn't want to think about it right now. She couldn't—she was close to the breaking point as it was. They all were.

Beth listened, beyond the booming of whatever approached, but could hear nothing inside the Heritage Centre. That was good in one respect. It meant no creatures were in here with them. But, if Aiden wasn't responding, it meant he wasn't here, he was dead, or he didn't want to be found.

She hoped it was the latter.

'Josh, you and I will look upstairs,' Beth said, forcing herself to act. 'Jim, take a seat on the steps. We're going to need to do more running soon, and I need you to get your wind back.'

'I'm fi—'

'No!' Beth snapped. 'You *aren't* fine, and we don't have time to argue about it. Get yourself together. Keep an eye on Pete. But be ready to leave when we need to.'

Jim frowned, but he nodded reluctantly. Beth and Josh then thundered up the stairs, yelling out Aiden's name.

The search was a short one.

As soon as they reached the hallway upstairs, they heard a door open to their left. Aiden's head peeked out, a look of horror on his face.

'I... I didn't know it would be like this,' he said in a whimpering voice. Anger surged through Beth. *What the hell did you think it would be like?* She couldn't vocalise that right now, however. She needed his help.

'Is there a way to stop it?' she asked him as calmly and evenly as she could.

'I didn't mean for all this to happen,' was his only reply.

Beth took a step forward. 'That doesn't matter right now. All that matters is stopping it. Now, tell me, do you know if we can? Can we close the door?'

Aiden was slow in responding, and Beth held her breath, waiting for his reply.

He nodded slowly. 'I think so.'

38

WILLIAM KEPT himself hidden central to the mass of people moving back into town. The Order's numbers had dropped en-route, with many of the grey-robed protectors giving their lives protecting him from the monstrosities that attacked. Their numbers were still strong, though, and William knew this town well.

He knew which backstreets would best keep them off the main roads, and William successfully led the group to the main street, where they huddled in a secluded alley. From the relative safety of the thruway, he saw that bitch Beth and her troublesome brother disappear inside of his home. The Heritage Centre.

And then he realised their plan.

Aiden!

The young man was born to study and learn, and was therefore perfect for William to have around as a tool to distil information from the sacred texts and scriptures. Aiden would also know how to stop the ritual and close the door.

Beth and Josh had likely figured that out, too.

Aiden was a believer, but this madness was testing even William, and he did not think the young man could hold his nerve through what needed be done. That was one of the reasons he was always kept at arms-length for some of the more hands-on matters.

However, William knew where they all were now. There would be no hiding.

39

JOSH FELT a palpable sense of relief.

The change in his sister over such a short time was frightening. Beth's skin had paled, her eyelids were distinctly purple, and there was now a hint of dark veins showing on her face—faint black lines beneath the skin that criss-crossed about the flesh. Josh was damn sure he wouldn't give up on her, but he was terrified there would be no way to stop what was happening.

And it was his fault.

As much as Josh could say he wasn't aware of the Order's full aims, he knew that was just an excuse. He had simply been seduced by what they had promised: the praise they had lavished on him while they had called him 'special,' which was something he'd never considered himself before. He had also been seduced by a beautiful woman who knew all too well how to play him. In the end, Josh had known the whole thing was fucked up, but he had gone along with it anyway, ignoring his own conscience and intuition.

But Aiden's words sparked a genuine hope that he could go somehow get redemption in the eyes of his sister.

He knew it might cost him his own life, but that was a payment he felt was probably fair.

Josh quickly ran over to Aiden, who shrunk back into the room from which he had just exited. However, giving Aiden no time to slam the door, Josh planted his foot to the base and stopped the door from closing. He then grabbed Aiden by the collar and pulled the cowering young man out into the hallway.

'Listen to me, Aiden, and listen good,' Josh snarled. 'No games, and no fucking around. How do we stop it?'

'The symbols within the seal of Moloch,' he quickly said. 'The seal is what keeps the door open. Destroy what is within and you close the door. Everything will revert back to how it was.'

Was that it? Could it really be so simple?

'And everything returns to normal?' Josh asked.

'Well, the two worlds will separate.'

'And people in the town will be safe?'

Aiden shook his head. 'Only if they are within the seal. That is the point where the connection is, where the two places align and merge because of the ritual. That is the gate, and when it closes you have to be within it to come out of the other side. Everyone who isn't inside will be trapped here.'

Josh thought back to when the initial change occurred, and how he felt that shockwave push out from the symbols the Order had put down.

'But no one besides the dead sacrifices was inside before,' Josh said, 'and everyone in town still got pulled through.'

'Because the seal was whole. That's what keeps every-thing held together. Imagine a flat piece of paper, drawing with lice, that has a red spot in its centre. Now, that paper is taken and placed in a tray of water.'

'And we are the lice?' Josh asked as Beth walked over to them both.

Aiden nodded. 'Yes. And the water is the other world. The paper will slowly become submerged as the water covers and engulfs it, which will submerge the lice as well. That flat paper is soon completely drowned in the water. The lice can scurry and swim around in their new environment. But, by breaking the seal, you are in effect tearing out the centre, the red spot, and yanking it free. The lice on that red spot go with it, back to their original environment and free of the water. But everything else, all those lives swimming and drowning, remain. You could wait until the ritual ends, though. It isn't indefinitely long. The worlds will slowly separate. Then the paper is lifted out as one, and everything on it will come back too. But, by waiting...' He looked to Beth.

'We can't wait,' Beth stated. 'Whatever is happening to me, whatever is growing in me, it's happening quick. I can feel it. It's going to keep the doorway open permanently, right?'

Aiden nodded. 'Yes. Have you seen that thing in the sky? The eye? The Master told us of it. That is Vao. It is something unknowable. Infinite. Its gaze is creation itself. It knows everything, but it is madness incarnate. The Master believes that it is Vao who created our reality, from a dream. We are but a mistake, a product of a wandering mind, that had evaded detection from most of the Great Ones thus far. Vao sees everything, but doesn't really *take note* of everything. It would be like us looking down at a colony of ants. How much notice do you take of each individual ant? So, to draw Vao's attention and undivided focus, we planned to create a new great being. One like Ashklaar—the creator of our Master—but this Great One would be born from a life native to our realm. And therefore, diverting its gaze, Vao would see through the gate into our realm. Into its own dream. The two would then permanently be joined.'

'By the power of that thing simply looking at us?' Josh asked, not bothering to hide the disbelief in his voice.

'By the power of its conciseness. The first, original consciousness. One that has existed forever. And, through its dreams, realities have been born. Our universe, and our galaxies, spread out from one such dream. Others have as well.'

'That sounds like complete horseshit,' Josh said.

Aiden shrugged. 'It was told by the Master, he who communes with Ashklaar.'

'Ashklaar? That thing up on the cliffs?' Beth asked.

Aiden's eyes went wide. 'You saw it? What was it like? How did you feel in its presence?'

'Disgusted,' Beth said. 'I don't know what to make of everything you're saying, but it doesn't matter. Horseshit or not, Josh, we can't ignore what we are seeing.'

Josh knew she was right. 'Agreed.'

Beth turned back to Aiden. 'So, we need to destroy the symbols within the seal. How do we do that? Does it involve a sacrifice or something?'

Aiden frowned. 'What? No. Why would you think that?'

Josh and Beth cast a glance at each other. 'Are you kidding, Aiden?' Josh said. 'How could we *not*? Look at what started this whole thing. Every single thing you people do seems to involve death and flesh and blood.'

'Oh,' Aiden said, nodding slowly. 'I guess you're right. But no, you just need to destroy the markings. Kick away what joins the circles of Moloch. But we need to stay inside the outer marking of the seal if we are to return home.'

Josh grinned. 'We?' he asked. 'You expect us to let you come along?'

Aiden's eyes went wide in panic. 'You have to!' he shouted. 'You can't leave me here. I helped you!'

'You helped *create* this hell, Aiden!' Josh snapped back, and Aiden's head dropped.

'I did,' he replied. 'But so did you.'

That caused Josh to pause. The little fucker had a point. Josh turned to Beth for guidance. She looked bad now, and he could see small lumps smattered across her skin. The fucking booming and rumbling outside was becoming louder and louder, causing fresh panic to surge through him. The sounds were now happening rapidly, with virtually no time between each immense crash.

'He comes with us,' Beth said, looking around in a panic. Josh wasn't about to argue. But he had one more question that needed answering.

'And how do we stop what is happening to Beth? There has to be a way.'

But he didn't get a reply, as they all heard Jim call from downstairs.

'We've got company!'

40

J<small>IM CAME RUNNING</small> up the stairs with Jess.

'What is it?' Beth asked.

She had a feeling it was something to do with the crashing noises getting closer and closer. Then, however, she heard voices downstairs, coming in from the back entrance, William Kent's at the head.

'Find them!' he shouted.

Josh turned to Aiden and, with anger in his voice, quietly asked, 'Didn't you lock *any* of the doors in this place?'

Aiden hung his head again. 'Until I heard you, I was too scared to come out of my room.'

'We need to get out of here,' Beth whispered. 'Back to the clifftop.' They quickly moved farther down the hallway. 'Is there another way out?'

'Pete?' she heard Kent exclaim in surprise from downstairs. 'Where are they?'

Pete's response was woozy and mumbled. 'In here... somewhere.'

She turned to Aiden as they moved. 'Talk. Because

they'll kill you, too, when I tell them how you are helping us.'

He looked terrified. 'The door at the end leads to the roof. There's an external fire stairwell that will take us to street level.'

'Well we can't go back down there,' Jim said, pointing to the stairs behind them. 'From the sounds of it, there's far too many of them'

Jim was right—Beth could hear the sound of multiple footsteps from downstairs. Footsteps that soon started to thunder up the stairs after them. The noise outside, however, those booming footfalls, was almost deafening now. Something massive was close.

The group broke through the door at the end of the corridor, where a flight of wooden steps in a narrow stairwell opened up flanked either side by concrete walls. They rushed up the steps to a metal escape door at the top. When they reached it, Beth noticed that the thundering noises—that now sounded on top of them—suddenly stopped. The group pushed the escape bar on the door and ran through and out into the open air. The door swung shut behind them, but—given it was an escape door with no external handles—there was no way to lock it from the outside. Beth and the others found themselves on a flat area of roof about five metres by five metres squared. The floor underfoot was exposed concrete that had a slight camber to it, running off towards rainwater collection gutters at either side. Ahead was a waist-high parapet, a section of which was cut out. Black metal escape stairs ran down out of view from this point, hugging the side of the building tightly. Either side of the flat roof, and behind them, was a vertical section of wall. This continued up about ten feet and met with a slate roof which ran down at an angle away from them.

It was clearly an escape route in the event of fire, and the way down was just ahead. However, the group was frozen to the spot. Jess barked savagely at what loomed above them.

A titan.

A nightmare given form. It was so large that, because of how close they were, Beth and the rest of them could not make out its full form, only what filled their view. Beth screamed. They all did.

They were looking up at the underside of... something. It was like the massive underside of an arachnid, with patches of dull whites and greys set in against the blacks of an outer, harder, armoured exoskeleton. Enormously thick legs layered with spines ran around the outer edges of the body, dropping down past the edges of the building and out of sight.

The underbelly of the titan, however, had massive ridges that ran together towards a huge, gaping hole. The abdomen area around the hole had thousands upon thousands of eyes covering it, ranging in size from as small as stones to the size of houses. All of the eyes were a cloudy yellow, each with multiple pupils inside. And that huge hole, that yawned and twitched, was wider than the building on which they stood. It was a mouth, but devoid of teeth of any kind, and the thick purple flesh inside curved up, like a dome, before disappearing into a dark void that hid the crest.

The smell that wafted down was awful—like a constant gust of rotted meat. And from the mouth, long and writhing tendrils fell, each attached to the inner walls of flesh. The wriggling tendrils also numbered in the thousands, and seemed to be able to drop, extend, and retract at will. They moved independently of each other, as if each one was alive and separately conscious of the terrible whole. The tentacles were a dark pink and lined with small teeth.

Other protrusions dropped from the yawning hole as well. These were bigger, wider, and fewer in number. The immense trunks were made of a thick and translucent skin that had veins visible beneath the surface. The ends of the huge tubes expanded and contracted, as if taking in air. Beth saw that the tendrils were lifting up captured prey from the ground. Some were unfortunate townspeople, while others were creatures native to this world. Each was stuffed into one of the long trunks, which in turn contracted around their prey, trapping them within their mass.

Beth could see a liquid inside that slowly dissolved whatever was within the appendages. The contraction of muscles also helped to mash the bodies, and the mess that remained flowed upwards, off into the wide void that blocked out the sky.

It was a hideous but awe-inspiring sight that left the group all frozen to the spot.

Soon, the door behind them burst open, and the pursuing cult—led by William Kent—spilled out onto the terrace. Beth noticed that Pete, still looking woozy, was among the group.

'Get them!' William ordered, but no sooner had he given the command than he and his followers all looked up to what blocked out the sky.

A number of the searching eyes on the underbelly fell onto them, and Beth suddenly felt like a bug in the sights of a predator.

Masses of the tendrils started to descend towards them, writhing and curling hungrily.

Everyone scattered and fled. Given the danger, the members of the Order now seemed to care little for capturing Beth and her group, and instead ran in fear and panic. The problem, however, was that the roof they were on was small and crowded, and the door behind them could not be opened to escape through. They were all trapped up here.

Soon, the fleshy tendrils plucked up their first victim.

Pete.

He was snared about the waist and hoisted up, thrashing and shrieking as he went. One of the clear protrusions came to meet him and Pete was thrust inside as the disgusting tube swallowed him up. Despite running for her life while dodging the grasping tentacles, Beth couldn't help but glance up to watch what was happening to Pete within the translucent tube. He was sucked up farther and farther, becoming little more than a dark smudge as he moved higher. A smudge that soon had a distinct red tint to it.

Another cultist was taken. Then another.

As Beth ran, a thought struck her.

This could be it. A way to ensure the plan of the Order— and the birthing of this new entity—was stopped.

She could sacrifice herself.

If she was dead, the doorway could never be made permanent, as she would not be able to birth the monster the Order wanted.

She turned and saw that Josh, Aiden, and Jim—who had Jess bundled up in his arms—had managed to make it to the escape stairs and were calling over to her.

Arms suddenly locked around her waist, and Beth was able to spin to see that William Kent had hold of her. He tightened his arms around her.

'You're coming with me,' he said through gritted teeth. 'Enough games.'

Beth, in turn, grabbed him around the back of the neck

and linked her arms together. With his hold around her waist, they looked to be in a dancing position, except for the look of disdain they both had for each other. But Beth then smiled.

'We're going nowhere,' she said. Confusion fell over his face as Beth cast a glance above her. One of the tendrils was quickly lowering down. William followed her gaze, then panicked and started to squirm.

'What the hell are you doing?' he yelled, trying to worm from her grasp, but she held tight, determined to take this fucker with her. He was strong, but Beth clung to the taller man like a leech.

'You deserve this,' she whispered to him. 'And it's going to hurt.'

'Let me go!' he screamed and fought harder. Beth took a breath, knowing this was what had to happen. The tendril fell closer, and Beth turned towards Josh—to tell him to run. But her stomach dropped as she saw her brother sprinting towards her, ducking between the grasping length of flesh that tried to grab him.

No! Leave me!

Josh quickly reached them and swung a punch at William. It connected clean, and the cultist fell back and straight into the clutches of the fleshy rope. The tendril wrapped quickly around William's midsection. He screamed in panic and terror.

'No! Help me! Help me!'

'I fucking told you,' Josh said to Beth. 'You aren't killing yourself. Now come on, we need to stop this.' He dragged her along behind him, back towards the escape stairs.

'No,' Beth said. 'This isn't going to work!'

But Josh either wasn't listening, or he didn't care.

41

WILLIAM FOUGHT and struggled for all he was worth. His bladder released as he was hoisted up into the sky. The snake-like appendage that held him squeezed tightly, the teeth on the flesh digging in to his skin. He screamed as it lifted him higher and higher up into the air. To make things worse, he saw that the girl and those with her—including that treacherous Aiden—had made it safely to the stairs and were descending down to the ground below. Some of the Order were fleeing, too, climbing down the stairs after the escapees. They did not seem to be giving chase, however, simply running for their lives. William wanted to be angry at them and their cowardice, but he was just too scared at what was coming. William prayed that something—anything—would happen to save him.

He was then brought to the opening of one of those vile trunks and pushed up into it. The edges of the open flesh contorted to his shape and sucked him farther inside, where a hot, thick liquid overcame him.

William was drawn up as the substance started to burn his skin.

The pain was immense and beyond anything he could comprehend. William could almost feel every cell burn and sear away. His skin slopped and sloshed, mixing with the liquid that forced itself down his throat, and the sides of his prison closed in as well, pressing from all sides. The boiling goo was momentarily pushed away from him as the other walls pressed around his form, leaving no room for anything around him. William felt his body start to compress, and red, runny mush was forced from his mouth. The contracting tube sucked him farther up, then slowly released, allowing the trapped liquid to again cover him. He kicked and flailed as the searing pain returned.

Though William's vision was fading, he saw one of his flailing hands before him. His fingers had congealed together, the flesh runny like wax, while some of it floated away into the substance around him. Red meat was exposed as the skin was stripped. Blood clouded what he could see.

And the pain. *Christ, the pain.* It broke his mind. Every fibre was melting and boiling and flaking. William could no longer scream—his jaw was no longer attached and now floated before him as it dissolved.

The contractions started again, pulling him farther up and pressing into his liquefying body even more. A gooey eye squeezed free. He felt his head split. Not crack, but rather, it slopped apart at the cranium, like a soft-boiled egg.

Eventually, as his body dissolved around him, William was granted the mercy of death, and his liquefied remains were sucked upwards to be consumed by the nightmare.

42

KEEP GOING, Josh told himself. _We're going to make it._

After reaching the bottom of the stairs, Josh had expected a fight with the remaining cult members, but it turned out they were all just too terrified at what they'd just seen and wanted to escape with their lives. One of the cultists was snatched up just as they reached the bottom of the stairs—the danger wasn't over. The remaining members of the Order disappeared inside of the Heritage Centre again to hide, running in through the back door.

A sound idea, Josh thought, but Beth had ordered them to keep away from the Order, shouting that they couldn't be trusted.

So, they kept close to the outer walls of the building, pressing themselves against the vertical planes in an effort to keep out of view. Then they slipped through into an alleyway between buildings and waited for a few moments while they assessed their options.

The creatures in the street beyond were still being plucked up by those writhing tentacles. They waited for what they thought was their best chance, when the numbers were thinned enough, then sprinted across the street and into another alleyway, successfully avoiding being grabbed.

The group quickly and quietly made their way down a backstreet, still pressed tightly against the walls of the houses, and eventually managed to move out from under the titanic beast. Then they dashed inside an empty house, close to a footbridge. Despite there being a sickening blood-stain on the floor of the living room, it seemed safe and empty. The pictures on the mantelpiece above a fire showed an old couple who looked happy. Now, Josh knew, they were likely dead.

Josh hadn't liked how Beth had tried to let one of those tentacles take her. It fucking scared him. She couldn't just give up like that. If anyone should be sacrificing themselves for the good of everyone else, it should be him.

Then he remembered he had unfinished business with Aiden. Josh quickly walked over to the young man.

'How do we stop what's happening to my sister?'

Aiden, who had been peering from a window, turned to Josh. 'What? What do you mean?'

'You *know* what I mean. How do we get rid of what's growing in her? What they did to her up on the cliff, how do we reverse it? How do we abort it? Tell me.'

Aiden's eyes fell to the floor. 'I... I don't know.'

Josh grabbed him quickly by his shirt and forced him back into a wall. 'You have to know!' Josh shouted. 'You know everything about this shit. Now tell me! No games!'

'I'm telling you the truth,' Aiden replied, holding up his hands in submission. 'The Master told us most of what we know about how to keep the doorway open. It never talked about how to stop or reverse it.'

'Then guess!' Josh yelled, and slammed Aiden's head against the wall.

'Josh!' Beth shouted, but Josh was in no mood to listen.

'Tell me how to stop it!'

Aiden's wild eyes flitted around the room in panic. 'Perhaps, when breaking the seal... if we get her back home, and away from this world, then whatever is inside of her will die.'

'And that will work?' Josh asked.

'I don't know,' Aiden stressed. 'I honestly don't. Not for certain. But if the link to this world is gone, then maybe what is in her will die. I can't know for sure, though. None of us can.'

Josh felt anger and helplessness rise inside of him. 'Maybe you don't know, but I know someone that will. Someone who can reverse this.'

'Josh,' Beth said, softly, coughing as she did. 'It's over. Let me go.'

He turned look at her. His sister's skin had now taken on a sickly, yellow pallor. 'No,' he stated. 'You didn't give up on me, even though you had every right. It isn't over.'

'It is,' Beth stated firmly. 'You don't owe me anything, so just let me go.'

Josh shook his head. Tears flowed from his eyes. 'I can't, Beth. Not knowing you came here for me. All I've ever done in my life is run. Run away from people who cared about me. I just couldn't cope with letting them down and failing them.'

'You never failed me, Josh.'

'Bullshit,' he said. 'I've let you down every step of the way. Ever since Mum.'

Beth cocked her head. 'Mum had a heart attack, Josh. That wasn't your fault. Finding her dead like that must have been horrible for you.'

'I didn't find her dead, Beth,' Josh said, sobbing now.

'When I found her, she was alive and clutching her chest. She begged me to call for help; her face and lips were all blue. But I froze, Beth. I fucking froze. I was so scared I couldn't fucking move. I wanted to help, but I just pissed my pants and watched her die.'

Beth could only look at him in disbelief.

'I've never told anyone,' Josh went on. 'But I could have saved her if I'd just stepped up. So, I mean it when I say I just let people down. I couldn't bear to be responsible for anything like that again.'

'You were fourteen,' Beth said. 'It wasn't your fault.'

'It was,' he stated. 'But I won't let that happen to you.'

A silence hung between them, broken after a few moments by Aiden. 'Sorry to interrupt, but what did you mean when you said there is someone who can reverse this?'

'The one that started it,' Josh said. 'We go and see your precious Master and put an end to it all.'

'The Master?' Aiden's face fell in horror. 'You can't. It will kill us!'

Josh looked over to Beth again, but when he spoke, it was directed at Aiden. 'We'll find a way.'

An almighty crashing and rumbling noise drew their attention again, and everyone quickly gathered around the living room window. Casting his eyes up towards the Heritage Centre, Josh saw the massive beast start to move its many legs and turn itself around. As the creature did, three of its thick legs swept into—and through—the stone building, collapsing the structure with a deafening roar. The stone blocks fell in a cloud of dust and rubble that swept down the street. The giant creature started to walk away, each thudding footfall sending shockwaves through the ground around them. The wave of dust rolled past the window, clouding the air outside.

'Christ,' Jim muttered. Jess sat whining in the corner of the room. 'We truly are insignificant here, aren't we?'

And they were. Gnats in a world of giants and horrors. But the titan that slowly lumbered off had seemingly cleared a lot of the dangers. That meant now was the perfect time to run.

'Then let's get out of here,' Josh said. 'It's time to go home.'

43

JIM WAS STRUGGLING to keep up with the others. His heart hammered in his chest and he worried he was pushing it too hard. But stopping wasn't an option. The activity on the streets now, due to the titan cleaning up during its feast, was minimal, and their progress to the footbridge was unimpeded. The group soon made their way back up the steep hill that led to the clifftop.

A stinging pain ebbed out from his chest.

Come on! Just a little farther!

Jess ran along beside him, easily keeping pace. She kept casting him worried glances.

Creatures roamed on the side of the river they soon emerged onto, but nothing moved fast enough to cause any real concern. The group soon made it up to the street at the top of the bank, close to Jim's house. It felt strange seeing the home he had shared with Ada for all those years now with a completely alien backdrop behind it, with the strange, moving stars in the sky. Concentrating, Jim noticed something else moving between the stars as well. Though it was hard to make out clearly, Jim thought he could see a vast living mass of unimaginable proportions. It moved over the pulsing light of a star, easily sucking the ball of gas into its much larger form. The star blinked out permanently.

Jim quickly looked away. What he had just seen could surely not be possible. He had a little understanding of how light worked, and how long it took to travel from stars so far away. So, if he could actually see whatever it was that had devoured the star from this great distance, then it must have been nearly the size of a solar system, or even bigger.

Ignore the madness, Jim, he told himself, knowing that if he thought about it too much it would drive him crazy. His heart hurt with every beat, but the group managed to push closer and closer to the clifftop.

Perhaps, against all odds, they were going to make it. Though he was slower than the others, his ageing body and tired heart had managed to keep up with them so far. He could now see the base of the towering cylindrical pillar, black with slivers of blue and white light escaping. The immense living column had acted as a beacon to them, visible from everywhere in town, and now they were close. Close to the symbols and markings that would send them home.

Jim let himself smile with relief. Who'd have thought an old fool like him could survive something like this?

Then, he heard something coming from behind him.

Jim turned to look back and saw an object closing in—a horrible, flying thing that was focused on him. It made a terrible and loud buzzing sound.

Before it grabbed him, Jim was able to take in its full, terrible detail.

The buzzing was caused by multiple wings that moved so fast they were a blur. These wings held aloft a fat body of greys, browns, and greens, with eight dangling legs. The body, which had masses of tumorous clustered eyes devoid of pupils also bore a huge, bulbous, and hideous head. It was the vertical, open mouth that terrified Jim most of all in the brief instant before it grabbed him.

The creature flew into Jim and its mouth snapped shut around him, covering him from his knees up to shoulders, and pressing tightly, compressing Jim to breaking point. He felt small, stubby teeth dig into him, and Jim let out a scream as he was taken up into the air.

'Jim!' he heard Beth cry out from below, but it was no good. The giant insect—if it could be called that—flew quickly and erratically away, swooping round in an arc and carrying Jim from the clifftop, off towards the giant black mountains in the distance.

44

BETH COULD DO nothing but watch as Jim was taken by the flying creature. Jess barked continuously, and then began to howl.

Her mind tried to come up with a way to help her friend. Surely it couldn't just be over for him? Not like this. Perhaps they could chase the creature, keep up with it, and see where it landed? Maybe Jim would still be alive and they could help him.

But she soon realised that was futile. The thing was moving too fast, and within minutes it became a small speck on the horizon.

'He's gone,' Josh said sadly. 'We need to keep going.'

Beth turned to glare at him, fire in her eyes. 'Just like that?' she asked, not hiding her rage. 'Just forget him and keep going, eh?'

Josh looked forlorn as he nodded. 'I'm sorry, but yes. We need to get you home. This should prove that we are always in danger here.'

'I never doubted that, Josh. Just look at the nightmare around us.' She pointed off to the giant tower. 'Look at that thing. A fucking titanic column that is apparently *alive* and some kind of God.' She then gestured to the mountains in the distance, and the huge demons on their edges. 'Look at those. Monsters of a size we can barely comprehend. I mean, we've just seen something I can barely comprehend destroy a building, and that was only after it sucked up people like they were candy. We've seen an entity tear a person apart with its *mind*. Oh, and then there is *that* fucking thing.' She pointed up to the sky, and to the swirling mass of stars that formed a terrible, cosmic eye. Even glancing at it set off a horrible tapping sound inside her head, so she quickly looked away. 'I don't need reminding of how dangerous this place is, Josh.'

'I know that,' he replied. 'But there isn't anything we can do for Jim. I'm sorry about what happened, truly, but by standing around, we just increase the chances of something like that happening to us. To you. And I won't let it.'

'I'm not yours to save, Josh,' Beth said.

'You are this time,' he said. 'You've always tried for me, even though I threw it back at you. Well, I need to fix my own mess this time. You aren't going to die here, Beth. I won't allow it.'

Beth suddenly bent double and a stream of black bile spewed from her mouth with surprising force. She then fell to all fours, wheezing and feeling incredibly weak. Josh was quickly at her side.

'Are you okay?' he asked, fear and worry evident in his voice.

'I'm not going to survive this, Josh,' she said. 'Believe me, I wish it were different. But we have to stop what's happening here.'

'I will,' Josh said, then lifted Beth to her feet. He threw

one of her arms over his shoulder so that she could rest her weight on him. Josh started to move forward again.

'Come on, girl,' he said to the whimpering dog with them. Jess wouldn't follow, however. 'Aiden, bring the dog. We aren't leaving her.'

Aiden did as ordered, grabbing Jess by the collar, and the hound reluctantly came with them, her head hanging low as she walked.

Beth looked back, off in the direction Jim had been taken. Whatever was going to happen to him, she prayed it was quick.

45

JIM FELT his ribs crush under the pressure of the slimy mouth. Short but sharp teeth punctured his body in numerous places, and he felt blood flowing from each wound, which only seemed to stimulate and excite the creature. The ground below was miles away now, and was no longer the town of Netherwell Bay, but instead an alien landscape of blacks and reds.

There was no going back for him now. He was going to die in this nightmarish realm. He knew that. Despite the pain, he tried to think of Ada.

The flying creature dipped down and Jim saw they were heading towards an outcropping from a black mountain whose peak towered above even them.

As they neared, he saw the flat plateau contained something on its surface. A mass that seemed to be alive, squirming and writhing. As he neared, Jim realised what it was: a pit, filled with lifeforms. Maggot-like creatures, yellow and grey, with bulbous eyes along their fat bodies and mouths at the head that dripped and oozed. As the huge insect that held him swooped closer, it buzzed louder, almost deafening Jim. The intermingling maggots below, that all looked to be half the size of a human, turned their open mouths up towards Jim.

They were the young of the creature that carried him, he realised. And this was their nest.

'No!' Jim screamed and began fighting and straining anew, but the grip of the mouth around him was too powerful. He was lowered helplessly to his doom as the giant insect landed on the edge of the pit.

Jim frantically wriggled his legs—exposed from the bottom of the vertical maw—in a desperate attempt to get free. The creature dipped its head.

Jim could not see what was happening, only stare into the maddening expanse at the top of the insect's head. He could see those eyes. Hundreds of them.

Everything in this damned place seems to have way too many fucking eyes. It was horrifying.

Then, as Jim was dipped lower, he began to feel it.

His right leg became snared at the shins as something contracted over it. Spindly teeth dug into his skin and pulled. He screeched in pain as the flesh was stripped away in a quick motion. Jim continued to wail in agony. The thing that held him then lifted him up again, chattered, then lowered him back down. More mouths took hold below. Some reached up to the knee of his left leg, others working on the exposed bone of the right, snapping it off. He yelled helplessly and tried to think only of Ada, not the pain he prayed was temporary. Jim was hoisted up a little yet again, and the monster let out another chatter. Its body shook, then it lowered him again.

Jim had the awful feeling it was playing with him. Somehow, if insectile creatures were capable of it, it was actually enjoying his pain.

This time, however, after dipping him down, the huge mouth opened, finally releasing him. Jim dropped a short distance into the squirming and disgusting mass of the nest.

As soon as he made contact with their firm, wrinkled bodies, the enormous maggots swarmed him. Their puckering mouths—lined around the rims with sharp and spindly teeth—started to feast. One creature went straight for his stomach, burrowing into his gut. Others clamped over his arms and what remained of his legs. The agony of being eaten alive was immense. Jim could feel his flesh being sucked and stripped from his bones, causing a fiery suffering that flooded through him. Nerves were exposed, then torn free. His left arm was pulled violently away, popping from the socket. Meat and tendons kept the arm attached momentarily, but the stringy lengths of flesh soon split and the greedy monster pulled away its prize.

Jim could see the wriggling abominations all around him, fleshy and pulsating lengths of veiny fat and puss littered with small and irregular bristly hairs. The squeaky chatters the things emitted were horrifying.

The old man prayed he would just die, but his body held out—against his will—for more pain and torment.

He could feel his insides being sucked out from the vile larva that had forced its head into his guts. It moved and feasted, pushing his intestines and internal organs about as more and more of him was greedily gobbled up. Jim could feel every single sensation, as countless bites chewed at him and pulled away more and more flesh.

His vision started to fade. While the pain never let up, Jim knew he was quickly dying. He cast a look down his body, what little of it he could see that wasn't covered with these things. It was now merely exposed flesh and bone, a skeletal outline that glistened red.

Ada.

Jim peered up to see the proud, insectile parent looking down. But it wanted its fill too, it seemed, and quickly leaned forward, opened its mouth slightly, and gently took hold of what was left of one of Jim's arms. He was pulled free of the nest, his body raging in pain, then thrown up into the air. The horrifying mouth of the creature opened wide below him. After catching him, the mouth snapped shut around him and blocked out Jim's vision for the last time. The last thing he saw was the fleshy and gummy insides, and Jim's head was pressed deeply into the stinking pit. He couldn't scream. Pressure came in from all sides, and what was left of him squashed together in a sickening mess.

46

BETH STRUGGLED TO WALK, even with Josh supporting her weight. He was leading her back towards the seal, where the grass had been removed and the symbols of the Order were marked out. They had to pass that infernal black tower as well, and Beth felt a sensation emanate from it, a draw, as if there was a connection there somehow.

She thought of what grew within her.

There were faint murmurs on the clifftop, uttered by members of the Order who had stayed. However, it was painfully obvious that these few would be of no concern. All were curled up on the ground, and none were in any condition to even move. One had his thumbs buried into his eyes, and blood and clear liquid had dried on his cheeks like the slop from runny eggs. Another had clawed the face from his skin, down to the skull beneath. They sobbed and muttered insane things, their minds broken. They all had their heads turned up to the great eye in the sky.

Other than the cultists, and the dead bodies of their brethren and those creatures that had died during the earlier attack, there was something else up here as well. A body. The huge corpse of a beast—Beth would have guessed it over twenty feet tall if standing. It had black skin on a relatively thin frame, with four arms sprouting out of each side. At the ends of the arms were long hands with three fingers. A stumpy tail was nestled between two strong-looking legs, and the head of the dead thing was a thick elliptical shape, and was a mix of holes, ridges, veins, and exposed bone—seemingly a random pattern of madness. It lay on its side, stomach split open, and black intestines streaked the floor before it as if they had been pulled out by some unknown assailant.

However, one thing Beth could not see was the Dark Priest.

Even if there was a way to make it happen, there was no chance the entity would agree to help them. They reached the seal and Josh moved Beth to the centre, where he then let her drop to her knees. Aiden and Jess joined her inside, and Josh stepped away. He looked around, searching the area.

But the dark entity was nowhere to be seen. Beth kept casting glances over to the huge body that lay on its side, just to make sure that it was actually dead. The corpse hadn't been here earlier when they'd fled from the clifftop, so something had clearly killed it recently.

'Come out!' Josh screamed up into the air. 'I know you're here. Come out!'

'Josh!' Beth scolded. 'Stop shouting. God knows what you'll bring down on us.'

But he wasn't listening, and simply paced around frantically. 'It's still here,' he said. 'It has to be. There has to be a way.'

'*Wretches,*' a weak but distorted voice suddenly called out from somewhere beyond the large corpse. A figure slowly emerged from behind the dead beast, stumbling as it walked, keeping a hand on the armoured flesh of the husk in order to keep upright.

Black blood oozed from its mouth, an arm was missing at the elbow, and there was a nasty dent in the cranium. Lastly, the right leg was twisted and bent inwards.

It suddenly became clear what had killed the large creature on the ground, though the battle had obviously not been an easy one. Beth forced herself to a standing position.

'You don't look well,' Beth taunted.

'*Your human bodies are weak. I was forced into this shell at birth. This was not my destiny.*'

'Well, now you're fucked.'

The entity, however, just laughed. '*I will heal soon. Just as a heart regrows inside of me now, these superficial wounds will right themselves. This weakness... is only temporary.*'

That was something Beth did not want to hear.

Josh wasn't inside the seal, and he stood instead between her and the slowly advancing being that had started all of this. Beth started to move over towards her brother, steadying herself on her feet. Aiden cowered in one of the inner three circles within the symbol, seated on the ground and holding on to an angry, barking Jess.

'Tell me how to fix her!' Josh demanded. 'How do I get out what's growing inside her?'

The entity just laughed again. '*You don't, wretch. Nothing will stop what is happening to her now. The birthing will proceed as planned. A new Great One will come into existence, Vao will cast its gaze down onto us, and the worlds will be connected as a doorway is permanently opened. And then, Ashklaar can claim all the souls it desires.*'

'Bullshit,' Josh shouted. 'There *is* a way. There has to be. Tell me!'

The thing kept limping closer, but Josh wouldn't back down. In response, the Dark Priest raised its remaining hand and thrust it forward. Josh was thrown back a little— he stumbled a few steps before falling to the ground. The attack was much more muted than Beth had expected. She had seen the entity pull a person apart with its mind, and now it could do little more than shove someone. It really had been weakened.

Beth stepped up from the dug-out area and moved next to Josh, helping him to his feet. It took a lot of effort on her part, and she realised just how much weaker she had grown as well.

'Get back inside the seal,' Josh said. But she started to gently pull him back towards it as well, hoping to get him within its outer edge before she destroyed the symbols herself.

'Come on,' Beth pleaded. 'You need to get out of here.'

Josh looked to her, then back to the entity. He shook his head. 'No.'

He then broke free of her weak grasp and sprinted towards the cackling monster.

47

IF THE LIMPING demon wasn't going to willingly tell Josh how to help his sister, then Josh knew he would have to extract that information physically.

He also knew he was insanely outmatched. However, the being was hardly at its strongest, and Josh wasn't about to let Beth die—he had to try. But even as he sprinted, Josh's mind —some small part of it—told him he was running to his death.

The entity gave a look of surprise before raising its remaining arm again. But Josh was quicker. He leapt into the air and slammed into the body of the demon, tackling it hard before any attack on him could be made. Both of them tumbled to the ground, with Josh landing on top of the monster. His hands quickly found its face, and he pushed his thumbs into its eyes. Black fluid pooled around his appendages and sloshed to the ground. The entity howled in pain.

Josh hadn't known it could feel pain.

'Tell me!' he screamed. 'Tell me or I'll rip your head off!'

But the dark entity's hand quickly found Josh's throat. Despite fighting against it, Josh felt the grip tighten.

'*Wretch*,' it seethed again. '*Your sister is now ours. And you will die.*' It began to slowly increase the pressure of its grip. No matter how much Josh fought, this thing was simply stronger than he was, and it pulled his head closer to its own, sneering as it did. Thinking quickly, Josh quickly dropped his face forward and took a mouthful of flesh between his teeth. Yanking back, he tore away a chunk of cold meat from the creature's cheek, which caused more black bile to pour free. The pain forced the entity to relax its grip just enough for Josh to slip free and roll to the side. He quickly pushed himself up and swung a kick, but the dark entity blocked the blow with its arm. It then arced its hand around and Josh was thrown through the air again, back towards his sister. He landed in a crumpled pile at her feet, the wind knocked out of him.

That throw had been noticeably more powerful than the last.

'*I will tear you apart!*' the entity said with a snarl, and brought up its arm again, aiming an open hand at Josh.

But... nothing happened. The entity just stood frozen, with a confused expression etched on its pale and scarred face.

Josh turned to Beth, expecting to see her looking down at him, weak and unsteady.

But that was not what he saw.

His sister was standing strong, feet set apart, planted into the ground. Her body was locked in place, unwavering, and her arms were held out towards the demon. Her skin was now mottled and blotchy, with the black veins beneath even more pronounced. Her eyes were clear white. But she was standing firm.

'You first,' Beth stated, her voice ethereal, echoey... not quite human. She then quickly moved her arms apart, and Josh turned to see the dark entity cry out in agony before it was ripped in two. The head clung to the larger right side, which was pulled clean away from the left. Bones split, the legs separated, and black blood and meat showered the floor.

Josh was in awe.

But a horrible realisation overtook him. Beth was changing. And these changes occurring were now more than just surface level.

Beth wavered, her breathing suddenly heavy, and then she dropped to the floor, wheezing and drained. She turned to look at him and smiled sadly.

'It's over,' she said.

'Not yet,' Josh replied. 'Not until I save you.'

Josh pulled her to her feet again and hugged her. She felt cold in his arms. Eventually, she pulled away, and he looked into her blank, milky eyes.

'This was never about *you* saving *me*.' And with that, she swung her arms, launching Josh through the air yet again. He landed in a heap back in the seal. As he hit the ground, he rolled into Aiden, who still held Jess.

'Beth!' Josh cried, looking back up to his big sister.

'It's okay,' she said. 'I've got you. I always did.'

Another sweep of her arm. The blood, guts, and markings that had made up the symbols burst apart while Josh, Aiden, and Jess remained inside of the seal's boundary.

Josh yelled out again for his sister. He then felt a sudden and intense wave close in around him.

48

Beth saw her brother—along with Aiden and Jim's dog—suddenly snap from existence. The exposed earth beneath glowed red like hot embers.

After Beth had destroyed the seal, an immense wind and current had pulled inwards, gusting past her and almost blowing her from her feet. She'd felt a static shock, though the whole thing lasted only a few moments. Then, everything settled.

They were gone. The doorway was closed. The red circle had been pulled from the paper.

Beth remained now in this other world, alone. And though she knew that she could not stop what was going to happen, at least it would happen removed from her own world. There would be no permanent link, and no way for the nightmare reality to seep through and bring about a hell on earth.

Beth looked around, feeling weak, faint, and alone.

She heard a faint laughing.

It was that thing. The Dark Priest. Though it had been

torn asunder, its head turned to look at Beth, and she could see the jaw rise and fall as the cackling continued. Feeling a wave of anger, she strode over to it.

'Something funny?' she asked through gritted teeth. 'Because the way I see it, you failed. *You're* dying. I won. My world is safe.'

It coughed black blood and spoke. '*I can never die. I will be whole again soon. And I am home now. Your world's safety is only a temporary reprieve. Soon, thanks to you, my creator will bear another child.*'

Beth glanced up at the titanic, black column that touched the sky. Was *that* the kind of thing she was going to give birth to? A living nightmare?

'Actually, no,' she said with a smirk. 'I still have time to put a stop to that. I see plenty of ways to die around here.'

The entity laughed again. '*Fool. Like me, you cannot die. Not now. It is too late for that—you are too far gone. Regardless of what you try, your body will knit back together, and what is destined will take place.*'

Beth clenched her teeth. 'No, the thing inside me will die. I know it. I'll kill it.'

The laughter grew louder. '*How little you know. You talk as if what is inside of you will be purged from your body when it's ready. But there is nothing growing in you that can be pushed out. You are to be the Great One. The birthing is your... transformation, my Sister.*'

It closed its eyes and continued to laugh. More anger rose in Beth.

That can't be true. It can't.

She brought up her foot and quickly and savagely drove the sole of her shoe down into the face of the entity, again and again, hearing cracks and squelches. With each blow, her fury built. The release felt good. Beth only stopped when the laughter died and all that was left of the Dark Priest's head was a pool of black mush.

'It isn't true,' she said and began to cry.

49

JOSH GOT TO HIS FEET.

He looked around, but he didn't recognise what he saw. The dirt beneath his feet was now higher than the ground around it by a few feet at least.

The general shape of the landscape off in the distance was as he remembered it to be, but instead of seeing the buildings and streets of Netherwell Bay, there were simply the slopes and hills of the topography. No roads, no pavement, just clays and soil. The buildings had all gone, as if they had never existed.

Netherwell Bay had been wiped off the face of the earth.

The sea behind him was normal, not a boiling or blood-red mass. And there wasn't a single nightmarish creature in sight.

'It worked,' he heard Aiden say. 'We got back through. We made it!'

Josh clenched his teeth, feeling absolute anger and pain at what had just happened, at leaving Beth behind. He swung a punch at Aiden and sent him sprawling to the ground. The young man cried out, then clutched his cheek, his eyes wide with shock and fright.

'My sister didn't make it,' Josh replied coldly. 'And it's *your* fault.' Josh advanced on the fallen man, who begged and pleaded, crab-walking backwards as Josh came forward.

'Don't,' Aiden said. 'Please. I'm sorry. I'm truly sorry.'

Josh stood over him, ready to tear the weaselly little fucker apart.

But he stopped himself. Though his fists were clenched and rage coursed through his veins, Josh knew he wasn't a killer. He'd known that when the Order had tried to make him murder someone only a few days ago.

He would let this cockroach scuttle off. After all, without his masters to serve, Aiden would likely be lost and useless. Josh turned away from the sobbing man.

Tears streamed down his face. It was supposed to be *him*. He was the fuckup. Beth didn't deserve what happened. *He* should have been the one to give his life for her. *He* should have looked out for his sister for once. But no, he'd failed again, and Beth had been forced to clean up his mess.

The madness of the last few days, hell, the last few years, had been unbelievable. But Josh knew he couldn't let his sister's death be for nothing. While the sect in this town was gone, the Order at large still remained.

No more drifting through life. No more ducking responsibility.

Josh had purpose now. He would make all of those fuckers pay. Alone, if he had to.

'Come on, girl,' Josh said to Jess as he started to walk away. The dog followed, head held low. She cried.

Josh knew her pain.

50

THE MOMENT BETH had crushed the head of the dark entity underfoot and strolled out of the town of Netherwell Bay unchallenged, she'd felt the changes within her speed up.

She walked and walked and walked, making her way through the alien hellscape, seeing nightmarish things. Eventually, her body had stopped responding and she fell. A surge rippled through her, blasting out an invisible energy that gave off a booming sound so great Beth thought her head would explode.

Then, she felt a weight on her. Not a physical feeling... but something else. Looking up to the skies, she'd gazed at the great cosmic eye, and somehow felt its maddening and infinite gaze focus in on her. It had taken notice.

Over the course of what felt like days, her form bloated and expanded. Beth felt every part of the transformation. Her limbs stretched, fingers worming themselves into the ground like the roots of a plant. She noticed the change in her skin—thicker, darker, with diamond-shaped scales forming. Seeing her own body slowly morph and elongate was terrifying.

The process was horribly slow and prolonged an unimaginable agony. Beth expanded further, wanting to die, and her body bloated out into a massive and pulsing mess of flesh and congealed limbs. Over the course of many agonising weeks, the disgusting lump she had become grew upwards. Her tumorous form rose into the air as her roots burrowed deeper into the ground. Soon, her sight was lost as her own flesh swallowed her face. Then, Beth took on the shape of a fleshy pillar.

Her skin darkened. Hardened. She grew and grew. Her mind broke.

In the years that followed—hundreds and thousands of them—Beth's new form grew to touch the sky. A new and expanding knowledge coursed through her, giving Beth a greater purpose and meaning far beyond what her original mind could have comprehended. Over the aeons she changed to stand shoulder to shoulder with Ashklaar and others like it in this world. She reached up to Vao, while at the same time casting dominion down over those below her. Beth was long lost, a faint echo mixed in with the tortured souls who had been consumed since the new and great formation.

She had become something else now. Something greater.

Something infinite.

51

ONE YEAR after the incident at Netherwell Bay...

JOSH SAT WAITING in the pub.

It was Saturday, and the place was quite lively. However, he was situated at the back, away from the gathered crowds who had come to watch the football match on the large screen at the front of the pub. He'd deliberately picked an area that was private enough for what he needed.

But the woman he was due to meet was running late. He'd never met her before, though he was *very* interested in talking to her.

He took a sip from his lemonade. No alcohol anymore. Not with so much to do.

Jess sat by his feet, watching the archway that separated this quieter space from the main body of the pub beyond.

'Think she stood us up, girl?' Josh asked, and gave Jess' head a quick scratch.

Another sip.

Then Josh spotted someone moving through the crowd. A tall woman with long, red hair and a strong build. He knew it instantly.

This is her.

Besides the scars on her face—slight burn marks that, while not too severe, were somewhat noticeable the closer she got—the woman had a definite aura about her.

She had been through something terrible. He could sense it.

The woman stopped at the other side of his table, standing above him and looking down.

'You who I'm here to see?' she asked.

He nodded. 'I am. Did you bring it?'

She dumped the rucksack she had been carrying onto the table with a thud. 'The book is in there. Pulled it out of hell myself.' Looking at her, he didn't doubt it. 'You were in Netherwell, then?' she asked. 'When it happened? When it vanished?'

Josh nodded. 'I was, so I'm all too aware of the Order. And I have a little inside knowledge on them, too. Something your friends might be interested in. Care to sit?' He motioned to the empty chair. After a moment's hesitation, the woman before him took it.

'Those people need to pay,' she said. 'They took people very close to me when trying to steal this book from me.'

'Sounds like them,' Josh said. 'And I agree. They're the reason my sister is gone. I have a score to settle.'

'Okay, then,' the girl said. 'If we want stop them, this book can help. The people I know can help as well. If you want in, then you are swearing to help us put a stop to all this shit for good. But, well, you know the risk. You've seen it before, haven't you.'

'I have,' he confirmed. 'And I'm in.' Josh then extended his hand over the table. 'Josh Davis.'

She looked at his hand for a moment, then smiled and shook it.

'Ashley,' she replied. 'Ashley Turner. Welcome aboard.'

THE END

HORROR IN THE WOODS

A NEW VOICE IN HORROR.

LEE MOUNTFORD

If you go down to the woods today...

For Ashley Turner and her three friends, it was supposed to be an adventure-filled weekend. A chance to get away from the hustle-and-bustle of city life, and experience the peaceful tranquility of nature.

But when they ventured into those woods, their trip turned into a horror far beyond what they could have ever imagined.

Because these four friends have wandered into the territory of the violent, grotesque Webb family. A group of psychopaths who have a taste for human meat. And they are hungry!

Ashley and her friends must face this evil head on, and worse, discover the shocking secret behind the family's existence...

In the vein of THE EVIL DEAD, TEXAS CHAINSAW MASSACRE, and WRONG TURN - HORROR IN THE WOODS will leave you exhausted and drained. A brutal, violent tale that hurtles along at break-neck pace—one that horror fans should not miss!

Buy Horror in the Woods now...

TORMENTED

Dare you enter the Asylum?

Adrian James is running from his past with nothing left to live for. At rock bottom, with a blade to his wrist, a mysterious stranger intervenes and offers him a chance at salvation.

Adrian accepts, and he enters Arlington Asylum of his own free will. Once inside, however, he soon learns that he will never escape. And worse, there are strange experiments taking place here, and a secretive medicine is being administered, one that causes certain... changes... in the patients.

The insidious secrets within the halls of Arlington Asylum are slowly revealed, and it is beyond anything Adrian could have possibly imagined. A literal hell is unleashed as impossible and terrifying creatures indulge their sadistic desires.

Adrian and his friends must escape this nightmarish place and warn the outside world before it's too late, but they must face down the demons of hell to do so.

TORMENTED is a gruesome and violent horror story, influenced by such greats as John Carpenter's THE THING, Clive Barker's HELLRAISER, and Jeremy Gillespie's THE VOID.

Buy Tormented now...

THE SUPERNATURAL HORROR SERIES

Separate stories. The same, terrifying universe.

The Demonic: A woman returns to her childhood home to lay to rest the ghosts of the past. But in this house the ghosts are real, and evil has found a home.

The Mark: A satanic cult. A woman's brutal assault. Can one woman face her darkest fears before a demonic entity is unleashed from the depths of hell?

Forest of the Damned: A group of paranormal researchers investigate the infamous Black Forest, hoping to find proof of the afterlife and learn more of the infamous Mother Sibbett. But what they find is far beyond even their worst nightmares.

Buy each book individually, or all three in one volume for a reduced price:

The Supernatural Horror Collection

ABOUT THE AUTHOR

Lee Mountford is a horror author from the North-East of England. His first book, Horror in the Woods, was published in May 2017 to fantastic reviews, and his follow-up book, The Demonic, achieved Best Seller status in both Occult Horror and British Horror categories on Amazon.

He is a lifelong horror fan, much to the dismay of his amazing wife, Michelle, and his work is available in ebook, print and audiobook formats.

In August 2017 he and his wife welcomed their first daughter, Ella, into the world. In May 2019, their second daughter, Sophie, came along. Michelle is hoping the girls doesn't inherit her father's love of horror, but Lee has other ideas...

For more information
www.leemountford.com
leemountford01@googlemail.com

ACKNOWLEDGMENTS

Thanks first and foremost to my editor, Josiah Davis (http://www.jdbookservices.com), for such an amazing job.

The cover was supplied by Debbie at The Cover Collection (http://www.thecovercollection.com). I cannot recommend their work enough.

And the last thank you, as always, is the most important—to my amazing family. My wife, Michelle, and my daughters, Ella and Sophie—thank you for everything. You three are my world.

Made in the USA
Middletown, DE
27 July 2020

13753896R00191